KT-159-887

ALISON BRUCE

THE MOMENT BEFORE IMPACT

CONSTABLE

CONSTABLE

First published in Great Britain in 2020 by Constable

This paperback edition published in 2021 by Constable

Copyright © Alison Bruce, 2020

1 3 5 7 9 10 8 6 4 2

The moral right of the author has been asserted.

All characters and events in this publication, other than those clearly in the public domain, are fictitious and any resemblance to real persons, living or dead, is purely coincidental.

All rights reserved.
No part of this publication may be reproduced, stored in a retrieval system, or transmitted, in any form, or by any means, without the prior permission in writing of the publisher, nor be otherwise circulated in any form of binding or cover other than that in which it is published and without a similar condition including this condition being imposed on the subsequent purchaser.

A CIP catalogue record for this book is available from the British Library.

ISBN: 978-1-47212-389-3

Typeset in Times New Roman by Initial Typesetting Services, Edinburgh
Printed and bound in Great Britain by Clays Ltd, Elcograf S.p.A.

Papers used by Constable are from well-managed forests and other responsible sources.

FSC
www.fsc.org
MIX
Paper from responsible sources
FSC® C104740

Constable
An imprint of
Little, Brown Book Group
Carmelite House
50 Victoria Embankment
London EC4Y 0DZ

An Hachette UK Company
www.hachette.co.uk

www.littlebrown.co.uk

To Abi Henry.

I said that my next book would be thanks to you.
Here it is.
And for everything, including this, thank you so much.

PART ONE

Prologue

Celia Henry had remained at her father's graveside after the other mourners had dispersed. She hadn't been ready to break the silence.

The days between his death and the funeral had passed in a slow and muted blur. A no-man's land. A halfway house between losing him and letting him go.

Cards and messages of condolence had arrived.

She had opened each and stood it alongside the others. She filled her kitchen windowsill with them, and let her unfocused gaze wander between them and the garden each time she washed the dishes. And, for those days, the kitchen had been her sanctuary, the place where she'd let her thoughts run unchecked, and where it had been safe to admit that she dreaded the funeral.

Most of the family didn't come because of the short notice and the cost of flights from Montego Bay. And Celia had been glad; their apologies were sincere, and she would visit when she could, but she hadn't been ready to be descended upon by cousins and elderly, emotional aunties. His brother Alton, her uncle, had travelled up from Dalston, but the rest of the mourners were locals, and many were the same faces who'd been at her mammy's funeral the previous year.

And when it was all over Celia had stood at the graveside alone, a weary woman saying a wordless goodbye.

Chapter 1

And now, almost eight years later, Celia Henry was aware that the same kind of silence had hung around her since the crash. It had descended when the news broke, and had deepened as the full impact touched the residents of Mawson Road. Of course, she'd carried on since then; she'd worked and shopped and still talked with her neighbours, although, on the subject itself, she said nothing. It was not the time for gossip.

She knew she wasn't herself, and she hadn't been since she'd found out the date of the trial. Or, more specifically, in the hours afterwards when she'd first asked herself whether she would attend. Whether she should.

Why would she?

She hadn't been at the scene. And although she knew them all, she wasn't family. The date had grown closer, and she had convinced herself that she should let it go.

Right up until last night she had told herself that she wouldn't attend.

She hadn't slept well, and rose and dressed while still telling herself that it wasn't her place.

Eventually she relented.

***

The walk from Mawson Road to Cambridge Crown Court would take no more than twenty minutes, but she still left home with an hour and a half to spare. Breakfast, usually a 9 a.m. mix of fresh fruit and good intentions that lasted until mid-morning, had been skipped . . . would be skipped.

After all, it wasn't yet eight and it was still too early.

She closed her front door by tugging it shut by the lip of the letterbox, making sure that it was no louder than just the unavoidable click of spring and latch. She had never been a loud person and disapproved of the noise that spilled in from Mill Road.

But this was different. She still needed her cocoon of silence.

The decision to arrive an hour before the court doors opened was deliberate; a mix of preparation on one hand, and on the other, enough time to slip away again unnoticed if she changed her mind.

In her handbag were two sandwiches and three slices of hummingbird cake, not home baked as usual, but one of four purchased from the Hot Numbers coffee shop on the other side of Mill Road.

And yesterday, without planning it, she'd tidied.

Tidying before a court case had been her in the days when she'd needed to shut the door behind her and forget about home until a trial was done. That had been a long time ago, but the order of sweeping and straightening and putting away still felt comfortable.

And, as she walked, she realised why she wasn't herself; she had awakened the person she used to be.

Everything about the building was as she remembered. She nodded at Tony, the elder of the two security guards.

He smiled in recognition. 'Working again?' he asked.

She shook her head.

'Ah, that's a pity, you were one of the friendly ones. So many come in without even a word.' He ran a handheld scanner across her as he spoke. 'I recognise their faces, but they look past me like I don't exist.'

She remembered his line of patter. 'Photographers are the worst,' she added. Her voice sounded rusty and she realised they had been her first words of the day.

'Exactly what I was going to say,' he chuckled, then switched to a sterner expression as other people arrived. She doubted he'd crack another smile between now and the end of the day.

She glanced back at the doorway, then hurried towards Court 1 before anyone else tried to speak to her. She chose a seat at one end of the back row of the public gallery where it would be easy to slip away, but, more importantly, where her presence would be least noticed, and waited as the court gradually filled. She recognised several of the court officials and knew all of their roles. She knew the traditions and the order of proceedings. The others in the public gallery remained restless and responded to each movement and new sound. The woman in front of her was upright, but visibly nervous, and her reactions were marginally sharper than those of the others. A mother, she guessed, but had no idea whose.

Celia placed her bag on her lap and folded her hands around it. She didn't care that she would not be taking notes; instead she would close her eyes for the first testimony and then listen to them all, no matter how many days that took.

Then Nicci Waldock was led in and Celia felt the air tighten.

Chapter 2

'So, you had a habit of looking out for your brother?'

'Yes, I did.'

'You wanted to protect him?'

'Of course.'

'What did you think you could achieve?'

'I don't know. Maybe I thought that worrying about him would keep him safe.' And, before the words dried, he added, 'I was mistaken.'

Jack Bailey had begun his shift at the 'Five Miles from Anywhere, No Hurry Inn' at noon. The pub stood about half an hour from Cambridge in a riverside hamlet whose population swelled in spring and summer months, thanks to visitors in cabin cruisers and narrowboats. Now every mooring was occupied and the slope between the bar room and the river was dappled with groups of people sitting at picnic tables laden with drinks or sunbathing on blankets. Weekend days in the hot weather were usually frantically busy, more so when there was a band playing. He had already been around several times to collect glasses. The punters were supposed to take only the plastic ones into the beer garden – health and safety and all that – but people often started in the bar and then wandered outside.

From time to time he scanned the crowd and glanced towards the car park. His brother Charlie had been typically vague. 'Yeah, well, we might come down in the afternoon. See what the weather's doing. Will you let me know who's playing?'

There were multiple bands, three today, three tomorrow. And Charlie had commented each time the line-up had been adjusted, so Jack knew that the question was redundant. It was more likely to be about who would be going, and who wouldn't.

Nicci would be there, of course. Charlie had been knocking around with her since primary school, and, as far as Jack knew, they had managed to get all the way through adolescence without anything beyond friendship occurring between them, but they remained close to inseparable. Of course, the dynamic had changed since they'd both started at uni, although it would have changed a lot more if one of them had decided to study further afield. But no, they had both stayed in Cambridge and had plumped for Anglia Ruskin, with Charlie studying Sociology, and no career plans beyond that, as far as Jack knew.

Jack suspected that Charlie's indecision about today had more to do with whether Nicci's new friend Ellie decided to tag along. Charlie's keenness was so poorly disguised that Jack was certain that the romance was doomed before it had even begun.

Jack made his way right around the building just to get a better view of the car park. If they did arrive, he'd be pleased to know they'd done so safely. Charlie might technically be an adult but, to Jack, he was permanently somewhere about fourteen.

Jack was back behind the bar when they finally showed up, six of them not three. They stood in the middle of one of the few remaining clear patches of grass. Three girls, three boys. Five of them conferring, with only the sixth, Nicci, standing apart. She had her back to him and seemed to be staring across at the river, ignoring a conversation which involved glances in Jack's direction, towards the band and back at the spot where they stood.

Jack knew them all.

He turned away, emptying the glass washer of clean glasses and refilling it with dirty ones. The next time he looked at them was when they approached the bar.

'I wondered if you'd had a change of plans. You missed the first band, you know.'

Charlie's expression was caught between warmth and awkwardness. 'Yeah well, we were running a bit late. All good now though.' He tapped his fingertips on the laminate-topped bar. 'Four pints of Coke, two of lemonade. Thanks.'

'Just soft drinks?'

'Yeah, for starters.' It was Rob who had cut in. Rob had been three years below Jack at school, but they'd been on the same football team and had been friends for a while. Until Jack and Gemma had briefly dated. He could still picture the darkness in Rob's expression. The protectiveness. It had been a life lesson; never date a friend's little sister.

Why didn't schools offer that kind of real-world advice?

'Good to see you.' Jack managed to sound neutral. Gemma stood nearer to him than her brother. It meant that he was looking past Gemma when he spoke to Rob and he could feel her languid gaze resting on him. 'Do you want a tray?' She had one arm draped across the shoulder of the third man, Callum, the only one of the six who Jack barely knew. Callum was pink-skinned and scrawny, and nothing like Rob or Gemma. Jack knew they wouldn't be an item.

When the others took their drinks outside, Gemma hung back. 'I hoped you'd be here.'

He worked every weekend; it was a pretty good bet. Jack grunted, 'Why?'

'Nothing really. A chance to clear the air.' She smiled, tilting her head back. It was challenge rather than warmth that flashed in her eyes. 'Isn't it time we were friends again?'

'It's good to see you, Gem.' Jack picked up a bar towel and began wiping down the beer pumps, giving his work most of his attention and casting just a swift glance at Gemma now and again.

'Come on. What's the problem, Jack?' She waved one hand in the direction of the beer garden. 'You and Rob could make up.' She patted the bar and her voice rose a little. 'Or maybe not, but you should be out there with us right now, having a laugh.'

Only the muffled sound of the band made it inside, so the sight of Charlie waving his arms around as he amused his friends, probably with a ridiculous anecdote, was accompanied by the unrelenting thump of a song Jack didn't recognise. 'Who's driving?'

'No one. We're sleeping out.' She made quote marks with her fingers as she added, 'Festival style.' She pretended to think. 'You could join us when you're done.'

'I don't think so.'

'Jack . . .'

'The air's clear.' He nodded in the direction of the beer garden. 'And even clearer out there.' He saw a new customer approaching the bar and turned away from Gemma before she had a chance to reply.

Chapter 3

'According to medical reports you have fully recovered, but you claim your memory of that afternoon and evening is incomplete?'

'Yes, it is.'

'You can remember being by the river, and everyone who was present, but not everything that happened?'

'Yes, but what I do remember is accurate.'

'Accurate, but incomplete? It is hardly the same as the truth, the whole truth, is it, Miss Waldock?'

Nicci couldn't remember how she and Ellie ended up at the Cam's edge, but she remembered them standing on the grassy bank and watching the slow flow of the ageing river. They must have wandered away from their friends and were now under the partial shade of a willow, and, in either direction, the moorings were occupied by a long line of narrowboats and cruisers. The ground sloped sharply, making her feet press forward in her sandals. 'Can we either sit or keep walking, El?'

'As long as we're not hanging out with Gemma?' Ellie asked.

'I'll be sociable, just give me some space first.'

'I'm not a fan, if that helps.' Ellie looked warily at the sun-wilted grass. 'I can see duck shit.'

'Well don't sit on that bit.'

'Do ducks pee on grass?'

Nicci chose a spot that looked no more sinister than hay and dust. 'Don't know, don't care.' She patted the ground. 'Just sit, will you?'

Ellie seemed reluctant, but did as she was told.

'Are you going to turn down crime scenes because they look too messy?'

'We'll have suits. Anyhow, that'll be work.'

Nicci raised an eyebrow. 'So you won't be fussy if you're being paid?'

Ellie gave Nicci's leg a playful flick. 'You know that's not what I meant. Besides, it's a long time before we'll start applying for jobs.'

Ellie was neat and precise in everything she did. She had plenty of skills that could make her a good CSI, but Nicci wondered whether she had the stomach for it. Nicci herself was the exact opposite; less organised, sometimes clumsy, but rarely fazed. 'Meaning what, that you are thinking of a different career?'

Plenty of the students on their course wanted to work in crime-related fields; some would be applying to join the police, others, like Nicci, wanted to be crime scene investigators, but most still seemed undecided. And, as Ellie had said, it was still early days.

Ellie seemed to consider the question carefully before replying. 'I'm thinking about leaving.'

'Leaving what?'

'The course. Cambridge. Everything.' She sat cross-legged with her hands in her lap and her straight blonde hair draped evenly across her shoulders; from a distance she probably looked serene. Up close she did not. Her gaze was unwavering, and her eyes were wider than usual. Her cheeks seemed pinched.

'But why?'

'It's wrong for me.'

‘That doesn’t make sense; we’ve almost completed the first year. And your grades are great.’

‘It’s not about my grades, Nic.’ Ellie looked away, maybe across the water to the flat, scrubby fields on the other side, or maybe at nothing.

‘Then what?’

Ellie shook her head and said nothing at first. Only the side of her face was in view, but it was enough for Nicci to see the pain.

‘Ellie, look at me. Why haven’t you told me about this before? Or has something happened?’ Nicci shuffled closer and put her arm around Ellie, but was immediately shaken away.

‘Don’t, someone will see.’

‘What’s happened?’

‘I don’t know. Maybe nothing.’ Ellie took a few steadying breaths. ‘If a man fell in the river now, what would you do?’

Nicci could swim, but nowhere more adventurous than the local pool or in thigh-height water on a sandy beach. ‘If I swam out, we’d both drown. The best bet would be to throw a ring or a rope.’

‘But you’d do something?’

‘Of course.’

‘How do you know you wouldn’t just leave him? People do, or they’re too busy filming it to shout for help. How do you know you wouldn’t be one of those?’

‘I just don’t think I would, but I guess some people freeze . . . What’s this about?’

‘I know I don’t have what it takes to get involved.’ She pressed her lips together as she fought back tears, then mumbled, ‘I thought I would, but I don’t.’

Nicci began to speak but Ellie shook her head fervently.

‘No, Nic. I don’t want any of it. I don’t want to stand up in court to give evidence or make statements to the police. I don’t want the responsibility.’ She had begun to shake.

Nicci spoke quietly and urgently. ‘Whatever has happened, it can be sorted. Just tell me.’

'I saw something,' Ellie whispered.

'What?'

'It was cloth, torn, like a rag. And I thought I recognised it, but I couldn't place it. I didn't realise what it was until today, but it turns out that I knew all along. I just turned my back.'

'Ellie, what are you talking about? Tell me everything.'

Ellie was already scrambling to her feet. 'I can't get involved. It's too much.' Fear and indecision were written on her face, and she was no longer looking at Nicci. Nicci wondered how long there'd been a shadow behind her friend's smile, and how many times it had gone unnoticed.

Nicci followed Ellie's gaze and twisted around in time to see Callum crossing the grass towards them. 'Oh great,' Nicci muttered.

But Ellie wiped her flushed face with the back of one hand. 'Forget about it, Nic.' And then, to Callum, 'Have we missed the shots yet? I didn't realise how long we'd been chatting.'

'Gemma wants us to stay together.' Callum glanced from Ellie to Nicci, and back again. 'It's why we're here, isn't it?'

'Of course,' Ellie nodded. She reached out and pulled Nicci to her feet. 'I'm sorry,' she said, too quietly for Callum to hear. The colour had faded from her cheeks and a film of sweat had formed across them and travelled down her neck. She looked as though she needed to throw up.

She looked reluctant when Callum took her arm, but said nothing as the three of them crossed the grass to join the others.

Chapter 4

'How did you first meet Ellie Daniels?'

'We started university at the same time and happened to rent rooms in the same house.'

'Did you become close?'

'Not sex. No, I didn't think of her that way. But we were friends. Definitely friends.'

'And on Monday 28 March, when you saw Miss Daniels by the river with Miss Waldock, did either seem upset?'

'No, they didn't. That happened later.'

Gemma had pestered Callum into walking over to collect the girls. It was less than a hundred yards, but it wasn't the distance that bothered him, it was the principle.

So far, Callum would have described the day as disappointing. Ellie had painted a picture of the pub by the river, and the kind of drunken party atmosphere where he'd been able to imagine that anything might be possible. Instead it had almost instantly turned into a complicated knot of subtext and uncomfortable silences. He'd had no idea that Nicci and Gemma shared a mutual dislike for one another which had existed since childhood, and now Ellie found it hard to warm to Gemma because of her ridiculous loyalties to Nicci.

He strode towards the river bank. He could see Nicci and Ellie talking, leaning in towards one another. Sharing secrets probably. Hopefully not discussing how he felt about Gemma.

Ellie had known about it all along; they'd discussed Gemma often enough. In fact, there had been evenings when she'd joked and told him that he needed to find a second hobby, one which was completely Gemma free. She'd made that joke as recently as last night . . . he slowed, and considered that for a moment.

Last night she hadn't quite been herself though and the evening had ended rather abruptly.

And now he had had to run after her – at Gemma's insistence – to bring the group back together. Ellie and Nicci looked up at him, and he tried to ignore the conspiratorial silence that hung between the two girls. 'Gemma wants us to stay together,' he said.

Surprisingly, Nicci looked happier about it than Ellie, but neither objected. Ellie walked quickly; it was only a short distance but he had to rush to keep up. He was half a stride behind her and as close to speaking distance as he thought he was going to get. 'Don't forget to talk to Gemma,' he whispered.

Usually she would have replied with, 'I won't', or 'Of course'. But she didn't answer until he looked at her and asked again. Then she nodded.

'What's the problem?' he muttered.

She shrugged. 'It doesn't matter.'

He suddenly wondered whether her pace was about avoiding him, and he sensed that she didn't want to talk to him at all. 'You'll speak to Gemma though?' he persisted.

'Of course. I said I would, didn't I?'

Callum sat on the grass, leaning back on one elbow and holding what looked like a pint of Coke in the other hand. His glass now contained about one-third Southern Comfort. He wasn't usually much of a drinker, but he worked part time in a bar and knew from first-hand experience that a few less inhibitions had fuelled plenty of encounters. He'd also seen many drunken falls and failures, but, he figured, the trick was to stop before it went that far. He would lie back, take it easy and wait until he was sure the time was right.

The six of them sat in an arc, facing in the general direction of the stage. The three boys sat in the middle, with Charlie and Nicci to Callum's left and Rob, Gemma and Ellie to his right. Callum nodded at the stage and asked Charlie, 'Who's up next?'

Charlie seemed to have memorised the running order of the bands, and didn't need to check. 'Crackleford.'

'Never heard of them.'

'Documentary pop, like very new, new wave?' Then he added, 'You're not into music, are you?'

'Sometimes. It depends.' For Callum music was little more than something added to video games and movies for extra effect. On a par with title sequences and power-ups.

Charlie tilted his head so that no one but Callum could catch his words. 'Gemma loves this band. Just thought you should know.'

Callum wasn't sure whether Charlie was being kind, or just laughing at him. He took a couple of gulps of his drink, half closed his eyes and watched the drummer reposition his stool and the snare.

Sometimes, Callum reminded himself, it was wise to pause for a moment just to take stock. And, at least until the band started, he thought he might have a chance of hearing snatches of the conversations around him. But Gemma and Ellie spoke in low tones and the only words he caught were inconsequential; about hair and fashion, and nothing to do with him.

Gemma looked across just once, and, when their eyes met, she smiled and raised her fingers in a small wave. Ellie looked at him too, and he raised his eyebrows at her, just enough to give her a subtle reminder. Her expression was blank and unsmiling, and her only response was to lift her glass, and tilt her head as she drained its contents.

The band began to play then, but Callum continued to watch

the two girls with growing curiosity. Gemma leant closer to talk in Ellie's ear, and then Ellie did the same in reply. Ellie looked tense. Gemma seemed irritated, there were no smiles, but there was no shouting either. Somewhere during Crackleford's second song they stopped talking to one another and, from then on, only watched the band.

Callum began watching the band too, with Gemma and Ellie unmoving in his peripheral vision. He had no idea what had changed between them, although he was sure that neither of them spoke again, or even moved.

But, the next time he looked at Ellie, her face was flushed and he saw her start to sob.

Chapter 5

'So, Mr Hayward, you drove to the pub because your sister Gemma asked you to?'

'That's correct.'

'But there were enough spaces in Miss Waldock's car?'

'Yes, but Gemma wasn't sure how long she wanted to stay, and, like everyone else, I thought it might be a laugh.'

'But later, you left without her?'

'I'll always regret that, but Nicci's the one on trial here, not me.'

Under Rob's jacket was a bag, and in the bag were two one-litre bottles of Southern Comfort and another of tequila. The plan was to buy mixers at the bar, add the whiskey, then later switch to shots. No one expected that to end without someone chucking up. But Rob hoped that no one would have the appetite for the tequila, and he'd been preoccupied with thinking of ways to try to divert Gemma from mixing her drinks. If she became determined, then he doubted he could.

Rob dug in his pocket for a twenty, then tried to pass it to Callum. 'Do me a favour? Go to the bar and get another round in. We need the drinks diluted a bit more than this.'

Callum shook his head. 'I've brought my own. Didn't want

to pay pub prices. Do you know how much profit they make on mixers?'

Rob had no doubt that Callum would have told him, and in far too much detail. Two minutes in Callum's company was all the motivation Rob needed to head to the bar. By the time he had crossed the grass, he'd reduced his intended order to three soft drinks, one each for himself, Gemma and Ellie.

The barmaid had white-tipped nails, several rings on her fingers and another on her thumb. A heavy charm bracelet swung from her wrist. He wondered how she managed with so much jewellery getting in the way. She tilted each glass and added syrup then soda water. 'I said, did you want lemon with that?'

'Sorry, no,' he shook his head, 'we're good.'

She flashed her thick lashes in the direction of the grassy slope and the river. 'Our barman's watching you lot.'

'Jack? Why?'

'He hates it when people bring their own drinks in. It don't bother me, I just think, the more the merrier. I get paid either way. But it don't even matter that he knows you, he'll soon chuck you out.'

'I'm buying drinks now, aren't I?'

'Don't tell me, tell him.' She pointed an embellished finger at the window. 'Rottweiler alert.'

The afternoon had been overtaken by evening, but trade didn't appear to be slowing. Candles glowed on tables and the lighting from both the stage and inside the pub was just enough. Rob caught sight of Jack weaving between the benches and people lounging on the grass as he collected glasses. Jack wasn't close to their group yet, but Rob could see he was heading in their general direction.

Rob picked up his drinks. 'Thanks.'

The atmosphere of the afternoon had changed; he noticed it as soon as he stepped outside. The band had finished playing, and as though the audience had forgotten to readjust their voices, their volume had grown. At first he heard laughter, but shouting too. He'd taken a few more steps before he pinpointed the source of anger, and as he hurried towards his group from one direction, Jack cut across from the other.

It was Charlie and Gemma who were shouting. Ellie was on the ground in the same place as before, but Nicci was with her, holding onto her as she sobbed. Callum was nowhere to be seen.

And Rob didn't notice the laughter after that.

Charlie and Gemma were toe to toe. 'Because there's always a drama when you're involved,' Charlie yelled. 'You wind people up . . .'

'I haven't wound anyone up.' She waved her whole arm in Ellie's direction. 'I'm looking after her.'

Rob was at his sister's side at pretty much the same moment as Jack reached Charlie. 'You're all pissed,' Jack said. He looked disgusted as his gaze swept across the group and his attention settled on Rob.

It had taken Rob a few seconds to see what was going on; like Jack, he'd run his gaze from Charlie and Gemma, to Nicci and Ellie. And he knew at once that Jack's take on it would be different to his own.

Jack turned by a few degrees, enough to square up to Rob. He glowered, his eyes narrow.

'What's the problem, Jack?' Rob asked. 'It is a pub.'

'You all need to quieten down. Forget the alcohol until you've sobered up, and buy the rest of your drinks in the pub.'

'No need to be so uptight, man.' *Man*, Rob never used that word in that context, but he did it then to prove a point, to highlight how Jack's attitude was unnecessary. It was *their* weekend, their fun. Not Jack's. So what if there had been a little too much alcohol and emotion? 'You're making a scene, Jack.'

'I'm making a point. This is a pub with entertainment for customers, not a music festival.' Jack turned to his brother. 'I told you, you don't just rock up with beer and a tent. It's taking the piss.'

'There are bands on tomorrow and you knew we planned on being here both days.'

'This is my job, Charlie . . .'

'Exactly, you could have sorted it out for us.'

'I haven't been here long enough to ask for favours. And I need this job, so don't eff it up for me.' Even though he stopped short of swearing, he still lowered his voice for the 'eff' and it spat out in an angry whisper that would have carried right down to the river.

Rob glanced at the pub. 'Jack, leave it.'

'Butt out, Rob.' Jack's expression darkened further, and he carried on speaking to Charlie. 'It was going to be you and Nicci, and maybe Ellie. Instead there are six of you, pissed and hysterical. Sort yourselves out or go home.' Jack turned back towards the group and moved so that he stood between Charlie and the others. His voice softened, but Rob still caught his words to his brother. 'What the hell is wrong with Ellie?'

'I don't know. Ask Gemma, not me.' Charlie feigned amusement. 'Or are you still avoiding Gemma? Is this whole arsy attitude about you being uncomfortable because she's here?'

Rob could imagine that it was. Jack dating and then dumping his sister had soured everything between them. Whenever he thought about it, he still felt the anger rise. Jack had remained sheepish ever since, and now, even when Gemma was mentioned, Jack didn't glance in her direction.

No surprise then when he ignored Charlie's barb.

'I'm sorry Ellie's in a state.' Jack spoke slowly, with forced calmness. 'But Ellie needs to calm down or go home, Charlie. She's your responsibility. And Nicci's.' He spun around to face Rob. 'And you should know better. Get this under control, or you're all out of here.'

Jack strode away, and then the attention of the others fell on Rob. They stared at him as though he had the answer to everything. He didn't need this. It wasn't his fault that the day had become screwed. 'Fuck this,' he muttered, and wheeled away.

Chapter 6

'So, would you say your memory is clear, or not, Miss Hayward?'

'There's nothing wrong with my memory. I can't remember what I never witnessed in the first place.'

'So you can't identify the moment when the mood of your party deteriorated?'

'Ask Nicci. She saw what was happening. She caused this.'

Perhaps if Rob hadn't stormed off like that, then everything might have been different.

Or would it? When she looked back, it was impossible to see it any other way, although, from then to now, she had tried incessantly. Incessantly, to the point of obsession. And each time she reached the same conclusion; if nothing had happened that afternoon, then someone would still have died.

But she always kept that thought to herself.

The events of that day were a collage: big blue sky, dust between the blades of grass, the slow, dark water and, superimposed on all of that, were people. Those she knew. More she didn't.

She lay on that grass, eyes closed, the sun on her face, thoughts drifting. The afternoon would be dull. But less dull than coursework. She'd pushed her assessments to the back of her mind, but Callum kept trying to talk to her about cartilage and tendons. He was like having a wasp on the food. Finally, she opened her eyes just enough to see that he was already looking at her. There was a thin film of sweat on his pink skin.

She wondered how long he'd been watching her.

'Where are the others?'

He glanced around as if it was the first time he'd noticed that anyone was missing. 'Oh yeah, Nicci and Ellie went off for a bit. They're down there,' and he pointed over his left shoulder. 'Doesn't matter, does it?'

And, just because she didn't want to have any common ground with Callum at all, she replied, 'It does matter actually. We're all supposed to be hanging out together. We wouldn't be here at all if Ellie hadn't suggested it.'

'I suppose. But you never seem bothered about her.'

'No,' Gemma lied, 'I think she's great, it's Nicci who has the attitude.' She nudged him. 'Go and get them, Cal. We'll have a better time if we're together.'

She only said it to make him move away from her for a minute or two, to give the air around her the chance to refill with oxygen.

She remembered watching him walk towards the water. She remembered hoping that he'd stay down there, or, at worst, come back with the others and be a bit less intense.

He was harmless though; just annoying.

She lay back again and closed her eyes. She thought she might pretend to be asleep.

In the seconds before earthquakes and tsunamis, survivors have reported seeing animals running, driven by instinct. There had been a change in the vibrations of her world that afternoon, but Gemma hadn't heard them. Or she hadn't stopped to listen. Afterwards she recognised Ellie's hysteria, Jack's irritability, her brother's restlessness, Callum's discontent and the tension that jumped between them all for exactly what it was: the misfiring of energy. And she went with it, they all did.

And so it went: from unremarkable to frenetic, from a mundane day to a different life.

Ellie was upset. First she held it back, pretending she hadn't been crying and making opaque comments. And then suddenly her composure was gone, it disintegrated, and she was nothing but tears and garbled words.

And Jack and Charlie started to row, but somehow that grew and became Rob and Jack. Then Jack left, and it was Rob and everyone else, and he was leaving the pub where he claimed he'd never wanted to be.

And Callum was still being a fucking pain in the fucking arse and Gemma didn't want to pretend to be having fun either. And she didn't understand why Nicci was even there. Couldn't Nicci see she was being used by Ellie and Callum because she had a car? And then Charlie pitched in, and said he'd only wanted to be there for the music, and what was the point now?

What was the point?

By then they were all in a maelstrom that cut them off from everything but themselves.

The five of them in the car park. Propelling her towards Nicci's old Honda.

No one had decided they would leave; instead it was a kind of emotional gravity that pulled them in that direction. An unspoken acceptance that they were done with the place and needed to head back to Cambridge.

Gemma shrunk away and hung back long enough to try Rob's number. It connected, but with all the shouting, it took a few seconds to know whether she was talking to her brother or just his voicemail. 'What the hell, Rob?' she shouted when she heard him.

'What do you want?'

'Come back and get me.'

'No chance. I'm done, Gem. Find your own way home.'

'Rob?'

'What?'

'I don't want to go with them.'

But the line was already dead. She should have known; if Rob had decided to leave, then he wouldn't be coming back for her. She was about ten feet from the others and none of them was interested in her – except Callum, of course. In fact, they would leave her there if she let them.

All she wanted now was to get back home.

Charlie was already getting into the passenger seat of Nicci's car. Gemma pushed forward, climbing into the back, stupidly positioning herself between Callum's whinging and Ellie's panic. And then Nicci started the engine.

The doors had barely closed when Callum leant across her. 'Ellie, shut the fuck up,' he yelled, trying to grab at Ellie's hand.

Gemma pushed him aside, but Ellie was straight back at him. 'Get your hands off me, you fucking weirdo.'

Charlie shouted at Nicci, 'Just drive.' Then he turned to yell between the gap in the seats. 'That's enough, just keep it down.'

'I know what I saw,' Ellie screamed. Gemma didn't know what she meant. But she heard it correctly; they all heard the same. Charlie banged his hand on the side of Nicci's headrest to get Ellie's attention. 'Ellie. We'll go to the police, if that's what you want.'

For a moment his gaze met Gemma's and she saw *just humour her* in his expression.

Nicci slammed the car into gear and it lurched towards the exit. She over-revved in each gear before changing to the next. The engine strained and the back end of the car drifted on the first bend. Gemma reached out and steadied herself with both hands on the seat in front.

The next bend had a sharper curve, but Nicci drove at it, barely touching the brake. The car drifted again and all three of them on the back seat swung hard to the left. 'Slow down.' There was panic in Callum's voice. 'Fucking slow down.'

They hit the straight and it should have been okay. Gemma still hung on to the front seat and was catching every glimpse of anything picked out by their headlights on the unlit road. The sporadic road markings. The shiny fragments of gravel on the road surface. The flash of rabbit eyes on the verge.

The moment the line of the road slipped away from them.

She didn't remember screaming. She remembered silence and the slow, unavoidable impact of car on tree.

She felt herself fly forwards. Her weight multiplying, piling into herself until her outstretched arms found no more give in the seats in front. The force corkscrewed through her arms and she saw the bones break. Then she ricocheted back into her seat, her arms following, flapping grotesquely. Ulna and radius jutting out of the back of each forearm.

Yes, in the midst of it all she remembered the right fucking names.

And then they were still. And some were silent. Others, she was aware, were not.

She closed her eyes. 'Hey, Siri. Phone Jack Bailey. Mobile.'

Chapter 7

'Mr Bailey? Take your time. Just tell the court in your own words.'

I didn't see them leave, I know that.

I've thought about it since and I'm not sure the last time I caught sight of them. I'd walked away in anger. Maybe I looked back at them as I went back into the bar, but I don't think so. I was furious and I think I just shut off from all of them. And certainly the last time I spoke to Charlie was when I was down there arguing with him on the grass.

So I went indoors, and was busy behind the bar and clearing the tables. I made a point of not going back outside, or even looking through the windows.

I always keep my mobile in my pocket when I'm working. Just in case there's an emergency. There sometimes is on the river; people actually do fall in. Anyhow, it was on silent, but I could feel it vibrate.

It was a number I didn't recognise. Gemma obviously still had my number, but I'd deleted her from my contacts list a long time before.

I answered, but it was hard to hear exactly what was happening at the other end, partly because of the background noise in the pub, and partly because of the noise from the phone. But I immediately knew that it was something urgent. Someone was shouting, more like screaming really, clearly distressed. I ducked outside.

And I didn't recognise her voice, except I knew it was her if that makes sense.

What I mean is, as soon as she said her name – yelled her name – I knew it couldn't have been anybody else. 'We've crashed. Jack, we've crashed. We're in the lane. Help us.'

I ran to the edge of the car park. I couldn't see anything. 'Where are you?' I yelled.

She said, 'Not far, not far, we'd only just left.' And then she was screaming, not the way people scream in films. This was animalistic. Desperate. My instinct was just to run. I didn't know how far, but heading back into the pub would have been going in entirely the wrong direction. And I just wanted to reach them.

I put the phone on speaker, torch too, and I just ran. 'Have you called an ambulance?'

'They're coming.'

'You're sure?'

'Callum did it. Just get here, Jack.'

I didn't try to ask her anything else. I shouted her name. There were only sobs then.

I should have brought more help. Or grabbed a car. Or phoned 999 myself. But I didn't do any of those. Somehow I knew I'd reach them. That help was coming. And that none of the voices yelling out belonged to Charlie.

That road bends and there are hedgerows. I saw the red of a tail light, and in front of it, the white light of headlamps creating fragmented shadows in the trees. By then I could hear nothing above my breathing, and, for a moment, it seemed abandoned.

I remember wanting to stop running, telling myself to slow, but I rushed towards it in any case. In the last yards I saw a figure moving towards me. A spindly, ragged silhouette breaking cover from the dark side of the car. Callum. 'Don't,' he told me. I was still a few yards away, but mentally I was already there.

'Help's coming,' and he muttered it a couple of times more. He dropped into the verge just in front of me. I stumbled past, reaching out and using the back of Nicci's car to bring myself to a stop.

I yanked open the nearest door, the one behind the driver. Ellie's body sagged towards me. There was blood . . . so much blood. It had pooled in her lap. It looked black and glossy. And she was limp. I think I spoke to her, although I don't know why.

I think I spoke to all of them.

Gemma was murmuring, and somewhere behind me, Callum was calling out.

There was no movement from the front of the car. 'Charlie?' I think I said his name over and over. I had a clear view of him through the gap in the seats. He was slumped back against his headrest.

He didn't look dead. Not from that angle, but I knew. I knew, but wouldn't accept it. I couldn't just give up on him, could I?

I reached across Ellie and nudged his shoulder. I don't know why I did that. I ended up with her blood on my hands, on my clothes. And I could see branches protruding through his window, so I tried the driver's door instead of his.

Both airbags were hanging out. I thought Nicci was dead; she was collapsed against the steering wheel and I reached over her to Charlie.

The front passenger side was wrecked and I hadn't seen it properly until then. The metal around his legs was mangled and the lower part of the door was staved in. The dashboard had buckled inwards too. His right hand had landed in the gap between the seats, as though reaching for a lost coin or dropped phone, and the fingers of his left were tangled in the splintered tree, looking like they wanted to brush it all away.

His eyes were closed and that was the only blessing.

I heard Nicci groan, and, in the distance, the sound of sirens.

I didn't help her. At that moment I thought it was cruel that she was the driver and still alive, when Charlie was dead. I didn't help any of them.

I just leant over her and held Charlie until they pulled me away.

Chapter 8

'This case is nothing to do with intention. I am willing to accept that there was no malice. But there was recklessness. Miss Waldock was marginally over the drink-drive limit when first arrested, marginally under when tested again. She cannot therefore be charged with drink driving, but our limits are higher than those of many other nations and, as expert testimony has demonstrated, this may well have been sufficient to impair her judgement, leading to reckless speed and slower reaction times.

'The driver of any vehicle has responsibility for the safety and welfare of their passengers and other road users.

'Miss Waldock, the deaths of Charles Bailey and Eleanor Daniels are attributable to the decisions you made, and the actions you took on the evening of 28 March. You must take sole responsibility for the resulting consequences.'

Celia had sat through every day of the trial. Speaking to no one. Taking no notes.

She picked up her bag and left before the verdict. There would be no surprise, and she had no desire to hear the sobs. Of relief. Of anguish. And probably the gleeful baying that often followed. It usually came from those people two or three degrees separated from the victims, and smothered the silence for those who needed it the most.

She had known, to some extent, every person in that car: Callum and Ellie had been her lodgers, and she'd seen Gemma, Nicci and Charlie in Mawson Road since they'd been small children.

She'd known most of the families too.

Being there had been a self-imposed duty, a loyalty to the children who'd grown up playing in Mawson Road, and those who'd come there later.

She walked back. She neither rushed, nor stopped along the way. She unlocked her tidy house and made coffee. The place felt deserted and she knew it would take a while before it felt like home again. It had always been the case when she'd been in court for long periods of time.

The heating would be slow to stir and the TV would stay idle for a few more days. But this wasn't anything like those other times when the people in court had invoked no more feelings of attachment than characters in a play.

This time she stood at the front room window and finally allowed herself to cry.

PART TWO

Chapter 9

Three years later

Nicci's dad had driven to collect her from HMP Peterborough. He had insisted, or so her mother had said. Her parents had shared the front of the car, and she'd sat alone in the back. They'd driven through heavy rain, the kind which fills the windscreen faster than the wipers can move. She'd expected the world to look different, but her view of it was limited, and by the time they'd become snagged in traffic on the A14, she'd decided that not much had changed.

Her mum was first up the path and unlocked the front door. She'd invited him in, but reluctantly, then the three of them had positioned themselves like three corners of an equilateral triangle; as far apart from one another as one three-seater settee and an armchair allowed.

Nicci had managed to claim the end of the settee closest to the door. Her father was firmly of the view that, in powerplay situations, the weakest spoke first. Her mother preferred to avoid conversation with her ex-husband altogether. They had been sitting in this silence for the past five minutes, and Nicci had already decided that she was damned if she'd be the first to speak.

Inevitably it was her mother, and her first words were a lie. 'We're so pleased you're home.'

'Thanks.'

Her father would speak now.

'Have you considered what work you might apply for? We want to make sure that you reintegrate as soon as possible.'

She tilted her head to one side and pretended to think. She bit back the urge to ridicule the word *reintegrate.* Especially coming from him, the man who'd treated this home as though it was solely his asset, and them as unwanted tenants. 'Did you move back while I was away?'

'Of course not. Harriet and I . . .'

'Ah yes, the mistress.'

'My wife . . .'

'Whatever, Dad. I'm going to my room. Same place is it, Mum?'

'Yes, of course. Everything's there.'

Her father was on his feet before Nicci reached the door.

She glanced at him. 'I'll come down when you've gone.' Then offered a small smile to her mum. 'Love you.' And she did love her, but she wished the woman had more fight, more determination and a whole lot less subservience to a whole heap of things that didn't matter, including her dad.

He followed her as far as the foot of the stairs. 'You should be thankful. It would be far easier for me if I'd washed my hands of you.' Any second he'd start banging on about his precious career, his promotion to DCI despite her, and how she needed him if she wanted to get her life back on track.

He wouldn't follow her up, she was sure of that.

She'd expected to be awed by the big things like the open roads, the sight of shops or the smells of the city. Instead she noticed the mundane. She concentrated on the stairs; it had been a long time since she'd felt carpet underfoot. And, when she reached her bedroom door, her hand found the curve of the handle and still knew exactly how hard to push. She couldn't have predicted or even described these little things, had no idea they even existed in her memory. But here she was. Touching remnants of the person she used to be when the parts that really mattered – Charlie and Ellie and a future filled with possibilities – were all gone.

'Shit.'

She stepped away from her own room, and turned for the bathroom instead. She stripped, ramming every garment into the tiny bin which stood under the sink; she dumped this out onto the landing then locked the bathroom door. She rummaged through both cupboards, the one on the wall and the larger one under the sink. If she'd had scissors, she would have chopped her hair off too, but her mum had been smart enough to remove every sharp or dangerous object.

In the end she lay in the bath as it filled, letting the taps run until the water lapped the overflow. She sank deep into the water; eyes closed, ears submerged.

She was glad to be out, but she doubted she was free.

Chapter 10

The nearest supermarket was a two-minute walk, but Celia still preferred to go in daylight unless there was an emergency. Running out of coffee counted. Even at 9 p.m. There was nothing else she needed, but she still made an efficient trawl of the aisles, just in case.

The shop was pretty much deserted, but as she passed the magazine racks was vaguely aware of walking around a figure who was browsing the latest editions. This only registered when, minutes later, after Celia had finished her raid on the instant-coffee jars, she approached the checkout. The magazines near the entrance were in clear view, and Celia realised that the same figure stood in precisely the same position. She could see that the titles were the usual mix of celebrity angst and real-life tragedy; nothing all that attention-grabbing in her opinion.

'Madam?' The assistant beckoned her over.

She placed the coffee down and took her purse from her bag, but she wasn't too distracted to miss the figure turning in her direction. And when she looked across the shop she saw Nicci for the first time since her release.

She'd always been slim, but now she was gaunt, her eyes looked too big and her cheeks too pale. She recognised Celia and froze for a second before turning away again. Celia wished she'd been quicker to smile. All Nicci would have seen was Celia's curious expression, and the last thing she'd wanted to do was to make Nicci feel like a freak.

'Nicci?'

Nicci had turned back to the magazines, but, as soon as she heard her name, she headed for the door.

'Nicci, please wait.'

Celia abandoned her shopping on the counter, and rushed onto the street. She expected to see Nicci hurrying away, but instead she was waiting on the pavement. 'What do you want?'

'To ask how you are.'

'I saw you in court. You were there every day. Were you covering it for a newspaper? Because I tried to find what you wrote, but I never could.'

Celia shook her head. 'I don't write news stories any more.'

'Why?'

'It was time to change direction . . .'

'So you were there for what? Entertainment?' Nicci looked frail, but her voice was strong and sharp with anger.

'No. I knew you all in one way or another.' Celia hesitated. 'I felt as though I needed to be there.'

Nicci's expression hardened. 'I've seen plenty of people like you. Showing concern, reaching out to help, but really they're only doing it because it makes them feel good. Do you feel good right now, Celia?' She took a few steps backwards, keeping her defiant gaze locked on Celia's.

'Can we sit somewhere and talk?' Celia took a couple of steps towards Nicci.

'No.' She gave a small, disgusted smile, then turned and ran.

Celia continued to stand in the same spot for several minutes more.

She'd been a reporter for twenty-two years. Mostly she'd covered crime cases, murder and rape trials, fraud cases, modern slavery and child exploitation. She'd spent countless hours with investigators and criminals, and many more with the victims.

It didn't matter which side of the law they were on. Some broke down, some didn't.

Nicci had struggled in court. She'd been isolated, filled with fear and intimidated by the process and formality of the courtroom, but she had also managed to keep her emotions in check. Celia had assumed that prison would have been the hardest part, and perhaps it had been, but Nicci looked as though she still had a long way to fall.

Chapter 11

Cambridge's Central Library opened at 9.30 a.m., and Nicci had been waiting since nine. That half an hour shouldn't have been a big deal, except Nicci had been awake since a few minutes after four. She'd slept for less than three hours, a pattern that had been consistent in the three weeks since her release.

Every morning she woke with her heart racing and a lurching feeling in her stomach, and then lay awake until dawn, dog tired and praying for a few more unconscious hours to blank out her agitated thoughts. It was reading that helped her fall asleep in the evenings, but those books were fiction, and never held her attention first thing in the morning.

This morning she'd had a few clear-headed moments thinking it through, and the answer, she realised suddenly, was that she read at the end of the day, to do just that, to end the day. Fiction was fine then, but when she woke, all her worries were about the future, and for that she needed enlightenment, not distraction. And that realisation was followed by another; that the course she'd been studying, crime and investigation, was still unfinished business.

She showered for the first time in almost a week, and left the house at eight. She knew it was too early, but it was also pointless to wait at home. She took a circuitous route, overtaking traffic-bound commuters. Passing cafés already open and serving hot food. And catching smells that seemed to alternate between croissants and fumes.

She was far better at walking than waiting, and the half hour outside the library doors seemed to drag out for as long as all the hours that had gone before. Finally the doors opened and she was let in by a sallow-faced man in his forties. He didn't smile, but neither did she.

'I'm looking for your forensics books?'

'Upstairs, in science.' They were standing at the entrance and, from there, there was only upstairs.

'Thanks.' Judging by his flat-eyed response, she guessed she'd sounded suitably sarcastic.

They had a reasonable selection, not as comprehensive as the university's, of course, but she found two books she recognised from her first-year reading list, *Crime Scene Management: Scene Specific Methods* and *Crime Scene Management and Evidence Recovery.* She took them to the nearest table and opened each to the contents page. She wasn't searching for any particular chapter, but topics jumped out at her: fingerprints, exhibit handling, blood-pattern analysis. Her cohort would have graduated by now, even allowing for resits.

An hour later she took the two books to the desk. She showed them to the librarian, a thin woman who looked a few years older than Nicci. She gave Nicci a bland smile. 'Do you have your library card?'

'I need to apply for one. Do you have a form please?'

'Of course. You'll need ID.'

Everything Nicci had was in her pocket. She fished around and pulled out her debit card.

The bland smile didn't waver. 'Something with your address? Driver's licence or passport?'

Nicci shook her head. 'No.'

'Your student ID, if it has a photo?'

'I'm not a student.'

'I see.'

Perhaps it was Nicci's imagination, but the smile seemed to tighten.

Nicci held up the debit card. 'This has my name on it.'

'No photo or address though.'

'Yes, but I can draw money out, that would prove it's my card, or I could phone the bank, that would be enough, wouldn't it?' Nicci held the books more firmly, she wasn't prepared to go home without them.

'I'm sorry. Those are the rules. We are open until six today.'

Nicci didn't own a passport, no bills were in her name and her driver's licence was long gone. 'What about a birth certificate?'

The woman blinked slowly. 'I'd need to check.'

Nicci took a breath. Perhaps it was going to work out after all. 'And then, if that's okay, could you keep these for me until I get back?'

The smile returned. 'It will take about ten days. The card will be posted to your home address.'

Nicci shook her head. 'But I need these today.'

'That's not possible.'

'There must be a way. You could sort this out if you really wanted to.'

'You can read them here. Now, do you mind if I serve someone else?'

'I do actually. I just want to borrow these books.' It was all Nicci could do not to shout. 'How can it be so complicated?'

Someone tapped Nicci's arm just then. 'Miss?' The sallow-faced man had appeared at her side; he positioned himself so that she needed to turn away from the counter and the waiting customer in order to face him. 'I'd rather not have to ask you to leave. It would mean a ban.' There was a sliver of sympathy in his tone, just enough to keep her on the right side of her temper. 'Bring in what ID you can and I'll try to sort it out. And, in the meantime, you can spend as much time as you like here.' He nodded as he spoke, encouraging her to agree.

She closed her eyes; swallow, then breathe.

Then she looked at him again. He had waited, still and patient, with no hint of a smile. 'Okay,' she said.

She took the books back to the table and read until closing time, then she returned them to the shelves, but deliberately placed them back in the wrong section, determined that no one else could take them before she returned, although she intended to be back at opening time.

As she walked home she tried to remember everything she'd revised on fingerprints; she'd read that chapter twice over, and, as she strode out, she recited the different types of loops, arches and whorls, then the types of second- and third-level detail. She'd once known these facts by heart, and they were still familiar, but not in the second nature way that they'd once been.

Her mood shifted again as she crossed Parker's Piece and saw the familiar lights at the junction of East Road and Mill Road; she was close to home. She slowed. It was evening now and the spectre of another night of broken sleep began to loom.

Suddenly, she didn't want to go back home.

But she had no option, apart from whatever some loose change and about £20 on her debit card could buy. But, when she thought about it, that might be enough.

She stopped in at the supermarket, hoping to avoid anyone she recognised. The shop was busy, but with people too fraught with the tail end of their own days to even look in her direction.

She bought a 70 cl bottle of own-brand vodka, and opened it as soon as she was outside. She hated neat spirits, so she swallowed the first couple of mouthfuls quickly, knowing that, by the third or fourth, the taste wouldn't matter any more.

She walked as far as the nearest closed shop and sat in the doorway, drinking more slowly now. There was no hurry to go home. No hurry to go anywhere.

Chapter 12

Celia's office faced the front of the house, and her first-floor sitting room lay directly above it. From both vantage points she could see the day-to-day life of Mawson Road. It had a rhythm. And unexpected activity would disrupt it, or make it settle into a new beat. To her mind, places were creatures of habit, just like people.

Night time had a rhythm of its own. Sometimes students might come back late, their voices loud and unfiltered. Or a taxi might stop, its engine idling while the occupants paid and left. A lone drunk at midnight was unusual. This one was across the street, standing on the pavement, bent over with her hands on her knees.

'No, no, no.' Celia moved quickly, pulling a jumper over her head and grabbing her house keys. She always left a pair of loafers by the front door, just in case she needed to slip on some shoes to go outside. But as fast as she was, Nicci had gone by the time Celia had left the house. 'Dammit girl.' It was aimed at herself more than at Nicci.

She watched more closely after that, and over the next couple of weeks she saw a pattern begin to form. Nicci walked in the direction of Mill Road in the morning, and back home in the evening. She always moved quickly; head down, hood up. After the first few days she began carrying a red bag, it was flat and rectangular, like a thinner version of a messenger bag. She wore it across her body, but always clutched it across her chest, rather than letting it flap around. It didn't look heavy, but Celia could also tell that it wasn't empty.

Each evening Nicci would pass Celia's window, and then return soon afterwards, dressed the same, minus the bag.

In the mornings Celia's last view of Nicci would be as she turned left onto Mill Road, towards the city centre perhaps. In the evenings she turned in the opposite direction and it was harder to guess where she may be headed, but Celia knew that, at some point between 11 p.m. and 1 a.m., Nicci would find her way back home through a haze of what might be either drink or drugs. And Celia would tell herself that it wasn't her problem, but still keep an eye on the street until she'd seen Nicci safely back past her window.

Celia hadn't tried to intercept Nicci since that first night. She told herself that she'd been rash to try to intervene. That it wasn't her concern. That the connection she felt to that group of teenagers, that accident, that court case . . . wasn't as personal as she'd let it become. But she still found it hard to fall asleep each night.

Nicci was vulnerable and also on probation.

This thought played on Celia's mind. She knew the family a little, and she'd watched Nicci's parents when they'd come to court; most days they'd stayed away. She doubted that Nicci's mother would be out looking for her.

Celia continued to tell herself that none of it was her problem, until the night when she couldn't sleep at all.

Enough was enough.

Nicci left in the morning, then returned in the evening as usual.

Celia was already dressed in outdoor clothes and ready to leave the house by then. She knew there would probably be a minimum of a half hour wait until Nicci walked back again, but she stood at her window and didn't divert her gaze from the direction of Nicci's home.

Thirty-five minutes later and Celia was out of the house and following at a discreet distance. Nicci turned right onto Mill Road, and out of sight. Celia realised that she would have been better off waiting in one of the shops around the corner. She quickened her pace, wondering whether she had already lost the chance to follow, but, as the length of Mill Road came into view, there was Nicci, only about fifty yards ahead.

The traffic remained busy, but on the pavements there were few pedestrians to hide behind. Nicci crossed the road then almost immediately turned left, down Gwydir Street. Celia followed and the scattering of other people was immediately gone. She didn't care, she was committed now, and just hoped that weeks of following the same daily pattern had left Nicci blind to the idea that someone might tail her.

Hot Numbers Café and a couple of antique shops stood at the start of the road; they were all closed for the evening. Ahead were two pubs, the Alex and the Cambridge Blue. If Nicci was not headed for either of those, then her destination was more likely to be a private house somewhere in the warren of streets up ahead.

Nicci walked noticeably faster than Celia; she had more youth and less weight on her side. Here, the street was narrow, packed with houses on one side of the footpath and parked cars on the other; visibility was poor and it wasn't about to improve.

There were no sharp bends, but the road curved gently to the left. Nicci hadn't looked back once, but suddenly she bolted. Celia stepped into the road, trying to get a better view. But Nicci had gone.

Chapter 13

Most days the library closed at six, and Nicci was home between quarter and half-past. Before prison she had shunned routine; she'd been a reliable student, but, beyond that, had hated the idea of being constrained by a diary and reminders popping up on her phone. Now the routine of spending the day at the library, and that was all day, every day, had allowed her to find a little peace.

A peace which lasted until she approached home, when a feeling of unease would begin to stir in her stomach. The feeling swelled if she saw her father's car parked outside, but he'd already visited once this week. That would probably be enough for him.

She slid the key into the lock, counted to three, then turned it and opened the door. 'Hi, Mum.'

She closed the door behind her, then stood still and waited. She didn't know where in the house her mum might be, but being called back to the hallway to explain herself was almost inevitable. This was a different kind of routine.

'You're back then?' This time the voice came from the top of the stairs.

Nicci looked up. 'Same as yesterday, Mum.'

'The library again? Do you expect me to believe that you spend whole days in that place? Doing what?'

'I told you.'

'You didn't tell me anything.' Her mum began descending the stairs. 'You said "reading and making notes". That's meaningless, Nic. Meaningless. Why do you hide it from me?'

'I'm sorry.' Nicci held her bag a little more tightly.

'I've been here all day. On my own. Does that even occur to you?' She stopped on the bottom step and pointed towards Nicci's shoulder bag. 'Why don't you want me to know what's in there?'

'It's private, but it's nothing bad. I just want to do some things in my own time. It's nothing to hurt you, Mum. We've already talked about this; I just need to find my feet.'

'It's always about you, about what you need and how you're feeling. Between you and your father, I feel as though I'm invisible. So don't try to manipulate me into doing more than I already am.' She pressed her lips together and glared at Nicci for a full minute.

'I'm not, Mum. And you don't need to stay home all the time.' There wasn't much else Nicci could add; there would be no right answer. 'It's staying home all the time that gets you down.'

There was a moment when she thought she saw a softening of her mum's expression, but she didn't relax. Nicci had been fooled like that before. And then, it was gone again. Her mum pointed at the bag. 'I looked, you know, when you were asleep. I found your other notebook too.'

'Why, Mum?' Nicci managed to speak as a lump formed in her throat.

'I need to know what you're up to. You should get real, Nicci. You have a record now and you're a stupid girl if you think there's any chance you can follow in your father's footsteps.'

Nicci shook her head, then pushed past her mum to head up the stairs. She had never had any intention of joining the police, or following her father anywhere, but she knew she couldn't risk arguing any more. Not when the words would come out scrambled with tears and denial and frustration.

'And I suppose you're going straight out again? I could tell your parole officer, you know. Or your father. And then where would you be?'

Nicci slammed her bedroom door and flung her bag onto the bed. She grabbed a warmer jumper from her wardrobe and pulled it on. She scraped her hair into a ponytail, and only stopped long enough to rub her face with her hands before shoving four £5 notes into the pocket of her jeans, and heading back out.

She was so focused on leaving the house behind that it took her until Gwydir Street to check whether she was being followed. There was no way to do it without being seen, so she waited until the curve in the road and then sprinted forward a few yards, ducking into a gap between two terraces of houses. She dropped to the ground and peeked out through a gap between the downpipe and the wall.

Celia.

Shit. The woman was less than thirty seconds away.

Nicci moved towards the back of the houses. She couldn't afford to be caught trespassing, but one of the properties had a low side gate, and Nicci climbed it easily. The daylight was fading rapidly, but it was still easy to see the rear fence, and she knew what lay beyond it. There was a large composting bin in the furthest corner. She ran towards it, scrambling onto it and over the fence before either her nerve or the wood panel had the chance to give way.

She heard a door open behind her, and a shout of 'Hey', but she was already long gone.

Nicci had known that Mill Road Cemetery lay on the other side of the fence before she scaled it. Luck was on her side, or so it had seemed at that moment. The cemetery had been her destination when she left home, just as it had been most evenings recently. It was just that she'd planned to use one of the official entrances.

She'd met some people.

It was no more or less than that.

They hung out around one of the benches. Talking shit, drinking cheap cider, smoking weed. Even without the alcohol and marijuana their conversations wouldn't have been memorable. And that was exactly the point.

She'd met Rolo and Spanner first. They were older than her by at least twenty years, or she hoped they were. They both had the same look: broken veins, leathered skin and ink bleeding out from their tattoos.

Rolo was all about *would have* and *could have*, about missed opportunities and the unkindness of circumstance. Everyone and everything had conspired against him; he had told her this in a variety of ways, always with a can in one hand and a reefer in the other. Spanner spoke less, and most of what she knew about him could be summed up by his visible tattoos; a lion on a crown on the inside of one forearm, and an old-school rose with the names, 'Michael, Danni and Nathan' on the other. 'I had them done for love,' he told her, 'but a tattoo becomes a ghost you can't escape.'

'Which one?' she asked.

He'd smiled ruefully. 'All of them.'

That had been yesterday's conversation, and today she wanted to ask him more. But neither Rolo nor Spanner was at the bench, just three people she thought she'd never seen before: a stocky woman and two older men. They all watched her through the dusk.

The shorter of the men spoke. 'You're back then?' He was lightly built and had the trace of an Irish accent. 'Looking for Rolo?'

'Or Spanner?'

'They've gone for some cans.'

That made sense. But Nicci stopped a few feet away. The Irishman and the woman both looked like drinkers, not the binge-drinking, volatile kind, but the type who mostly remained addled and slow. It was the other man, tall and wiry, who made her uneasy. She refused to look away, and smiled a little as she spoke. 'That's cool. I'll catch them in a bit then.'

His gaze was sharp, and caught hers before she had a chance to turn around. He pointed at the backs of the houses, at the fence she'd just scaled. 'Do you live over there? They're big-money houses.'

She shook her head. 'I took a short cut.'

'What do you want?' She saw his expression change; she was the new kid, about to be bullied to show the others the pecking order. There was nothing in particular that he wanted from her, and any answer she gave or anything she did would be an opening for him to bring her down. 'Nothing,' she shrugged, 'I just came to hang out. Buy a joint maybe.'

'You've got money?' He took a couple of steps closer.

She knew the score, and if there was a time to run, this was it. There was still enough light for her to find her way. And she was fast. Maybe he was faster, but she was agile and sober. 'Not for you.'

'Why would you say that, eh?' He strode towards her.

She stood her ground. 'I'm not here to see you, that's all.' The other two were further back, and the Irishman was shaking his head at Nicci. 'Run,' he mouthed, and flapped a hand as if shooing away a pigeon, or a cat.

She looked back into the tall guy's face. He swung at her, she tried to push his fist away, and her reflexes were enough to lessen the impact. She winced though, and cursed herself for letting him see the pain. 'Fuck you,' she yelled as another blow landed. Her words sounded muffled and she knew she was going down. She hit the ground and curled up in a single move. His first kick was clumsy, catching her in the shinbone.

There wasn't a second.

'Stop.' The voice was firm.

Nicci stayed tightly balled, but she opened her eyes enough to see Celia marching through the grass, her phone held in her outstretched hand, its light on them. 'I've found her,' Celia spoke to the phone, her voice projecting. 'I'm near the centre.'

He moved towards Celia.

She slowed a little. 'I am live streaming this. It will be evidence.'

‘Put it down, bitch.’

‘The police are on their way.’ And, on cue, a siren wailed from the direction of Mill Road.

It was enough for the woman and the Irishman to move. They turned towards the centre of the cemetery and loped away. The woman glanced back. ‘C’mon, Dave.’

His head swivelled from Celia, to his companions, to Nicci, then back to Celia at the moment he started to run at her. Nicci scrambled to her feet in time to see him knock Celia to the ground. Nicci rushed at him, determined to ram him before he could kick out. But Celia fell and he just kept running, the light from the phone flashing as he carried on across the graveyard.

Chapter 14

Nicci knelt beside her. 'Are you okay?'

'We need to go. There was no live streaming.'

'I don't suppose he knew what that was anyway.' Nicci helped Celia to her feet. 'And the police?'

'There are always sirens on Mill Road, but that one was particularly well timed.'

'What about your phone?'

'It doesn't matter.' Celia brushed herself down, and they walked side by side towards the Gwydir Street exit. 'You are on probation?'

'Yes.'

'So, how are you out at all hours without restriction?'

Nicci shrugged. She had no desire for this conversation, but no fight left either. 'It's fine as long as Mum doesn't report me for being absent . . .'

'Is that a perk of being a policeman's daughter?'

'No, the perk of an understaffed probation service.'

The exit was just a narrow gate that took them through to a few industrial units. The car park was lit by a single street lamp. Celia grabbed Nicci by the shoulders and turned her towards the light. 'You're going to bruise.'

Nicci didn't need Celia to tell her: her face and her leg were both throbbing.

'I can take you to Addenbrooke's?'

'No.'

'You're shivering. It's what happens when the adrenaline subsides, did you know that?' Celia led her by the elbow and began walking towards the houses. Nicci pulled her arm free, but kept pace anyway.

'What do you want from me?'

'I want you to walk me home. I'm elderly and could get mugged. And I want you to listen to me, just from here to my house. Will you do that?'

'You're not elderly, that's crap. But okay.'

'When you were a child, and you may not remember this, I was the only black woman in the street, and people would say, "you know, the Jamaican lady". I've been here since I was a baby by the way. And then later they would say, "you know, that reporter woman". I love my home, but I always know that I'm a little bit of an outsider in some people's eyes.'

Nicci stole a glance at Celia. Celia's voice was calm, almost melodic, and Nicci realised that she wanted her to keep talking.

'It's good to be an outsider, Nicci, but not so far outside that it hurts. Do you know what I mean by that?'

Nicci knew exactly, but she kept her eyes on the pavement in front of them and didn't reply.

'And if you stand on the outside, not by much, mind you, so you're just at the edge, you can see much more clearly.' She took off her jacket and swung it around Nicci's shoulders. 'Tell me about home. You live with your mother?'

'I make her miserable.'

They'd walked almost to the top of Gwydir Street. Once they reached the junction, Celia would be as good as home. Nicci hesitated; she wasn't ready for that yet. She turned to Celia and studied the older woman's expression: looking for the angle, the dishonest shift in her eyes or the undercurrent she couldn't quite hide. 'Thanks for coming for me.'

'I could see you were troubled. Standing by when someone is in distress is the worst thing.'

'Good men who do nothing?'

'Yes, that quote. I have a few favourites.' Celia sat on the low windowsill of the closed café. 'So how do you make her miserable?'

'My mum? Is this the reporter asking?'

'It is the nosy neighbour, that's all.'

'Mum used to boast about our perfect family, then Dad had a fling with a woman at Parkside. Then he married her.' Nicci pursed her lips as though there was something sour in her mouth. She doubted that the bad taste would ever subside. 'It still makes me angry, but he's too thick-skinned to realise.'

'And your mum?'

'She used to say that she kept it together for me. Then I got banged up, and she had all that shame to deal with. She visited me once in prison. Just wrote after that.' Nicci thought for a moment. 'I love her, but she's so hurt. She's just spikes. You tell me, where's the future in anything after what I did?'

When they reached Celia's house, she patted the windowsill, inviting Nicci to sit. This time she didn't pull away. 'Charlie and Ellie were your friends. You loved them, I could see that. So I don't believe you are a bad person, Nicci. You were responsible for something terrible, but is that supposed to make the rest of your life impossible?'

'It does.'

'I don't think so.'

'How? Nothing I do will ever . . .' Nicci's words faltered. Just next door was the shadow of the house where Ellie had lived. 'I can't . . .'

'You can't settle the debt?' Somehow Celia seemed able to read her.

'It's too big,' Nicci said quietly.

PART THREE

Chapter 15

Now

Jack Bailey stood just a few feet inside the door, reluctant to step in further.

The estate agent had hurried in first. They'd met on the pavement outside and he'd moved quickly from the start. He was still fidgeting now and talked continuously; perhaps he was nervous, perhaps he knew what was coming.

More likely he was oblivious – too wrapped up in his spiel and the rush to close another deal to have any sensitivity.

Jack pushed himself into the centre of the room, blocking out the other man's voice until it became nothing more than static. He turned slowly through a full 360 degrees. Grubbiness hung in the air and nothing looked the same. Beneath it all, he had no doubt that there would be layers he could recognise. But, right now, it didn't feel like his former home. There was only familiarity in subtle ways such as the angle of the light through the window and the barely perceptible slope in the floor; there was nothing for Jack here, just a job to be done.

He took a moment to stare at the estate agent.

Richard Simons.

He was skinny and had talked incessantly from the moment they'd met, exuding restless energy. It already felt exhausting to share the room with him, but he'd finally fallen silent and Jack realised that Simons was probably waiting for a reply to some question. Simons stared expectantly at Jack, his small, dark eyes flickering slightly and a wary smile forming on his lips. 'Is something wrong?'

Jack rubbed his palm across the arm of the sofa. 'Grease.' He pointed to the coffee table and the 'O's left by coffee mugs. 'When was the last time you came here?' He didn't need to walk through to the kitchen to see that a poor attempt at tidying had included stacking the discarded pizza boxes in a pile by the door.

Simons remained unabashed. 'It's been a while; we've been very successful at letting it out so there hasn't been any need for us to constantly visit.' He spoke with glib confidence, as though he expected Jack to accept the answer and happily move on.

'You told me that it was ready for viewings. We have been paying for a service; the property was in your care, maintenance was in your care. Every time tenants have changed, you have billed us for a professional clean.'

Simons fluttered his hand in the direction of the pizza boxes. 'It is in the diary for next week.'

'Well, the last tenants moved out a month ago and I seriously doubt that all of this mess has occurred in one tenancy.'

'Your father has been quite happy; I've spoken to him on the phone plenty of times.'

'But he hasn't visited, has he? He's taken your word for it on every occasion . . .'

'And we've successfully let it each time too.'

Jack stiffened and stepped closer to him. 'You will find, in your files, a complete inventory of everything that was in this house when you took on responsibility for its rental. My father wasn't involved in that, but I was, and in there you will also find photographs. Everything was documented and my father has paid for it to be maintained to that standard throughout.'

'You have to consider the wear and tear.'

'I know about wear and tear. Go through your records, Mr Simons. Every time we have been asked to repair or replace anything, we've agreed. I should have checked on you. I haven't had my eye on the ball, but that doesn't mean you can rip my dad off like this.'

'Hey! Nobody is ripping anybody off. What you don't appreciate is how hard it is to rent this place.'

'What, right near the centre of town? Students around every corner?'

'Yes, but the ones who are happy to live here . . .' His voice trailed off.

Suddenly Jack knew where this was going. He didn't jump into the silence, he just waited.

'We've been marketing this property for almost four years and, well, I haven't been here that whole time but let's just say it has a history.' Simons's energy was focused now, he was determined, like a small, yapping terrier. 'Yes, we rent it out every time, but they always find out. They ask about the owners, or they'll suddenly want to leave, ask to switch to somewhere else. There are few students who want to stay in a house connected with tragedy. They think it's a bad sign that there was a suspicious death.'

He stopped abruptly, no doubt realising that he'd crossed the line into urban myth, that his storytelling had found the wrong audience; someone who actually knew the case. He looked as if he was becoming nauseous, his unsteady gaze darting a couple of times towards the door and once towards the window. He wouldn't be going out either way in a hurry.

'There was no suspicious death in this house,' Jack told him coldly.

Simons looked cornered. His patter gone.

'Tell me,' Jack growled, 'what do you think actually happened here?'

Simons shrugged, gripped the fingers of one hand with the fingers of the other and then pulled them apart in a nervous, jerky motion.

'How old are you, Richard?'

'Twenty-one.'

'So, you're talking about a time when you were probably still at school? What do you do, Richard? Show them around and spread a nice little urban myth about the students who lived in this road. Who died. Who survived. How the road is still tainted with it.'

Simons shook his head with too much vigour.

'Perhaps you like to exaggerate, make it sound more dramatic, try to weed out which students would leave after a month and which students would relish the idea of living in a house with Charlie's ghost. Is that what you do?'

'Of course not.'

'You know I was there that night, don't you?'

Simons nodded, a thin line of sweat appearing at the top of his cheekbones.

Jack moved closer. He could feel his anger rising and at that moment he didn't care that the estate agent felt intimidated. 'You've taken money from my dad for jobs you clearly haven't done. You haven't cared about who you've put in here, or how they've looked after the place and, worse than that, you've been perpetuating a story about my family's tragedy like it's a cheap bit of entertainment. But it isn't. He was my brother.'

'We kept it occupied.'

Jack glowered at him.

Simons showed Jack his palms. 'I'm sorry, I get it. It's personal for you. It felt like an old story. I didn't mean anything.'

'Four years. That's not old.'

'Everything I've ever said was in the public domain. Students move in here and find out about it, and of course they want to know the story behind it. I think they're better hearing it from me than hearing it second hand from one of the neighbours. It's notorious.'

'The neighbours don't owe us anything. You, however, are employed to look after our best interests.'

Simons knew he was on thin ice but scratched around anyway.

Jack stepped away, pushing his frustration back out of sight. Simons wasn't a kid, but he was barely an adult either; he wasn't the person who deserved the brunt of the anger that had been rising in Jack for the last couple of months. When Jack spoke again his voice was quieter. 'Let's look at the rest of the house. I will list everything that is not as it should be and then give you a copy of that list.'

Jack led them through to the kitchen, flicking open and slamming shut each cupboard door in turn.

Jack pulled open the fridge, took the milk carton from inside the door and tipped the contents into the sink. The congealed milk fell from the carton in heavy lumps. He used his phone to make notes as they toured the rest of the house. He took photographs of everything that had been neglected and tried to ignore the fragments of memories that sprung up to chip into his concentration.

The house was not huge: three bedrooms and a bathroom upstairs, two reception rooms and a kitchen down? By the time they had made their way back to the front door, Simons had found the ability to apologise.

Jack found it more unpleasant than the initial refusal to accept any responsibility.

'I'm on it. We will make sure that we take care of everything,' Simons said, 'and I realise that we have made mistakes, that there have been oversights, so I'm sorry.'

Jack tilted his head to one side, his expression set into something that could be mistaken for a smile. Simons's apology had been forced and insincere; the minimum required to allow him to move on with his day. 'You have two weeks to rectify these problems.'

Simons nodded again. 'Two weeks,' he murmured. 'That will be fine, plenty of time for us to market it again before the next batch of students arrive. And you're right, it's old news, it shouldn't affect things now.'

Old news.

The clumsy paraphrasing lit a flame in Jack's gut. Four years; it didn't seem so long ago. There had been events between then and now that had drifted away from him, but that night had hardly faded. Four years was nothing when your family was living with it. He said nothing, he didn't need to. Simons could see it in the way Jack's jaw clenched, the way his shoulders tensed.

Simons shook Jack's hand. His fingers were cold, and he pulled his hand away too quickly, too relieved. 'We'll keep you posted. We'll let you know as things are rectified and as soon as it's ready. Don't worry, we'll look to get better tenants this time.'

Jack had intended this visit to be brief, a favour to his dad who had taken the out-of-sight, out-of-mind approach to being a landlord. Neither of them wanted to be here, but, for Jack, it suddenly made sense. He smiled slowly. 'I'll know when things are sorted because I will be here. And no, don't look for other tenants, I'm staying.'

Chapter 16

The last time Jack had seen Frank Bennett he'd been sitting in the bar of the Mitre pub, beer-splashed plans spread across the table. His offer to take Jack out to mark the end of six weeks of summer work at his architect's office had amounted to a bowl of chips, a can of Coke and zero conversation until the hour was almost done. Frank had thanked him then, offered his greasy hand to shake and wished Jack luck.

Neither had expected to see the other again and when Jack had phoned it had taken Frank several minutes before he seemed to remember. And now Jack stood outside the same pub almost seven years later. The Mitre's exterior had been given a facelift since then: the gold lettering remained but the frontage had been repainted in black to replace the previous shade, which had fallen somewhere between caramel and pale orange.

It now looked as though it was embracing its Victorian heritage.

The interior had been refurbished too, but Frank sat in the same spot with what could have been the same A1 plan spread out in front of him. Had he, Jack wondered, remained exactly here, occasionally lifting his pint or his paperwork as the builders had worked around him? Frank glanced up at Jack, but it was a couple more seconds before recognition showed in his expression. 'Blimey, you're not so scrawny now, are you?'

Jack managed a smile and they shook hands.

'When was that, son, four years ago? Five?' He slid the plan away to one side and gestured towards the vacant bar stool. 'That would make you . . . what, twenty-seven? Twenty-eight?'

His memory and his arithmetic were both out of whack.

'Almost eight years. I'm thirty-one.'

Frank puffed out his florid cheeks. 'Shit. Thirty-one? I'm closer to death than I thought I was. What brings you back here?'

'It's temporary while I decide what I'm doing next.'

Frank had lifted his pint but paused to shake his head before taking a sip. He lowered the glass by a couple of inches. 'Fucked up your marriage, did you?' He drank more deeply the second time and then placed the glass in the very centre of a circular beer mat. 'Shame that. I heard you had a kid too.'

I did, Jack thought but said nothing. *Maya*. Her name was also hard to say out loud. He still thought that it was a beautiful name, and he had chosen it after all. But the sound of it wouldn't be met by her chattering reply. He hated the void.

He pressed his lips together and waited for the feeling to pass; he reminded himself of the reason for the meeting. He drew a slow breath and then released it. He'd forgotten how it was with Frank; tactless comments fuelled by a talent for insight.

'But you qualified in the end, Jack, and no one can take that from you.' Frank poked his finger at the plan. 'Because being an architect is the career of a lifetime, right?'

'Yeah, right,' Jack echoed.

Frank looked at him expectantly. 'What is it you want from me?'

'Work, actually.'

'Really?' Frank chuckled. 'You know I don't do corporate headquarters and boutique hotels?'

Jack was surprised. 'I'm not looking for that kind of work. Not now.'

Frank leant forwards. 'Every year since you I have employed

a student for a few weeks in the summer; some go on to do well, others . . .' He shrugged. 'I can usually tell. But not with you, so I kept an eye open. You were doing too well to come back here. Especially to me.'

Frank lived alone for good reason and spotting other people's misfortune was a daily pleasure. Jack wasn't planning to divulge anything. 'If you're busy enough I'd like to take a few jobs off your hands. I'm just looking for some freelance work.'

'Hmm.'

'I don't mind what.'

'Really?' Frank reached down to his briefcase and retrieved three cardboard folders, each thin enough to appear empty. 'Two loft conversions and an extension to stretch out over an existing garage. Architecturally simple, but with each of them, what the customer wants isn't going to get through planning.'

'So, they need a mediator, not an architect?'

'Always the same. So, do you want them, or not?'

Jack took the files and shook Frank's greasy hand.

Chapter 17

Nicci Waldock's first client was due at 4.30. His name was Mike. He was older than her by a few years; thirty-two, thirty-three, something like that, she guessed; he was heavy-set, but it was mostly muscle, and of below-average height, which made his proportions compact. She had no idea what he did for a living, but he always arrived smelling as though he had just showered. And she appreciated that. Some of them came when seeing her was the last thing they did before they washed; their clothes wilted and their skin was always slightly sticky. Mike wasn't like that, but he wasn't a great talker either. She couldn't remember without looking at her diary, but she guessed she'd seen him seven or eight times and throughout he'd barely uttered a word. All in all though, quiet or surly was always better than mouthy or volatile.

Mike often arrived up to ten minutes early, which was her reason for standing not far from the window glancing, from time to time, in either direction along the street. She liked to watch them arrive, not for any pleasurable reason but because she wanted to be certain of who she was opening the door to. Mike drove a Volkswagen, a black Golf, and whenever she saw it turn into Mawson Road, she knew it would be anywhere between a couple of minutes and ten before he'd find a parking space and arrive at her door. It was normal for her to turn away then, to use those last few minutes to ensure that she was ready.

But on this occasion, someone else caught her eye.

From her front window she was just able to see the Mill Road end of Mawson Road. The street itself was a patchwork, different houses built at different times, gaps filled in, homes replaced. This end had once been called Union Terrace. It had been the poorer end, but the terraced workers' cottages that had once been simple two-up, two-down homes now shared the street with properties that had been updated and extended, rethought and replaced. And it was as Mike's Golf passed these that she'd spotted a figure as he turned the corner.

She didn't know what made her stare. His features were too indistinct from that distance and she recognised nothing about his silhouette or the way he walked, but still, there was something.

There were a few men standing outside the mosque. He stepped round them on the pavement but didn't slow; she saw then that he was carrying a bag of shopping. Groceries perhaps. Maybe he was just some local guy she'd seen walking around. Still she didn't turn away. Something about him was setting her nerves on edge and making her tense; little electric pulses ran up her spine.

The anxiety came swiftly. She felt her heartbeat first. It never thumped, instead it fluttered, filling her chest with small shaky bursts, breeding trepidation in her stomach and lungs. She steadied herself, one hand gripping the back of the nearest chair. 'I'm in here,' she whispered to herself. 'I'm safe.'

She moved her free hand to rest on the top of her chest. She needed to steady her breathing. She inhaled, trying for shallow but steady.

Enough oxygen but not too much. 'One, two.' And slowly exhale. 'Three, four, five, six.'

She should turn away. Lie down. Close her eyes. Instead she repeated the breaths, all the time staring across the street.

He stayed on the opposite side of the road. She reminded herself of her breathing and that, in a few more yards, he would be passing the house opposite and then be gone. But he didn't get that far. It was three houses sooner than that when his free hand reached out towards the gatepost and in that split second the combination of that particular move and that particular gatepost told her everything she needed to know.

She made a small audible 'Oh' just as Mike approached her house. A second later he knocked on her front door with his usual double rap and the sound made the other man turn.

His front door was ajar, and one foot had stepped into the shadowy hallway, but she could see enough. His hair was darker now, shoulders broader, but she had no doubt: Jack Bailey.

Nicci fell back from the window.

Mike waited on the doorstep while she counted. 'One, two.' And exhale. 'Three, four, five, six.'

Chapter 18

It took Nicci's full concentration to make it through her appointment with Mike. He made no comment, but she knew he'd seen her shaking hands and he didn't question it when she wound things up more quickly than usual. She closed the door in his wake and, in the next instant, was reaching for her phone.

'Craig? Hi, it's Nicci. I'm really sorry but I need to cancel.'

'It's short notice,' he told her gruffly.

'It is,' she agreed, 'and I'm sorry, but I don't feel well.' And as she said it, she realised that her free hand was pressed to her stomach, trying to suppress the queasiness that bubbled there. 'I can see you at the same time next week?'

'Not much choice really, is there?'

There was, of course, but she let him run on with his complaint for a few more seconds before stopping him. 'Would you prefer to go somewhere else?' She nodded at his reply, ended the call and put his next appointment in her diary.

She stood in the centre of her front room, at first keeping her back to the window but when that failed, she tried to settle in an armchair, this time with a view of the street. Neither position was working for her. The room had somehow lost its usual feeling of sanctuary and, instead, it felt airless and smothering.

She wanted to run.

She gripped her thighs, pressing her hands against the denim.

It would be better to throw this away than have it snatched from her.

To have nothing, to be nothing, suddenly felt like her sanctuary.

I need to run.

She drew a sharp breath, standing up and rejecting the thought in one movement. 'Come on,' she muttered, 'you know better than this.'

She slipped upstairs, not to her own room, but to the one next to it; Ellie's old room. She pushed the door and felt the change in pressure and the release of cooler air. The bed was bare now apart from a white sheet stretched across the mattress. She closed her eyes and tried to capture any hint of her friend's presence. She'd tried to do this whenever the house conjured memories of Ellie, but, as always, her friend was gone.

She locked the front door and then let herself out of the back. The garden was short, the width of the property and almost square. The fencing at the back and along one boundary was six-foot-high, but half that height on the other side. She locked the door behind her then stepped over the low fence into the adjoining garden. She let herself in through the back door without knocking.

'Celia?'

'I'm in the office.'

Celia had dispensed with the standard settee and two armchairs. Instead, her front room resembled a large version of most people's studies, and it was what could have been her study, the second bedroom upstairs, which resembled a standard sitting room with a two-seater settee and a television set.

Celia was at her desk. It was orangey pine and had been self-assembled from IKEA and it clashed with her fuchsia trousers and not-quite-matching smock top. When Celia dressed for an occasion she thought it through; on days she stayed home, Nicci was sure that thought never came into it.

Celia worked as a part-time lecturer and was surrounded by

what Nicci assumed to be essays spread across the desk. 'I'm sorry. I'm interrupting, aren't I?'

'Never a problem, my dear.' Celia had come from Jamaica in the mid-sixties, arriving with her parents when she was just a baby; she'd grown up in Cambridge but had still managed to inherit her parents' intonation.

She smiled but her gaze was watchful. 'You look unsettled?'

'I saw Jack Bailey.'

Celia barely moved. 'Did you now? Where?'

Nicci pointed towards the window. 'At their old house . . . his old house. Do you think he's moved back?'

'It's been empty for a few weeks now.' Celia turned slowly in her chair and looked thoughtfully along the street as though the front elevations of the Bailey house might reveal the answers. 'I can't think why he'd return.' Celia swivelled back and remained silent as she studied Nicci. 'How are you feeling?'

Nicci raised her hands then dropped them back to her sides. 'I remember the last time I saw him properly. Most people either had a go at me or looked away, too uncomfortable to make eye contact. Jack had a very direct way about him.'

'Yes,' Celia nodded. 'I remember.'

'He found me at the hospital. They were keeping visitors away, but he managed to bypass the nurse and slip into my room.' The moment returned to her with unexpected clarity. The sounds of sterility, the anaemic walls and Jack's hollow eyes staring into her own. 'He spoke quietly to me,' she said, almost to herself. Then to Celia, 'He told me that Charlie had deserved better. That they all had.' And of course, that was true, but she hadn't said that then, and didn't now either.

'Was that all he said?'

Nicci shook her head. 'He said that it should have been me that died. Then he told me not to string it out. Not to drag him or the others or their families through a court case . . .'

'He asked you to plead guilty?'

Nicci nodded. He'd walked away then. She'd closed her eyes and disappeared into her very first wave of shaking and nausea. She'd always known Jack, but the coldness and weight of his disgust had been new and immense. It had hung over her, she remembered thinking, as heavily as if his words had come from a parent or barrister. And, worse still, she'd completely understood his sentiment. But what he'd asked had been impossible. She'd waited for the next dose of painkillers and had slipped into semi-consciousness.

She levelled her gaze at Celia.

The crash had never been a subject for discussion. It had become an unspoken rule that Celia never asked for details and accepted that Nicci only ever shared as much as she chose to. Up until today that had been virtually nothing. But now a few words came. 'I couldn't bring myself to plead guilty.'

Celia tilted her head, 'Why?'

'Because I couldn't accept that I was, I suppose.' Nicci shrugged and her voice trailed away. The trial had been filled with evidence and virtually no mitigating circumstances. She'd stayed numb through most of it. A reaction that had been described as *emotionless* and *without remorse*. And, at that point, the idea of prison hadn't terrified her, not the way it should have done. 'There have been times when I've thought I should have listened to him.'

'We've been through this. You have a right to live here. These are the streets where you grew up. That makes them your home. It's fine to go outside . . .'

Nicci began shaking her head even before Celia had finished the sentence.

Celia rose from her chair and hugged Nicci. 'He'll work out that you are here soon enough. And when he does, we'll just cross that bridge like we've crossed every other one. Besides,' she whispered affectionately, 'you look so different now. You could walk down that street and he wouldn't notice. He'd be looking for a mousy blonde, not the determined young woman I've got here.'

She stroked Nicci's straight black hair a couple of times.

'That's not it,' Nicci whispered. She stepped back and her gaze met Celia's. 'When I saw him today – it was so unexpected – it was as though a jolt went through me. And then I knew.' She held Celia more tightly. 'He lied in court, and I think he tried to kill me.'

Chapter 19

Celia couldn't recall when she'd first met Jack's family. As far as she knew Pete and Fiona had moved into Mawson Road before they'd had children. But her first clear memory was stopping outside the newsagent's and chatting with Fiona as they both smiled at Jack in his pram. And then a few years on, seeing him leaving for school in his oversized uniform and a look of nervous bewilderment on his face. Her next mental snapshot was a few years on from that: it leapfrogged the years that followed Fiona's second pregnancy which had ended with stillbirth and landed on the image of Jack, glowing with excitement at the precious arrival of his little brother.

Celia sighed. Stories rarely followed their initial route and it seemed to her that they invariably took a less attractive course.

On the opposite wall to her desk was a dainty two-seater sofa with tapered legs that didn't look strong enough to hold any weight. It usually supported nothing more than a pile or two of papers, a cushion and a throw draped across the back. Occasionally Celia sat on it to think and to see the room from a different angle; it never felt entirely safe. Despite the risk, they both sat. Nicci perched on the edge with her feet tucked under her. She looked as though she was cold and frightened. Neither, Celia assumed, was the sofa's fault. She kept a kettle and mini fridge beside her desk and had made Nicci a tea.

Nicci wrapped her hands around the mug. She brought it to her lips but didn't drink, instead she stared blankly past the curl of steam that rose from it. 'I've never known what happened after we drove away from the pub. I heard the evidence, but it might as well have been someone else's story, or fiction even. There were some sounds, but I think my eyes were closed. I have tried to remember.'

She glanced at Celia then, perhaps to see whether she was believed. Celia nodded.

'All I see is nothingness. Not blackness. It is black I suppose, but as though that's the colour of the walls and they're a long way away and don't really matter. It's the nothing in the foreground that I want to see, but I can't. Does that make sense?'

'Yes, it does.' Celia nodded again. 'Go on.'

'There have always been voices; they are faint sounds. Muffled and indistinct. There have never been any words.' She shifted uneasily and the surface of her tea rippled close to the edge of the mug. She chewed on her lip. Her lipstick disappeared rapidly, leaving her mouth with asymmetric scarlet patches. 'There are no words, but I hear Ellie. She is the only one I recognise. Have you ever heard a rabbit scream?'

Celia shook her head. 'No, I don't think so.'

'They scream like children.' Nicci moved the mug and pressed it to her chest; she suddenly felt colder. 'Rabbits are silent their whole lives then they make this noise that shouldn't be possible. Ellie screamed like that; not like a rabbit, but with a sound that shouldn't come from a human. Her terror . . .' This time she shivered visibly. Celia pulled the throw from the back of the sofa and draped it around Nicci's shoulders. 'I heard that. It was enough to block my senses of anything else whatsoever. And I have listened to that sound so many times since. I used to wake up with it in my ears, convinced that she was in the room with me.'

'Does it still happen?'

'Rarely. I hoped . . .'

Celia could tell that she'd become hesitant. 'It's okay.'

Nicci took a breath. 'I hoped that, for Ellie, it was nature's way of blocking out everything for her. Stopping her feeling the pain until she died. I told myself that and it made the sound almost bearable.'

Celia wanted to hug Nicci, or at least squeeze her hand, but Nicci remained closed in on herself, gripping the mug and huddling over it. 'So, what changed today?'

'I think it was the shock of seeing Jack unexpectedly. I stared across the road at him. He disappeared into his house and I held it together at first. I had a client coming, I got through it but the screaming had already started in my head. It was the first time it had happened in so long. As soon as he had gone, I sat on the floor by the window, closed my eyes and waited for it to pass. But it was different this time. There was still nothing to see, but I could feel what happened after the crash. A man had his hand on the back of my head, his fingers woven through my hair, and I felt his grip tighten.' She stopped abruptly, then attempted to say more but, for several seconds, the words wouldn't come. She raised her left hand in a fist and slammed from left to right with her whole arm. 'Like this,' she managed to say. She repeated the movement several times. 'He smashed my head against the steering wheel.'

'And it was Jack?'

'A man's hand. That's all I know. And I only remembered when I saw him.' Finally, Nicci leant towards Celia and allowed herself to be held. 'I think I was meant to die.'

Celia didn't doubt Nicci, but she also knew the Jack who had grown up in her street, who had studied hard, loved his family. She couldn't imagine it.

Then again, life flowed in unexpected directions and could twist people in unseen ways.

Celia's gaze landed on her desk, the place she sat to write, but, more importantly, the place where she used to sit to write when her work had been so much more than puff pieces for glossy magazines. The place where she had planned and assembled and honed disparate bits of information into coherent stories. This wasn't for publication, it was just for answers, but she could almost taste the questions as they formed.

Wasn't she too old and too close to retirement to consider this again?

Celia rarely swore, but shit no.

Chapter 20

Jack moved into his former family home with just three cardboard boxes. The first contained his Mac plus a handful of books with Frank's three files stuffed in the top. The second contained clothes – he'd left most behind and just grabbed trousers and jeans, shirts, T-shirts and one heavy coat. And the last box and smallest held a few personal items, half that he hadn't wanted to lose and the other half that he hadn't wanted to leave with her.

He set up his Mac on the dining-room table, which he'd pushed close to the back window. When he sat at this makeshift desk, he could have had a view of the garden, but he'd purposefully shut the curtains. When the Mac was running and the books were lined up behind it, he took the box of clothes upstairs, transferring them in two bundles into the top two drawers of the pine chest.

The third box stayed in the hall.

Jack hesitated, staring down at it as he wrestled with the problem. It contained too much that was dangerous and too much that belonged to his old life. The idea of moving it further into any room or, in fact, to any point deeper in the house would be too much of an intrusion. In the end the box was left like a naughty child waiting outside a doorway. Jack avoided dealing with it for the first few days and, after that, it became a feature that he grew used to ignoring.

It took a week for the estate agent to make good on the promise of cleaning and while he waited for the carpets and the sofa and the armchair to dry out, he decided to walk from Mawson Road to Cambridge centre.

It was the first time he'd walked the route since his college days and although it only took about fifteen minutes, he felt his memory stirring with waves of recognition. Perhaps places were like people; they changed on the outside, they wore different clothes and they weathered and aged but underneath it took something catastrophic for them to completely change.

He stopped across the road from the new fire station. It was on the same site as it had always been but even with his love of architecture, he struggled to remember what had stood there before. If its previous incarnation had been beautiful, he was sure that he would have remembered but equally he would have remembered a hideous building, so he guessed the old fire station had been functional and nondescript.

He carried on walking around the town like that, glad to see some buildings that had been restored, struggling to remember the ones that had gone, and reminded of places he'd forgotten. Mostly oblivious to the people but sometimes reminded of the ones he hadn't seen for years, or the things that he'd done and the good times he'd had there.

He reached the market, bought a coffee and sat at one of the outside tables. The air was cool, and he seemed to be the only one not bundled in a coat. Don Pasquale's had been here when he was a kid. He rarely drank coffee then, and had never stopped here as far as he could remember. He'd walked by though. Now he sat with his coffee and watched the street.

Cambridge moved constantly; it throbbed like a big city though its heart was tiny. Tiny but strong.

He could pick out the tourists. They moved slowly, keen to take it all in. They looked up and around. They were the ones who pointed, or stopped abruptly to take photos, the ones who carried shopping in bright bags and often took illogical routes through the town. He stayed long enough to see some of them more than once, watching them appearing from Rose Crescent or Trinity Street, disappearing through the market stalls and re-emerging later, undecided about which route to take next. He didn't feel like a tourist. He knew the place too well.

And there was some comfort in the familiarity of the city.

But he didn't feel like a local either. Not any more.

Chapter 21

Jack had been out for three hours, hoping that was enough time for the cleaners. When he arrived back at the house it still smelt dank, not from carpet shampoo but a kind of grubby dampness, as though a wet dog had run through the place or shaken itself out on the carpet. What the place needed was air.

Jack left the front door open, then opened the front downstairs windows. He went to the kitchen to boil the kettle and found that the carpet cleaner had picked up his morning's post and left it propped up by the microwave, no doubt to save it from soaking up moisture from the carpet. There was only one item. Jack opened it and recognised the estate agent's logo immediately. It was a copy of a letter that they had sent to his father, half apologising for their shortcomings but managing to do so without admitting to any wrongdoing on their part. They'd signed off with a standard, 'Thank you for your custom and we hope you consider using us again in the future.' The apology was weak, as he knew it would be, but he also realised that the anger he'd been feeling towards them had been disproportionate; it had occupied him and blocked him from thinking about the things that really mattered.

He blinked and like the snapping of a shutter saw Sadie's face, the same elfin features that he'd fallen in love with, but he saw her as she'd been in the moment she'd delivered the death blow to their relationship; her gaze was heavy lidded and hard, her lips still slightly parted from the words that she'd just shot at him. He remembered the seconds afterwards when all physical sensation seemed torn away from him and he'd stood in front of her, shouting back, indecipherable as everything ruptured.

At first Jack had refused to leave. He hadn't been able to process what she'd told him. But, after two weeks of denial, he'd given up and moved into bed-and-breakfast accommodation. He probably could have called on some friends, begged a room for a few weeks, but the ability to confide in anyone had eluded him.

In the end, the only person he spoke to had been his dad, spurred by the realisation that he had a right to know. They were both losing family.

Dad, she's not my daughter.

Jack realised how it had panned out. When he'd come back to this house, he'd focused his attention on the shoddy estate agent and had been able to, albeit briefly, look away from the bigger, crueller picture.

Jack continued to hold the letter in his hand, to stare at it even though there was nothing more to read. The estate agent had capitulated, their resistance had evaporated and so had his anger. Without it there to distract him, all that was left was him and the house.

'Okay,' he said aloud, then walked from room to room, opening every single window. He moved quickly and the breeze from outside followed him, cold and dry. He took downstairs first and then the bedrooms. His was, as it had been before, the medium-sized room, the only one that faced the front of the house. The largest one had belonged to his dad and mum.

The final window he opened was Charlie's. It was the first time he'd stepped inside since he'd come back. The window was on the opposite wall to the door and he crossed quickly, pulled up the sash and made himself look into the garden. The gate was still painted the same dark blue although the bottom of the wood was now zigzagged with age and weathering. The metalwork was black with a bolt on the inside and a tradition latch with the lever that looked like the head of a spoon.

Charlie had always leant his bike against that back fence. Every bike from when he'd been about four years old.

There had been an eight-year gap between the two of them and Jack's memory was littered with his little brother's minor milestones, and, in this case, it was the moment the little red bike had had first one, then both stabilisers removed. The bike didn't have a stand, so Charlie used the fence. The next had been a silver racer, Charlie's favourite, which he'd stubbornly hung on to until he'd had to ride it with his knees out at awkward angles to avoid the handlebars. And finally, the dark blue Diamondback, an adult bike that ought to still be standing there.

Of course, it was long gone, but Jack couldn't shake the feeling that no bike against the fence just meant that his brother was out there, and at any second the gate would fly wide and Charlie would appear.

Probably breathless.

Probably grinning.

It made it feel as though Charlie was still within touching distance, and that hurt way too much.

Later, when he thought of it, Jack had no idea how long he'd stood at the window. It could have been most of the afternoon for all he knew; he'd lost himself in a train of thought that skipped and jumped and diverted from one topic to the next. But, in the middle of it all, something inside of him had twisted and snapped.

He'd fallen back from the glass, then turned and hurried down the stairs.

He left the house with the windows still wide open, stopping for nothing but his mobile phone. He didn't even bother to lock the front door. At that moment he didn't care.

He walked out onto Mill Road and found the nearest supermarket and purchased two one-litre bottles of cheap whisky, a brand he'd never heard of. It looked unpleasant but he wasn't planning to drink for enjoyment, and he opened the first bottle before he made it home. He took a couple of heavy swigs and swallowed fast so that he didn't have to taste it.

When he reached his house, he put the second bottle on the draining board, picked up a pint glass but then didn't bother using it, drinking straight from the bottle instead.

He sat in the damp armchair for just a few minutes. His instinct had been to sink into it and carry on drinking, but he was soon back on his feet and pacing.

The alcohol hit him hard and after a few more swigs he gave in to it all. He muttered at first, replying to himself with sarcastic barbs. Later he ranted and was no longer aware of his own words.

He'd intended the alcohol to numb the pain but instead it hit him with full force, and the question he had never been able to answer burned without reservation now: 'Why?' The single word made a guttural sound as it rose from the pit of his stomach.

Jack found himself staring into the third box of his belongings. The dangerous one. And he reached into it, too drunk to think straight but knowing exactly what he was drawn towards. The picture frame was plain, the photo just a snap with the camera on Sadie's phone.

He was holding Maya and she had her arms around his neck, gripping him in the ferocious way of a toddler, with no inhibitions, just enthusiasm. She wore a plum-coloured woollen jacket, pink leggings and black patent T-bar shoes. Her first pair.

This photo was his favourite. He'd made several copies, one to frame, one for an album, one for his dad. He'd only just framed the first when it had all gone awry.

'Maya,' he'd intended to whisper, but his voice sounded frayed and too loud. He let out a sob, and he gripped the frame in both hands. Was she okay?

I still want to see her.

You can't. She's nothing to do with you now.

Did she know he hadn't deserted her?

He took the photo to his desk and stood it alongside the monitor, in the exact spot where he knew his gaze would drift whenever he was thinking. His drunken logic was simple: in that photo she was still his daughter, and he needed that picture however much it hurt.

He took a couple of steps back and stared at it until tears made it blur.

A few minutes later he tried to climb the stairs, grabbing at the banisters and trying to pull himself up, stumbling, ending on his knees and crawling the last few steps. He knew he was going to be sick and grabbed the doorframe, trying to haul himself to his feet.

He staggered across the landing into the bathroom and the last thing he remembered was staggering again and knowing that he was about to fall.

Chapter 22

He woke before dawn with a hangover, which then swallowed three or four hours until a little after eight. He felt sick and bruised, his head throbbed but, apart from that, he barely felt connected to his physical self, more like a disjointed mess of nerves and nausea. He felt half-dead but also the most alive he'd been in months.

Jack had seen a shadow in the window of the house across the road. It hadn't startled him. There had been lots of shadows in lots of windows over the last couple of weeks. He guessed there would have been more if he'd kept regular hours.

A couple of days ago he'd walked for twenty minutes. Not far, as the crow flies, just an idle stroll down Mawson Street to the far end, the posh end, around the corner and up the road that ran parallel behind his house. He hadn't seen familiar faces in that time, but there had been a couple of instances when he was sure he felt eyes on him.

These were the streets that he had cycled along as a kid, where his friends had lived. He hadn't tried to find out whether they were still in their old homes. Pretty sad if you were still living with your parents at thirty-one. But then again, he was living in his dad's house without his father being there. That wasn't a whole lot more independent.

He'd been two streets from home when he'd run straight into

Patrick Hayward, Gemma and Rob's dad. There was a spontaneous smile of recognition that passed between the two men. Both smiles faded equally quickly. Patrick nodded and moved on immediately and, if Jack was honest, he'd felt relieved.

There was nothing to say to someone when every small connection was overshadowed by the one that devastated both your lives. Nothing to say about the crash. Nothing worth mentioning about any other subject either.

There was no other subject.

Jack knew it wouldn't be the last time he would be in that situation, not while he lived here. He needed to find a way to deal with it, a tactic. But right at that moment, his mind was completely blank.

What would he want somebody to say to him?

He didn't know.

He returned home in a more pensive mood. Between Patrick and the twitching curtains, people now knew he was back in Cambridge. Despite the students and the constant churn of residents, at the core of it, this was a close-knit community. It was only a couple of hours later when a knock sounded at the front door and he wasn't particularly surprised. But opening the door to find Celia Henry on his doorstep was not what he had expected.

She looked older and a bit plumper than the last time he'd seen her. His dad and she had been friends, and from time to time she'd come across the road and delivered a bag of Caribbean spices to make what she called 'mix me up chicken'.

'Celia, how are you?'

'I saw you were back,' she smiled; he didn't.

'I was waiting for you to come and say hello. Are you avoiding me or waiting for me to say hello to you first? If it's the second one, then here I am.'

He shrugged. 'Finding my feet, I guess.'

'What is there to find, Jack? You know where everything is.' He'd forgotten how her comments often contained subtle barbs; so subtle in fact that sometimes he had only been able to feel them and had been unable to identify where they actually lay. 'And you know what, Jack, the faces change but the streets are the same.'

'I know,' he admitted, 'but I didn't really plan on being here.'

'But the pull of our childhood home, it always brings us back. It's stronger than you think. I've been to Port Antonio. Of course, I had no memories of it, but it felt right when I got there.'

Cambridge felt anything but right, but Jack said nothing.

'So, I heard you had a wife and a child. They're not with you?' He could feel her gaze searching for any tell-tale signs. 'Did that not work out so well for you?'

Jack smiled ruefully. 'Something like that, Celia.'

'But she'll come to visit, I'm sure. The little one, I mean.'

Jack shook his head. He didn't want to get into this, but Celia had never been one to shy away from asking questions.

'You mean you don't see the little girl?'

'No.'

'That's such a shame. What did you call her?'

Jack blinked. 'Maya.' He'd chosen her name because he liked the sound of it. *Maya Bailey.* His surname was plain, and he thought Maya lifted it. The first and last names together sounded memorable, they belonged to someone who could go far. Maya meant love. Later he discovered that it also meant illusion. 'She's just turned two.'

Celia waited, as if expecting him to say more. It was a long few seconds before she spoke. 'And I can see I'm making you uncomfortable. Losing your mother and Charlie was enough pain to last you a lifetime, without everything else.'

He held her gaze. 'If you don't mind, I'm not really in the mood for visitors right now.'

'I just want a few minutes, Jack.' She stood a little taller then. When he'd been a child, she'd been a journalist, renowned for her perseverance. 'It's important.'

'Like a dog with a bone,' he muttered, then turned and walked to the sitting room, knowing that she would follow.

'I don't have to ask you any difficult questions. But I'm interested to know, am I the dog or am I the bone, because one's insulting and the other's becoming increasingly ambitious?'

'No offence intended, Celia.'

They sat across from one another. He knew there would be a few more pleasantries before she revealed the real reason for her visit. He saw her gaze briefly settle on Maya's photo, but she didn't comment. Instead she asked, 'Is your father well?'

'Thank you, yes he is.'

'He'll be pleased you're keeping an eye on the place. My goodness, some of the students you rented the house to. Let's just say, they weren't primarily here for studying. I did manage to contact him once and I warned him. I said, "Pete, there's people in that house that are probably wrecking it. You need to get your backside down here and sort it out." I thought he'd listen to me. I'm the one neighbour that knows something about students and the mess they get themselves into.'

But this wasn't just pleasantries, rather the precursor to something relevant. Jack nodded in the direction of Celia's and the adjacent property, which she also owned.

'Do you still let it to students?'

'It's still rented, yes.'

'I've only seen one woman there. Slim with black hair.'

Celia didn't respond. Instead she waited for whatever it was that he was going to say next.

'There seem to be a lot of people coming and going.'

'People?'

'Men mostly.'

Celia's expression closed off slightly. 'And your point is?'

'Nothing. I was just curious.'

'Was there a question in there somewhere, Jack? Because I didn't quite catch it. Thing is, I've had a few women in the street asking me questions like that, wanting me to tell them whether what they read between the lines is accurate. And I think mostly it's none of their business. But I'll tell you more than I'd tell them.' She interlaced her fingers and leant back until her head was fully supported by the back of the chair. It made her head angle backwards a little and she looked at him through steady, half-closed eyes. 'The woman living in my other house is Nicci. Nicci Waldock,' she added when a look of disbelief crossed his face.

'Why, Celia?'

'She needed to start again.'

'Across the road from our house? That's unreasonable.'

'Neither you nor Pete were living here, or even visiting. She's been with me for just over a year.'

'She shouldn't show her face around here . . .'

'She barely goes out for that very reason, but I'll tell you something, she should. She has a right to live here, she cannot spend the rest of her life . . .'

'What? Feeling ashamed for what she did?'

Celia unlocked her fingers and spread her hands on her thighs. 'I wanted you to know she was here before you heard it any other way. And that's for your benefit, as well as hers. There are gossips who would like to think they know that girl's business, they draw conclusions from the sight of men coming and going from the house. Maybe you are the same?'

'I don't care what she does; I care that she's here.'

'I am personally insulted at the idea that I may be turning a blind eye to some kind of brothel in my property, so I will tell you the situation, and once I have shared that with you, I would like you to give me the courtesy of an answer to a question of mine.' She remained calm and immovable as she waited for his response.

'Go on then,' he said at last.

'Nicci removes tattoos for a living. She was a mess and she needed a chance to get herself together.'

'Why get involved, Celia?'

‘You and Charlie and Nicci and a bunch of kids grew up outside my window. She was never a bad kid, Jack; you know that, don’t you?’

He’d never disputed it. Not until the crash anyway. He didn’t reply.

‘You get to know someone pretty well in a year, especially when they’re living in your house. I asked her what she wanted to do for work . . .’

‘She always wanted to be a crime scene investigator.’ Jack hadn’t planned to say anything; the words slipped out.

‘She still studies, but no. Instead she chose tattoo removal. She’s helping people get rid of something they regret. Don’t you see the metaphor there?’

Jack laughed coldly. ‘For fuck’s sake.’ He was on his feet at once. ‘Just go, Celia. I don’t want to hear any more of this shit.’

Celia remained implacable and, for a split second, he was sure he saw satisfaction glint in her eye. Without missing a beat, she responded, ‘Did you assault Nicci when she was unconscious?’

‘What?’

‘Did you grab her, and then smash her head against the steering wheel?’

Jack couldn’t physically recoil; he was standing too close to the chair for that, but he felt himself sway and the sounds of the room were drowned out by the thick pulse of blood in his head.

‘Did you attack Nicci while she was unconscious?’

He didn’t know whether he shouted then, which words poured out and which just screamed for only him to hear. The loss of Charlie. The death of his mother. His anguish about Maya. The truth of how he’d wished Nicci dead so many times. And the lesser of all of those: the accusation of violence. It was the final fray in a weak rope, and he felt four years of pain burst apart.

And through it all was Celia’s voice, rich toned and resolute. ‘When you saw Charlie was dead, did you attack her? Was it a moment of rage? Did you try to kill her?’

On and on, until the nausea from the hangover and the rage imploded and left him in silence.

Jack found himself standing close to Celia, glowering down at where she still sat.

She blinked slowly. 'So, I have to believe you are both honest people. I don't think she's lying, and I don't think you attacked her. But someone did.'

Chapter 23

Celia stopped briefly on the pavement outside Jack's house. Home was just yards away, but there were no answers there, so, instead, she pulled out her phone and headed for the city centre as she dialled. DI Briggs answered on her second ring.

'Briggs, can I come to see you?'

'Celia?' He didn't wait for a reply. 'You sound like you're walking. Would that be in my direction?'

'Very astute.'

'Give me fifteen minutes. Can you meet me at Espresso Library?'

The café was in East Road, just around the corner from Parkside Police Station. Celia arrived first and ordered two white coffees and a plate of sourdough toast. She sat away from the counter, next to a map of Cambridgeshire and a bicycle hanging from the wall. The café was about half full and not big enough to lose anyone, but she'd chosen this spot so that Briggs would see her as soon as he stepped through the door.

He arrived before his coffee had cooled too much. Their greeting was more hug than handshake, and he raised an eyebrow when he saw the table. 'Toast too? You really are pleased to see me.'

'It's a bribe.'

'I thought it was short notice for a social.'

Celia had known Briggs since the Hatton Murder in 1995 when they'd both been at the peak of their energies and ambitions. Their respective roles in the case had been small, but enough to secure a promotion for each of them. They had remained friends even after Celia had ditched frontline journalism.

'Let me guess; something about Nicci Waldock? Has she gone feral again?'

Celia scowled. 'You know perfectly well that's not fair. That girl was never feral.'

'In your eyes.'

'But yes,' she conceded, 'it does involve Nicci.'

'Oh good.' He pulled the plate of toast towards him. 'Jam or honey?'

'Just butter for me.' She waited until he put down the knife, and had his full attention before she spoke. 'Nicci's remembered more about the crash. She says she was attacked afterwards, that someone grabbed her head and rammed it into the steering wheel.'

'For what purpose?'

'I have no idea, but she thinks it was an attempt to kill her.'

'I don't believe that for a minute. Unless she thinks she can become the victim.' He screwed up his nose. 'It would help with the guilt, I suppose. She might not even know she's done it. I'm no psychologist, but I believe people who rewrite the truth genuinely believe it.'

Celia scowled. 'Seriously, Briggs?'

Briggs shrugged in reply. 'I could have just said that she's a bare-faced liar trying to pull some scam on you. Instead I'm being kind; trying to give her the benefit of the doubt.'

'No, you have one view of what happened, and you don't want to consider anything else.'

'A closed case is just that, Celia. I'm not even going to waste brain space on it.'

'I am not buying that for a moment. Unofficially you fret and churn things over with the best of us. It's more that you have never liked the furniture disturbed once the room has been arranged. Would it be so terrible to go back over the details, to look at her injuries, and see what you can see?'

'For what purpose, Celia? We're never going to reopen that one. She drove the car. People died. Trial, conviction, time served. It's done.' He bit into his toast and simultaneously gestured for Celia to wait. He chewed and swallowed before continuing, 'But, I'll admit, I don't get her angle.'

'Because there isn't one. She's as straight as a die.'

He tilted his head and watched the flow of traffic sliding past the window. He finished his toast and coffee. He didn't speak, but he didn't get ready to leave either. She waited. Briggs was one of the most reasonable people she knew, just as long as he was feeling receptive, and that all came down to timing.

He reminded her of a lift travelling from the basement to the roof. An uninterrupted straight line, direction and momentum in perfect harmony. But she also knew that, if she could make it pause along the way, if she could prise open those doors, then Briggs might consider stopping somewhere else.

He stayed deep in thought for several minutes and she waited until his attention returned to her before she spoke. 'I believe her,' she said softly.

'You would though. You have invested so much in her, and in the face of the opinion of plenty of people who will have written you off as almost as blinkered as one of those death-row penfriends who go on TV to refer to their wife-murdering fiancé as "misunderstood".'

'I'm not that bad.'

'I bet you want to ask me if I'm sure she was driving, don't you?'

'Maybe,' she conceded.

'Well, I am sure, and unshakably so. We weren't on the scene investigating a crash where the driver had done a runner. The fire crew had to cut her out, for God's sake, and then the ambulance crew had to save her life because of crash trauma.'

'All so you could put her away. That's what I call a team effort.'

'It was the right result. You know that.'

And Celia did, for, as much as she loved Nicci like a daughter, she agreed that there had had to be a price for the recklessness of that evening; death going unpunished was one of life's great injustices.

Then, just as Celia thought that there was nothing she could do to press Briggs's pause button, he pressed it himself. 'But . . .' he began, then let the sentence drift into nothing as he strummed his index and middle fingertips, pursing his lips as he thought.

Celia waited and quashed the urge to slap his hand or interrupt.

'But,' he repeated, 'if her seatbelt was in place on impact, which it was, there should have been an airbag between her and the steering wheel. I will look as far as her head injuries, and nothing more.'

Celia touched his sleeve. 'Thank you.'

They walked outside together and said goodbye at the corner. 'Good to see you, Celia. And, for future reference, I am offended by the furniture remark.'

She held his gaze for a moment. 'I hoped you would be.'

Chapter 24

Some trades traditionally ran in families, like removal companies and greengrocer shops. And farms still passed through the generations. She'd met plenty of police, nurses and members of the armed forces who had followed a parent's or a sibling's career path. The Maitland family was the only one she knew who had chosen to found a dynasty of pathologists and could trace their line back to Thomas Maitland, a Victorian pathologist who had studied and worked alongside James Paget at a time when the skill of being an executioner was also passed from father to son.

So, although she had rung and left a message for Dr Roy Maitland and had been invited to his Addenbrooke's Hospital office at 2 p.m., she shouldn't have been surprised when the Dr Maitland who called her through was an entirely different person.

He introduced himself as Dr Harry Maitland. If Celia had been given a forty-year-old photograph of his father, she imagined she'd be looking at twins. Since then Roy's tall and lean frame had broadened, his hair had thinned and his generally sober demeanour had overtaken him, permeating his words and face with heaviness. She knew immediately that Harry's personality had come from elsewhere in the family tree.

Harry stepped forward quickly to greet her, smiling warmly and guiding her deftly into his office. The room was cubicle-like with thin walls constructed of plasterboard and frosted glass. Most of it was taken up by his desk and two chairs, the comfortable one for himself and the smaller, more utilitarian one for guests. A single frame hung on the wall, housing the almost obligatory certificate.

'Dad's up to his elbows in the usual muck and bullets. Are you happy with me instead?'

'Of course, if you have the time.'

'Absolutely. We met once before. You wrote an article on my grandfather, Gregory, and my sister and I were hanging around, asking you questions on journalism.'

Celia could remember the article, but nothing about the background to it. 'That must have been a long time ago.'

'Yes, I was probably about twelve at the time. Of course, neither of us became journalists, but we are harangued by the press from time to time, so I'm sure it served a purpose.'

'Most things do.'

'Absolutely. Now the note I've received says "seatbelts and body trauma" . . . and I'm intrigued. How can I help?'

'I'm investigating an incident where there were five people in a single vehicle crash. It hit a tree and the front passenger died on impact. The driver suffered head injuries, but she has regained some memory of the immediate aftermath, and it seems as though another person may have been involved between the time of the accident and the arrival of the emergency services. I want to know whether she could have been moved into the driver's seat and then belted in to look as though she'd been there all along?'

'So, you don't have access to her medical records?'

'No, I don't.'

'Would this be the sort of accident that might occur on a country road after an afternoon of drinking at a village pub?'

'Yes, it would.'

'I know the case, I assisted with one of the autopsies actually. Dad worked on the other.'

Celia knew about Roy but hadn't realised that Harry had had

any involvement. 'So, you know the level of impact?'

'Yes. There are plenty of cases where people don't wear seat-belts and still escape serious injury, but this wouldn't have been one of them. Your driver would have been a good few yards down the road with all the injuries that accompany it, so we know that whoever was driving was stopped by their seatbelt. Can you get a look at the driver's injury report?'

Celia shook her head. 'I haven't tried yet. What will I be looking for?'

'Highly prominent bruising and soft tissue damage running from the right shoulder to the left hip. It would definitely have been flagged up if the injuries weren't there.'

Celia could feel the possibilities narrowing, but she wasn't ready to give up either. 'So, what if she was located directly behind the driver? Surely the injuries would be similar.'

Harry made a maybe-yes, maybe-no gesture with his hand. 'Things can be overlooked, especially at a scene with multiple deaths or injuries. The urgency is to save lives, not gather evidence. But, in this instance, it was the woman in the middle who inadvertently inflicted injuries on the passenger to her right, injuries that ultimately resulted in that passenger's death.'

Celia sighed. 'So no chance that my girl was in the rear.'

'No, absolutely zero possibility. And you may not know this, but seatbelt buckles react on impact, they can be opened but not refastened. First responders would cut the straps rather than release them, and that will be documented too.' He pushed his chair back a little, and leant forward as if ready to stand. 'Is there anything else?'

Celia shook her head. 'I'm sorry, I feel as though I have wasted your time.'

He rose and held out a hand. 'Bear all this in mind if you do see the crash report.' There had been an edge of formality to his manner as he sat at his desk, but, as he walked her to the corridor, that vanished again. 'Look, it is very easy to become side-tracked by possibilities; wishful thinking can send any of us in the wrong direction. It's very hard to fabricate anything in a complicated scenario such as that one, but, because it was complicated, it is also possible that something was missed. Or possibly not missed, but misinterpreted. I know your reputation as a reporter . . .'

'Former reporter.'

'Irrelevant. You will scrutinise everything as you always have and one thing to consider is the reliability of your witness's memory, when she's suffered, first, a serious injury, and second, emotional trauma. Just remember to let go if there's nothing to find.'

Chapter 25

Celia drove an old Fiat which had belonged to her parents before becoming her second vehicle. These days she covered less than a thousand miles per year, so the red Bianchina had been promoted to pole position, and the more sensible Nissan had been sold. Mostly, she had no complaints about the cramped interior or poor acceleration. But for twenty-five minutes since leaving Dr Maitland's office she had been sitting in her car, and the feel of the under-upholstered front seat was, literally, wearing thin. More importantly, it was interrupting her train of thought.

Sentimentality seemed to be at the root of all her problems.

She had witnessed the entire court case and, of course, there were inconsistencies; there always were. Understatement, yes. Exaggeration, that too. But she hadn't noticed anything that felt like a full-blown lie. And the whole process had been documented by experienced people, justified to their superiors, and laid out in a courtroom full of lawyers and expert witnesses trained to dissect every fact. If nobody had spotted anything then, why would she now?

She'd been fired up by the idea that Nicci may have been moved into the driver's seat post-crash, but her meeting with Harry had revealed a catalogue of flaws in that theory. As soon as she'd walked away from him, his words had turned into an earworm, and she'd passed through Addenbrooke's long corridors and back to the multistorey with them taunting her. *Wishful thinking, wishful thinking.*

Nicci's life had been stable for the last year. She hadn't, to Celia's knowledge, had any contact with Jack in that time, so it had been his arrival that had triggered a defensive reaction. And what mattered now was whether that reaction was really a resurfacing memory, or a calculated lie.

Either way, Jack had been the reason.

She shifted in the seat; the lack of springs was becoming intolerable, and the parking charge would be equally unbearable if she didn't move. She walked to the ticket machine to pay and was holding her phone to the contactless payment point when the name *Briggs* flashed onto the screen.

Come to Parkside. Ask for me.

Chapter 26

Celia didn't need to ask for Briggs; she walked through the front doors of Parkside Station and he was right there with his back pressed against the nearest internal door. He held it part way open as if every second saved was going to matter. 'You're already signed in,' he told her and those were his only words until they had walked the length of the building and up one flight of stairs. He had his own office, and it wasn't dissimilar to Harry Maitland's in size, contents and décor. In the middle of his desk there were two full boxes and a roll of papers held together with an elastic band. The same case number was written on each item and it wasn't a huge stretch of her imagination to guess what they contained.

He closed the door and then turned to her. 'First things first, don't think for a minute that Nicci wasn't the driver. She was.'

'I know.'

'Good.' He walked round his desk and pulled one of the boxes towards him. 'We do hold digital copies, but sometimes staring at a screen can't compete with holding the real thing.' He pulled a thin white A4 envelope from about an inch down the pile and held it out to her. 'You can't take them out of my sight.'

Celia took the envelope in one hand and placed the other on the back of the nearest chair. 'Do you mind?' Celia pulled it up to the desk and sat down. Briggs perched on the edge of the desk and she was conscious of him studying her expression rather than the envelope. She slid her hand inside and immediately felt the liquid smoothness of photographic paper. There were three shots; numbered and clearly part of a much larger batch of photographs.

They'd been taken in hospital and the first showed Nicci, battered, and either comatose or asleep. She looked dead. She should have filled the frame, but she didn't quite, and, in the periphery, it was possible to see an IV line and, beyond that, the red and green lights of monitoring equipment. She was dressed in a hospital gown and the bare skin that protruded was extensively bruised, but the most prominent injuries were to her face. Her bottom lip was split, and heavy, liver-coloured bruising spread from her nose and across the eye area on both sides of her face, with further dappled bruising at the top of her cheeks.

Celia looked at Briggs questioningly. He shook his head. 'Apparently those are consistent with this type of accident. The airbag deploys quickly and those marks,' he pointed to the dappling, 'are a result of friction burns from the bag.'

Perhaps the first photograph had been taken purely as a general shot, because the composition of the second was entirely different. It was well-lit, more accurately focused and had been taken from above with Nicci's face filling the full 10 x 8.

She could feel Briggs watching her with increasing expectation.

She simultaneously leant nearer to the picture and brought it closer to her eyes. She began at Nicci's forehead and worked her way around the face. But it was only on the second scan that she saw a tiny pink mark, almost a V or a short-legged X, protruding from her right brow. 'There. What is it?'

He grinned. 'It took me a minute as well. Hardly surprising it was missed.'

Celia turned to the final photograph.

'It's an enlargement of the same shot.'

Even viewed more closely, the mark was still subtle. But it was also distinctive. 'Do you know what made the mark?'

Without having to locate it, Briggs reached back into the box and retrieved a fourth photo which had been standing vertically alongside the other contents. It showed the interior of Nicci's written-off Honda, taken from the open door on the driver's side. The steering wheel was visible, but it wasn't a particularly clear shot. 'The steering wheel had stitches running all the way around the inside, but it also had a seam of stitches running perpendicular to those. With an impact to the steering wheel it would only have been those stitches which could have come into contact with her forehead. And look here . . .' He pointed to the upper edge of the right eye socket, and there, at the tapered end of her brow and in the midst of the other bruising was the same distinctive mark. 'The airbag had deployed correctly – I checked.'

'So, neither of those marks should be there.' For the first time in several years, Celia felt the unmistakable tingle of excitement that came when a vital fact hit home. She had believed Nicci, but this removed the last trace of doubt. 'What happens now?'

Briggs's face darkened. 'Nothing. I went to DCI McCarthy. She says there's no chance of reopening any part of the case. I understand why; it's old now and Nicci's culpability isn't in doubt . . . putting in bluntly, we have higher priorities.'

'How do you know? We don't have the full picture yet.'

Briggs flicked the photo Celia was holding. 'That happened afterwards. No one else was driving.'

'That's not the point. What if the truth is dramatically different? Nicci needs to know.'

Briggs dropped the photograph of the wrecked car back into the box, then perched on the edge of his desk. It was an unusually informal pose for him. 'Do you know Nicci's father, Paul?'

'They lived in the next street and I'd spoken to him, just in passing, and I crossed paths with him a couple of times while I was working. But, once he and Janet had divorced, I don't think I saw him again until Nicci appeared in court for sentencing.'

'He's a bully, both to his team and his family.'

'He and Nicci are estranged.'

Briggs nodded. 'That's good. Fortunately, it's a long time since I worked with him. But I know he talks about her sometimes; she's his anecdote for the repercussions of bad parenting. He talks about how his ex-wife made access difficult, how she put herself before the needs of their daughter and how inevitable it was that Nicci ended up going off the rails. He actually boasts, as if demonstrating how his wife messed up is more important than his daughter going to prison.'

'Nice.'

'He's a shit, and if he speaks like that about his own family, imagine how he treats his team.'

'Fair enough, but I don't understand how that all relates to this.' She waved a hand at the boxes.

'Or this,' he said, holding out his hand. She saw that he held a flash drive. 'Two big boxes and a roll of random papers. See what you can do, Celia. If you can find enough for us to reopen the case, then great. And even better if it helps Nicci.' Then, in a lower tone, 'And a bonus if it silences Paul Waldock.'

She plucked the memory stick from his palm. 'You know that last point's pretty immature, right?'

'Guilty, but not sorry. Just keep me posted.'

Chapter 27

Nicci stood in her front room and watched Celia disappear into Jack's house. The door closed behind them and she continued to stare at it for the next half an hour. Celia had shown no nerves about speaking to Jack and Nicci wondered what that meant. Celia was tough, that went without saying, but she wasn't foolhardy. Beyond that, there were just two possibilities; either Celia thought that Jack was no longer a threat, or that he'd never been one.

Nicci stepped further back from the window, frowning slightly as a question formed. *If Jack had attacked her, shouldn't she now fear for Celia?*

The memories she'd retained from the day of the crash were all separate from one another; she could go over each in isolation, but they never flowed. It was like going through the box of video cassettes her gran had kept in the bottom of the bookcase; she could slide one into the player, watch it, then eject it again, before moving on to the next. There was always a break between each, a jolt into reality and a feeling that she might not be watching them in the most logical order. Jack had been remote that day. And then angry with Charlie. Then damning of her ever since.

But she wasn't sure that her visceral reaction to seeing him had been fair.

Sure, Celia had known him since childhood, but Nicci had

too. She only thought about that time when Charlie accidentally stepped into her thoughts.

This time she chose to think of the brothers.

She and Charlie had started hanging out in primary school. She guessed they'd been about eight or nine. They hadn't really known each other until they'd been put in groups of four to make a poster about one of the local streets in the 1800s.

They'd chosen Mawson Road because they lived here. It used to be called Union Row and they'd drawn the nearby mill and workhouse. Then they'd started picking out popular Victorian baby names and saying them in posh voices. Nicci would say 'Oh, Frederick!' and Charlie would reply 'Yes, Henrietta!' They'd giggled at each new pair of names, trying and failing to suppress what quickly erupted into uncontrolled laughter.

She smiled at the thought, but immediately had to fight back tears too.

They'd been inseparable after that, so she'd known Jack since then. Not to hang out with – he'd been too much older – an actual teenager. She made a quick calculation; Jack would have been about sixteen; sixteen and probably really pissed off with the pair of them.

A tear had escaped onto her cheek in any case and she left it to run; it was a memory that deserved tears. Jack loved Charlie, and Charlie had adored Jack; no question about it. Jack had been moody at times, but never violent, never devious.

And on the day of the crash? If he'd seen Charlie like that, with Nicci at the wheel? She wasn't sure of the answer, but beyond that? She couldn't imagine Jack being a danger to either of them in the cold light of day.

She returned to the window then, wishing Celia had never gone to see him. She'd been in there for a while and it would be too late to stop Celia from asking Jack about the crash. Nicci wanted – needed – to know the truth but had no stomach for heaping any more trouble on Charlie's family until there was more evidence.

Nicci picked up her phone; calling would be quickest, but a text would be less intrusive. The front door opened again before she'd had time to decide, but, instead of heading home, Celia turned towards Mill Road without a backwards glance.

Nicci pressed dial, then heard the call divert straight to voicemail.

So, Celia's phone had been turned off. She didn't need to let Nicci know where she was headed, or why. 'Stop,' she whispered to herself, 'just stop.'

She paced back and forth, to the window and then towards the rear of the house. She didn't need to fear whatever Celia would uncover; Celia had known Nicci's faults and had helped her in any case.

She paced some more, fighting the self-doubt that was trying to settle and breed in her gut. Finally, she halted at the door. 'Stop, stop, stop,' she snapped. She gripped the frame and refused to let herself move.

Celia was solid and loyal.

Nicci let that thought settle; she'd seen the look her parents had both given her when, first her dad, and then her mum, had lost faith in her. It had felt as though they'd opened her up and found the real, and far inferior, version of their daughter inside. And there'd been no way back from that.

Celia would come home and, until then, Nicci would wait.

Rush hour in Cambridge was always a heavy, slow-moving affair. Mill Road was a single lane of traffic in each direction, but less orderly than most other roads in the city. The roads traversing it were one-way streets, with the traffic flow of each running in the opposite direction to the next. The plan was to stop drivers weaving through the back streets, turning them into dangerous rat-runs. The result was one heavily congested main road with cars, buses, taxis, bicycles and pedestrians creeping forward at every junction, all attempting to make it home with everyone unscathed.

Nicci had assumed that Celia would be walking or busing home and was surprised when she saw the lights of the Bianchina illuminating the glass in the back wall of Celia's tiny garage.

It was only a few yards up to her back door, but Celia walked with purpose and didn't spot Nicci just the other side of the fence. Nicci gave her fifteen minutes to settle in before stepping over the fence and knocking on Celia's back door. She waited a couple of minutes for a reply, knocking once more before using her own key to let herself in. 'Hello? Celia?'

A few months earlier Celia had purchased a 30-inch monitor for her desk. She had liked the idea of being able to enlarge proof layouts and digital editions of magazines when they came through. In reality, she had found it dominated her desk and made her feel hemmed in, so she'd unplugged it and stowed it away. But, in the short time she'd been home, she'd manoeuvred it out of the bottom of her 'everything-cupboard' and returned it to the end of her desk.

'Hi.'

Celia had been too absorbed in staring at the monitor.

Nicci startled her. 'I'm sorry.'

'No, no. I should have let you know I was home.' Celia hit the screensaver, then patted the chair next to her own. 'I need to talk to you. And there's a rug here. You're looking cold.'

'I was starting to worry,' Nicci told her. It was a lie; she'd been doing some kind of worrying ever since Celia had left all those hours ago.

'See that?' Celia pointed to a flash drive protruding from the front of her computer. 'That holds case files with everything leading up to your trial. Police reports, forensics, witness statements and more. I will tell you as much or as little as you like. But first . . .'

'Jack?'

'He didn't hurt you, I'm absolutely sure of it.'

Nicci nodded. 'I thought it through too, and you're right. But, I know something's wrong.'

‘With Jack?’

‘Maybe. Maybe just with the situation. Why did he come back?’

‘His marriage broke down. He has a daughter, but he said he doesn’t see her. That doesn’t always hurt people, but I think it’s hurting him.’

How much it was hurting was hard to tell with someone such as Jack, someone whose life had been punctuated by loss so many times over. She and Charlie had met Sadie after Jack’s first couple of dates with her. They hadn’t liked her, but neither of them had decided why. But, whatever Sadie had done, it had to have caused less pain than she had wrought upon him. She changed the subject. ‘So what else did you discover?’

‘I transferred every file from the flash drive to the computer, and I am willing to share it all, if you can face it. And as long as it doesn’t go further.’

‘It won’t.’

Celia sought no further reassurances and recounted her meetings with Briggs and Maitland. ‘I spent a couple of minutes looking at the documents before you arrived.’ Celia hesitated. ‘I haven’t looked through everything yet, but I know there are some disturbing photographs . . .’

Nicci straightened, she spread her hands out on her thighs to keep them still. ‘I need to see them.’ She looked at Celia as steadily as she was able. She’d had plenty of photographs pushed in front of her. Various officers had tried to make her remember. Or confess. Her eyes closed briefly. ‘Please, Celia, I need this.’

Celia still looked uncertain, but she nodded.

‘Thank you. There’s just one thing; I don’t want to see Charlie. Not like that.’

‘I’ll be careful.’ She moved her mouse so that the screen unlocked. ‘Are you ready?’

Chapter 28

Celia flicked between windows until Nicci saw her own battered face filling the screen. Celia pointed to the steering-wheel marks near Nicci's brow. 'Briggs spotted them.'

Nicci felt herself blanch. It wasn't because of any revulsion at her injuries. It was a mix of fear and relief that made her feel queasy, that, and the realisation that these tiny marks meant that she and Celia were stepping into the unknown. Celia copied the files again, this time onto her laptop, and she and Nicci sat in the same room, reading at their own speed. For the next couple of hours Nicci read reports and statements, and sifted through photographic evidence and forensic reports. Celia kept a note-book by her side and frequently made notes, shorthand probably, since Celia's gaze never left the screen. Nicci opened a window for Word and flipped back and forth to that, making her own notes too.

Eventually Celia pushed her chair back. 'I need a break. Drink?' Celia reached into the mini fridge, then gently lobbed a can of Coke at Nicci. 'Flick the side to stop it fizzing.'

'Does that work?'

Celia shrugged. 'Try it.'

Nicci placed the can on the floor beside her chair.

'If you don't open it, you won't know if it works.'

'I don't believe it does, and I don't want to make a mess.'

Celia waved her notepad. 'We're going to shake this up, and definitely make more mess than a few drops of Diet Coke, I hope you know that. Just open the drink.' She glanced at her notes. 'There was a great deal of focus on Ellie's change of mood and I know you can't remember much, but what's your gut instinct?'

'She wasn't herself when we were down by the river. She'd been passionate about our course, but suddenly she was talking about leaving. That didn't make sense at all. I've thought about that many times.'

'Any ideas?'

'She was doubting herself; she said she didn't know whether she was up to getting involved.'

'I read that, but I wasn't sure exactly what she meant.'

'No, me neither. But you've heard of bystander syndrome?'

'Yes.'

'Well, it felt to me that Ellie might be talking about that; the fear that she wouldn't step out of the crowd to help.' It struck Nicci that a good proportion of bystanders had no intention of stepping out of any crowd. Therefore, it wasn't about them thinking that someone else would help, it was about them never having given a shit in the first place. And if Ellie was worried about her conscience, then she had never been one of those. Nicci felt herself go cold. She remembered Ellie's example, *if a man was drowning*, and wondered how many people sitting by the river that day would have tried to help. And how many would have stood by as they lay in the wreckage.

Celia looked at her curiously, 'What just happened?'

'What do you mean?'

'Your expression changed. It darkened.'

'Something was preying on Ellie's mind, that's certain. I think she wanted to speak out, but couldn't.'

'You think she was frightened?'

'Maybe. But I don't know whether that would have been for

herself, or for the trouble she may have caused. Ellie liked having a fuss made of her, but never liked attention for the wrong reasons.'

'Who does?'

Nicci had spent three years in prison with plenty of people whose mindset was confrontational, who'd set out years ago to layer trouble upon trouble. She blinked the memory away, and a thought immediately arrived in the space it vacated. 'There is one thing – and I don't know why I have never looked at it this way around before – Ellie didn't want the others to see that she was upset. At the time I thought she was avoiding awkward questions, or because she didn't want to lower the mood. What if she was trying to be low key for other reasons?'

'You mean the problem related to someone who was there?'

'Exactly. Was there anything amiss between her and Callum when they lived together?'

'I've wracked my brains on that one, too. I don't think so. Callum came across as cocky sometimes, but that was just a front. He mooned over Gemma, but I assume he knew he was punching above his weight there. He talked about other girls, but I think that's all it was: talk.'

'So they didn't fight?'

'Him and Ellie? Not that I'm aware of. Probably the usual tiffs about tidying. He'd leave things lying around, but then she kept to her room most of the time.'

'Why wasn't this looked into during the case? I know they asked whether her hysteria could have caused the crash, but I don't mean that. I mean, what caused her to be that distressed in the first place?'

'I doubt it was considered relevant, although it was discussed in court.'

'Was it?' Nicci couldn't remember. Much of the court proceedings remained a blur. The days had been long and there had been too much to absorb. She had also been taking regular – probably too regular – doses of painkillers. It had been painful to sit for hours, so she'd numbed herself with the drugs available.

'It was brief. Jack, Rob, Gemma and Callum were all asked why she was so upset. Nobody had an answer. Then, here somewhere,' Celia clicked on several windows in succession until she found the right one, 'the accident reconstruction witness – a Ben Kohli – stated "that, given the nature of the crash and the injuries sustained by Miss Ellie Daniels, and her position within the vehicle, there appears to be no possibility that she physically interfered with the driver at the time of impact. However, it is feasible that she may have caused distraction to the driver, causing a momentary lapse in concentration which, in turn, could have contributed to the crash."' Celia scrolled down the page as she read. 'The judge queried whether there was any evidence to explain Ellie's distress. The prosecution argued that it would not have been relevant, and the defence agreed.'

Perhaps it was nothing. Perhaps she would have still driven them off the road in the same way, and with the same consequences. But Nicci's instincts knew better than that, and she paled.

There was a bigger picture and her own defence had shut it down.

She scrambled to her feet and felt her half-drunk can of Coke spin across the floor. She rushed through the door, and made it as far as the kitchen before she began to puke.

Chapter 29

Nicci cleaned her vomit from Celia's floor. Refusing to cry. Refusing to release any emotion whatsoever. And Celia had, as always, been reassuring. She'd gone to mop up the spilt Coke and raised her voice once or twice to make a comment, just to make sure Nicci knew she was there. Which Nicci always did.

When the floor was back to being clear and dry, Nicci stood and stared at her reflection in the kitchen window. It was past nine and dark beyond the glass. Nicci was not the person she'd been those years before. Then she'd been naive and frightened and too eager to please. Now she knew that she'd been let down, lied to and used, and that changed a person as much as everything else she'd been through.

And somebody knew something.

Rob and Gemma, Callum and Jack.

They were the only ones left from that day. And she only knew the whereabouts of two of them. She washed and dried her hands, then quietly opened the back door. 'I'm going home. I need a shower,' she called out, and slipped away before Celia could reply.

She changed her clothes, swapping one pair of narrow, indigo jeans for another, almost identical pair, and black T-shirts also like for like. She was home for less than five minutes before she left again. Her black Converse made no noise on the pavement, but she still waited until she was a few yards past Celia's before starting to run.

Nicci knew that Gemma still lived at home with her parents, two streets away in Tenison Road; she had caught sight of her several times over the last year. The family lived in a large bay-fronted terrace.

She banged on the solid front door. The nearest of the street lamps was a few houses away and the only other light came from a semicircle of glass above the door. She could barely see the red and black chequerboard tiles under foot, but she knew they were there. She couldn't quite grasp the metaphor, and was still distracted by it when Patrick Hayward opened the door.

He was almost as she remembered him. He had gained a few pounds around his face and waist, but seemed to have lost weight almost everywhere else. The effect was as though he was impersonating himself. She had never been sure whether he could be classed as good looking; he and his wife Andrea always seemed pleased with themselves and that had tainted her view. And, if he had been attractive, that moment had definitely passed.

Most people opened the door to unexpected callers with polite coldness; all the polite disappeared as soon as he recognised her. She remembered that he once had a good smile, but there was no sign of it now. 'What do you want?' he said.

'I've come to see Gemma.'

'Why?'

Nicci tried to see further into the house but there was nothing visible apart from a glimpse of sage-green textured wallpaper and a three-bulb ceiling light. 'Please can I talk to her? It's important.'

Each time he spoke his lips moved the minimum amount, then returned to a thin, hard line. 'Why?' he asked again.

Nicci shifted her weight from one leg to the other. 'It's important.'

'I heard you were back last year. If you wanted to see Gemma, you should have tried then.'

Nicci glared at him. 'And you would have blocked me.'

'Too right.'

'Fuck this,' she muttered, then shouted, 'Gemma.'

Patrick rushed to shut her out then, but not before Nicci saw a shadow move in the hall behind him. The door stopped just a couple of inches short of closing.

'Dad?'

It took a few more seconds of muffled whispering before she saw either of them again. Patrick Hayward let Nicci in, and he had his coat on before she'd made it to the end of the hall. 'I'll be back at closing time,' he said over his shoulder to Gemma and she didn't reply.

'Right,' she said, and turned towards the back sitting room. Nicci followed.

Nicci had been to the Hayward house a couple of times. The first at primary when kids were young enough to be invited to parties in bulk, when kids went because their mates were going, and not because of any real friendship with the birthday child. She guessed she'd been invited for similarly impersonal reasons. That time, and the second, when she'd tagged along when Charlie had dropped in on Rob, this room had looked pretty much the same; decorated with Victorian botanical print wallpaper. Rich shades. A dark but comfortable room.

The paper had been painted over, but there were still tinges of emerald slipping through the magnolia. The mock-Victorian furniture had gone too; in its place was a day bed and a cluster of side tables, book shelves and plastic storage crates. The room was overly hot, but Gemma wore a long-sleeved jumper and, when she sat, pulled a throw across her lap. Nicci refused a seat, and waited until she had Gemma's full attention.

Gemma's gaze passed from her hands, to the floor, to the opposite wall before finally settling on Nicci, but, even then, there was something off about her focus. 'What do you want?'

'Tell me about the crash.'

Her eyes were flat. 'You know what happened.'

'There's more. What happened in the car when I was unconscious?'

'Charlie and Ellie died.' She tilted her head. 'Is that what you mean, Nicci? Or do you want me to be a little more specific?'

'Why did you come that day? You never liked me or Charlie, and you barely knew Ellie.'

'I knew her well enough. Callum was on my course, and he lived with her.'

'So?'

'Callum was trying every trick in the book to get in my knickers. Including flirting with Ellie whenever he thought it might grab my attention. Juvenile, but also true. I doubt he'd ever had a girlfriend.' Her expression instantly jumped from indifferent to sharply amused. 'Probably a paid up member of the incel fraternity.'

'Why the hell did you hang out with him?'

She shrugged, 'It helped my grades. It was a perk of the situation. Besides, he helped Rob's grades too. Rob was in his final year at the time, but nowhere near as academic as Callum.' She tilted her head and seemed pleased with herself. 'They got on well actually.'

'With their exams, or each other?'

'Rob would have got what he wanted from the situation.' There was an edge to her tone. Possibly a hint at an unburied sibling hatchet. 'He usually does,' Gemma added.

Nicci had a flash of memory from secondary; Gemma leaving her friends at the corner of East Road, then she and Rob walking home in single file, ten feet or so between them, and neither acknowledging the other.

'Of course, you never finished your studies, did you?' One corner of Gemma's mouth twitched with a smile. 'I switched courses, I mean, what was the point of training to be a paramedic when my arms didn't work properly?' She paused, swallowed and continued to smile. 'But at least I do have a qualification. In fact, the university was very good to me. Did you ever study again?'

'No.'

'Well, I'm pleased about that at least.'

Gemma was angry and bitter, and Nicci understood. She kept her expression neutral; it was a skill she'd had to practise countless times. 'So why were you all there?'

'Callum told us about it. The others were going and I thought it would be a laugh. Rob agreed to take me.'

'But you really went because of Jack.' Nicci didn't leave space for a response. 'When did you first notice that Ellie was upset?'

'Why do you care?'

'Why let me in just to be a pain in the arse, Gemma? Have you always planned what you'd say to me? How you'd try to belittle me?' Nicci closed in on Gemma, then leant in close, so that their faces were just inches apart. 'I remembered something, Gemma. I remembered a hand, like this . . .' she reached out and wrapped her hand around the back of Gemma's skull, 'a strong hand.' Gemma wriggled but Nicci held tight. 'Someone grabbed my head and smashed it against the steering wheel.' For a moment Nicci pressed harder with the tips of her fingers, then released her grip. 'And you were there.'

Gemma's face grew ashen. 'I don't know what you're talking about.'

'Did Jack touch me?'

Gemma shook her head. 'No.'

'Did Rob come back?'

'No.'

'What about Callum?'

'No. No, Nicci. Please stop it. You weren't conscious, you don't know.'

'I don't know what?'

'You don't know what you're talking about.'

'My memory isn't wrong.'

'It doesn't matter. The whole thing is done, just drop it.'

'For fuck's sake, how is it done for you or for me? Look at us both. Why would I drop it, Gemma?' When Nicci had grabbed Gemma the first time she hadn't wanted to let go. She'd wanted to shake her or slap her. She stood abruptly, stepping away from the sofa and taking several long breaths. 'Tell me,' she growled. 'I need one straight fucking answer from you, because if you won't tell me, Callum will.'

'Callum's gone. He cleared off.'

'Then I'll find him, Gemma. And I'll go back to the police, make them open the investigation . . .'

The eye-roll was subtle. 'They won't listen to you.'

'They'll listen to Celia.'

That sparked Gemma's attention. She said nothing, but Nicci felt the room tighten around them. 'We have new evidence. We can prove my head injury wasn't caused by the accident. Callum will tell me.'

'He won't.'

For a single second Nicci saw that Gemma was angry with herself. And then, in the next second, more of the old Gemma was back. Cold. Detached. But no longer entirely in control. 'Well, you asked for it.' She leant back in her seat. 'Ellie and Charlie were alive in the wreckage, not for long mind you. But long enough for Charlie to blindly grab at you. It was the pain, his dying, involuntary thrashings. That's what you remember. Because you drank. You crashed. The thing is, you have supposedly paid for it. So now you have the same opportunities as the next person, whereas I . . .' she tugged at her sleeves and pulled each in turn above her elbows, 'I have this to look at every day. And the pain. Do you know about that? About the drugs and the nightmares. About waking up in the middle of the night with my whole body hurting, and my arms feeling like they are burning, like the bones are sawing against each other. I never get music stuck in my head, just the sound of my bones snapping again and again.'

Chapter 30

Nicci had come for breakfast, and they had sat at opposite sides of the kitchen table, Nicci with tea, Celia with coffee, and a pile of toast between them. Nicci had an early client and hadn't stayed for long. Celia wiped the table, and had toast crumbs on her hands, when someone pressed the doorbell. She rinsed, then dried them as she walked up the hall. The silhouette in the frosted glass was tall and broad-shouldered, but it didn't occur to her that it was Jack until she actually opened the door.

Celia was curious, but not surprised. As life had gone on, she recognised that more things made her curious, but fewer contained surprise. 'Jack?'

'Would you mind if I came in?' His clothes had a slept-in appearance but, from his face, he looked like someone who hadn't slept at all.

She opened the door wider to let him through. 'The kitchen, if you don't mind.'

She closed the door behind him, and followed him back down the hall.

'Sit down, Jack.'

He didn't accept the invitation at first, but stood next to the chair. He wore grey trousers and a pale blue buttoned shirt, with the sleeves rolled up to his elbows.

Celia pointed at the creases. 'I hope your meeting was yesterday. Or, if it is today, I hope you've come to borrow an iron.'

'I've come to apologise actually.'

'I see.'

'I am ashamed to have lost my temper like that, Celia. And I'm really sorry if you felt threatened at all.'

'I have experienced worse,' she replied levelly. 'Besides, there may have been some deliberate button pushing on my part, you know.'

'Well, I am sorry. That's all I wanted to say really.'

But, if it had been the only reason for his visit, he would have left then. His expression seemed sincere, but she knew that some people were well practised.

She smiled warmly. 'Now will you sit?' She re-boiled the kettle and put four slices of bread in the toaster, then placed the jam, marmalade and butter in front of him.

'I'm not hungry actually.'

'Did you have breakfast this morning, or just hang around, wondering how early it would be acceptable to call? I think you thought, "I'll wait until nine", because that's the start of the working day, and because you were on my doorstep at about one minute past.'

'Impressive.' He raised his hands by a couple of inches in mock surrender, and she placed the toast in front of him.

'Aren't you having any?'

'I already ate with Nicci.'

He looked uncomfortable.

'Don't worry, she's not here now. Coffee?'

He nodded. 'With milk thanks.'

'So, tell me what's on your mind.' Of course, she already knew, but how he expressed it made a difference.

'She told you that someone hit her head against the steering wheel. How do you know she didn't lie?'

'I've seen the marks in the injury photos; she's telling the truth.'

‘What if she made them herself?’

Celia passed him his drink, and then sat across the table from him. ‘And waited until after she’d served her sentence to mention it? Would that make sense to you?’

‘No,’ he conceded. ‘But I believed that all the details had come out in court. The thing is . . .’ he pushed the untouched toast away, ‘it seems cruel to me that you would want to stir this up. Nicci was driving. She and Charlie were great friends, but she still killed him.’

Celia flattened one hand on the table and ran her hand along the pine, feeling the grain against her palm. She was out of practice at pushing for information and she needed something to settle her unease. ‘I’ve found a problem with the evidence, Jack.’ She made sure that she sounded firm. ‘I’m not going to ignore it.’

‘And there are people, like my dad, who don’t need any more pain.’ Jack’s dark eyes watched her steadily. ‘So I wanted to tell you to leave it alone.’

Celia nodded. She understood; when people already had an acceptable picture of events, it often became difficult to trade *that* truth for *the* truth. ‘But?’

‘I don’t sleep well when there are things on my mind. I never have. So I lay awake last night wondering why you’d do this. But then I remembered Dad describing you as persistent and determined. It made me pause. Mind you, I don’t remember him saying anything about honesty.’

‘Or lack of it?’

‘Agreed.’ He took a sip of coffee and became occupied with thought. ‘Like I said, I wanted to tell you to leave it alone. And then I googled you. It was about four this morning and I read that you had won awards for “tenacious investigation” and a “dogged search for the truth”. So, for the next few hours, I lay there asking myself whether you deserved those accolades. And, if so, how I could be right to demand that you stop.’

‘The awards don’t matter to me, but my reputation always

has. I've never chased salacious headlines; I was never that kind of journalist. I don't want to cause anyone distress, and I'm not trying to prove Nicci's innocence – she was driving that car. But what if there was more to it?'

'Such as?'

'To be honest, I have no idea. Nicci needs answers though.'

He snorted.

'And why shouldn't she, Jack? She has a right.'

He scowled. 'How will you do anything, apart from create more pain?' But there was more consternation than anger in his tone. And he still showed no sign of wanting to leave.

'It's a risk.' In her experience there were always shadows in an incomplete picture. And even when the truth wasn't wanted, the lack of it was corrosive. 'People, in general, do deal with the truth, Jack.'

She didn't know whether he heard her, he seemed too deep in thought. She didn't hurry him, and eventually he pointed to the plate of toast. 'Is it still okay for me to have some?'

'Of course.'

She made more coffee while he spread butter and jam. She couldn't remember him ever being a frivolous child; he'd been serious and studious. Responsible. Fate hadn't rewarded him for it. 'You're going to follow this to wherever, no matter what I say, aren't you?'

'Tell me exactly what you want.'

'To keep me informed, to discuss with me before anything goes public. To let me be the buffer between what you're doing and my dad finding out. And I just want to talk to you: I don't want Nicci anywhere near my dad, or me, okay?' He nodded to himself. 'Yes, I think that's everything.'

Celia nodded too. 'That makes sense, as long as you don't try to block me from releasing information if I need to?'

'Just talk to me first?'

'Okay.'

'Okay,' he agreed and this time he stood. 'Thank you for the coffee and toast, Celia, I appreciate it.'

Celia walked him towards the front door. 'I'd like to speak to Callum, do you know where I might find him?'

'Sorry. He was studying to be a paramedic, but the last thing I heard was that he'd dropped out. Maybe he went back home.'

'I thought Gemma might know, but she doesn't.'

'Try Rob then. Trackside Gym, it's just over the bridge, on the left.'

'Are you in touch with him?'

Jack shook his head and looked at Celia with a wry expression. 'I would have thought you would have worked it out, Celia; I don't keep in touch with anyone.'

Chapter 31

Trains had started to run through Cambridge in 1845. The tracks had sliced through Mill Road, and the railway had brought crowds of sightseers followed by new prosperity to the area. In 1889 the first road bridge was opened and it had become a landmark in the area, dividing Mill Road into 'this side of the bridge' and 'the other side'. The bridge, damaged in Second World War bombing, had been replaced in 1980. It had needed to be taller than the original to allow for the electrification of the lines, and the new design featured solid sides instead of railings. Celia always thought it seemed out of place, more of a divide in Mill Road than a link. She found Trackside Gym immediately, and within sight of the railway line; it was only then that she realised that the name didn't relate to the gym's proximity to any athletics ground.

The building was one of several industrial units, and, as Celia approached the front entrance, she expected the industrial look to continue on the inside too. In fact, the gym was light and sleek inside, and fitted the image of a facility in a hotel, or perhaps on a cruise ship. Music filled the space, chosen, she imagined, for the optimum number of beats per minute rather than for its singalong potential.

Two fitness instructors were present, each occupied by a client. The nearest excused herself and walked over to Celia. She wore a crop top and had one of those stomachs that look as though they are too flat and toned to exist outside Photoshop. But there it was.

Celia realised that one eyebrow was still raised as she spoke. 'Is Rob around? I need to speak to him.'

'Sure.' The woman crossed the floor to what Celia guessed might be an office at the back of the unit. She held onto the top of the door frame and stretched out for the few seconds it took to convey Celia's presence.

Some people had too much motivation. Celia glanced around in case there was a chair handy.

The woman returned to her client and Rob walked across to Celia. He wore joggers and a loose T-shirt, but Celia could tell that he had the whole Photoshop thing going on too. 'Beth said you wanted to see me?' He was halfway through the sentence when recognition made him smile. 'Celia? I didn't realise it was you.'

'No problem. I didn't actually give my name.'

He looked at her expectantly. She'd had that expression when she'd bumped into a former colleague; been pleased to see them and had then been flummoxed about what she was supposed to say next.

'I'm trying to locate Callum Shaughnessy.'

His smile faltered. 'Can I ask why?'

Celia nodded in the direction of the office. 'Can we talk in private?'

•

The 'office' had a small desk positioned in the opposite corner to the door. Most of the room was taken up with a massage table in the middle. There were framed prints of abstract pale green leaves on the wall, and two chairs by the desk.

'Yes,' Rob said. 'Please have a seat.'

Celia hadn't realised that her glance at the seating had been quite so wistful. She was momentarily tempted to pretend to prefer to stand, but so much fitness in one place was tiring.

She noticed several certificates standing at the back of the desk. 'I thought this would just be an office.'

'No, it's my treatment room. Beth, Dan and I all trained together, they took sports science and I took sports therapy. They encourage people to injure themselves, then I fix them.' He laughed softly. 'That's the in-joke here.'

They took one chair each; Celia immediately relaxed into hers, and Rob sat more squarely, no doubt continuing to flex one group of muscles or another.

Rob had become serious at the first mention of Callum, and as soon as she was seated grew concerned again. 'Has something happened?'

'In what way?'

'My sister had a visit from Nicci Waldock. It upset her.'

Celia had contemplated finding an excuse, unrelated to either Nicci or Jack, as her reason for looking for Callum, but she'd also guessed that there were good odds that Gemma would talk to her brother. It was always hard to fish without making ripples. 'Nicci lives next door to me.'

'In your other house.'

'Yes.'

'I'd heard that.' He frowned deeply. 'My parents were angry when they found out. I guess you have your reasons?'

'I do,' she said, but didn't offer anything else. 'Nicci visited Gemma on impulse. It might not have been the best way to ask, but she was trying to understand more about the crash.'

'And she thought Gemma would want to help?' He looked doubtful. 'You know, she recovered well at first, then she plateaued. We bought the gym together. She was happy to invest, and I hoped it might help her improve her physical health, which might, in turn . . . you know, improve other things. But she rarely leaves home.'

'So having Nicci in her house would have been quite a shock?'

'I don't know actually,' he said. 'Apparently Nicci came to the door and Gemma decided to see her. So it was her choice.' He shrugged. 'I just don't know what she expected, but Mum said she wouldn't stop crying afterwards.'

'I'm sorry.'

'Don't be, it's not your fault. Perhaps it could have had the opposite effect.'

'How do you mean?'

He leant forwards, elbows on knees. 'Some of her problems are physical: limited movement, real and phantom pain . . . but some are psychological; maybe being faced with Nicci could have changed something.' He sighed. 'I don't know, when I say it out loud, it sounds like clutching at straws.' And then, with an abrupt change of direction, he added, 'Can I ask why you are looking for Callum?'

'He was in the car, conscious throughout as far as I know. Nicci has some questions.'

'Didn't you keep in touch with him after the trial?'

Celia shook her head. She had had less contact with Callum than any of the other students who had rented the house next door. 'He was quiet, he never spoke much.'

'Well, he dropped out of college after the accident, but, the last I heard, he was still around Cambridge. What has he done?'

Celia cocked her head to one side. 'Not "Is he okay?"'

Rob sat back in the chair. He looked at Celia and seemed to be weighing up how much, or little, he could trust her. She wasn't oblivious to comparisons with Jack; they were both suspicious of her for a start. There was a darkness in both of them.

'I never liked him. I found him uncomfortable to be around; there was something off about him.'

'In what way?'

'I've always been protective of Gemma; it's partly the age gap I suppose – and because she's my sister. I'm sorry if that's sexist, but it's the truth. Her first boyfriend really hurt her. But I had a different kind of bad feeling about Callum.'

Most years Celia had let the house to larger groups of students, and there had been four at the start of that year, but the other two, both girls, had left at the end of the first trimester. One had moved in with her boyfriend, and the other had decided to commute from home. Celia had taken the opportunity to redecorate the vacated rooms, so no one else had shared with Ellie and Callum. How had it been, she suddenly wondered, for Ellie sharing the house with just Callum?

'Celia, are you okay?'

'Yes, I'm sorry. What did you say?'

'About Gemma. Callum asked her out several times, but she clearly wasn't interested. He didn't seem to be able to see that, though, and trailed around after her. He was always at ours on some pretext or other, and Gemma was finding him increasingly persistent. He was constantly on the edge.'

'I hear what you're saying, Rob, but I know that Gemma visited Ellie and Callum at my house.'

'Did she?'

She couldn't tell whether he was surprised or disappointed. Both perhaps.

'She should have shut him down sooner.' Rob's voice became more insistent. 'But they were on the same course; she couldn't just avoid him.'

'And yet you all chose to go out together that weekend?'

'Because she still had feelings for Jack.'

Chapter 32

Rob had moved into his own flat a couple of years earlier. It was closer to the gym, not that his parents' home was more than three or four minutes' walk away.

The flat was small, but the air was clearer there and every time he returned to the family's house – like now – he felt himself grow heavier.

The energy drained from him.

He guessed he hadn't visited for two or three weeks. And in the intervening time he had dismissed them from his thoughts, but, as soon as he turned the corner and the house came into view, he began to feel stifled.

He'd kept a key and opened the door to the aroma of patchouli air freshener fighting against the lingering smell of cheese on toast.

The house had changed a lot since his childhood, especially with Gemma relocating herself to the old dining room. But as soon as he returned he felt the way he had when he'd been a child; he'd grown since then and that made him wonder how it would have been if there hadn't been the crash.

He doubted Gemma would have qualified as a paramedic or, if she had, she wouldn't have stuck at the job. She had claimed that she'd had the right mentality, but he knew her well and the idea of it seemed ridiculous. She'd been trying to please one of her parents, although he never knew which. Unless she'd been trying to please them both, which, in his opinion, was a challenge that ran close to impossible.

He timed his visit to the house when both of them were out. That was his normal routine, and he saw no reason to change it even though that had meant waiting over an hour to speak to Gemma, when he would rather it had been sooner. She was, as usual, in her chair in her room. The television was switched off and her iPad was a couple of feet out of reach. Her phone was on charge. He wondered if she'd had any contact with anyone so far today. He glanced at his watch. It was ten past two.

He took a moment to study her expression; he could tell that she had been worrying over something. She looked at him expectantly, but there was some kind of unrest behind her eyes; it was hard to pinpoint. Perhaps it was the intensity of her gaze, or the way her pupils were totally dilated.

'What's wrong?' he asked her.

'Nothing. Just wondered why you decided to come today?'

'I was thinking about the visit you had from Nicci. I could speak to her if you wanted me to?'

'No,' she said, 'but you didn't have to come here to ask me that.'

'I didn't, but the thing is, I've just had Celia round. No warning. She just turned up.'

'Did you tell her anything?' Gemma asked sharply.

Rob shook his head. 'What's going on? Nicci's been out for a year, why now?'

Gemma shrugged. 'Apparently she remembered something.'

'Like what?'

Gemma inhaled slowly, and Rob guessed she was considering her words. 'She says she remembers somebody banging her head against the steering wheel. But I was there, I know she was stone-cold unconscious.' She paused, stared blankly past him and chewed her lip as she thought. 'It's her mind playing tricks on her.'

'Is it though?'

Gemma raised one hand, palm upwards, then dropped it back to her lap. 'All right, so she remembers . . .'

And even though her sentence wasn't complete, they were both silent. Each probably completing it in their own way.

'What if this is the start of something?' he asked her at last.

She shook her head. 'It won't be.'

'How do you know?'

'It just won't be. She's discredited. It's an old case and there's no reason it would ever be looked at again.'

'Her father's police.'

'And that counted for nothing.'

Rob nodded, more to himself than in response to his sister. 'Why are you protecting Callum?'

If she was surprised by the jump in topic, she gave no indication. 'You know why. I'm safer that way.'

'But you're not, you're not at all.'

There was a hint of defiance about her. 'Well, I've been okay so far, haven't I?'

'Nicci going to see you, Celia coming to see me. I don't think it will stop there.' He sat beside her then, putting his hand over hers. 'Tell me, do you feel safe?'

She looked into her lap or perhaps at her hand in his, and then she smiled. 'Actually I do. Callum is nowhere near here and it's going to stay that way.'

Chapter 33

A tattoo becomes a ghost you can't escape.

She'd seen the metaphor as soon as she'd heard the words, and the idea of doing something, however small, to free people from their pasts was what had drawn her to the training. People had three choices with an unwanted tattoo: ignore it, remove it or cover it with something else.

Several of her clients had chosen a second tattoo principally for its ability to cover the first, and had ended up disliking the new one just as much because they knew that the original still lurked underneath.

Her first client of the day was Ted, on his sixth treatment, and close to saying a final goodbye to both Nicci and a badly drawn and badly aged image of Debbie Harry.

'I'm not sorry I had it done in the first place.'

He'd said that on every visit.

In general, people either emphasised how their regrets were either countless or non-existent. Either way they wanted to move on. Whichever the case, they spent a great deal of energy justifying that original decision.

But once the tattoo was gone, it was gone.

Yes, it was an excellent metaphor.

***

By noon she had seen four clients, had finished cleaning her equipment and had a free afternoon ahead of her. Celia had left a couple of hours earlier; Nicci had heard the small but distinctive sound of the Bianchina's engine idling as Celia prepared to drive away. Nicci hadn't seen or heard her return, and had no plans to bother her when she did.

She was making a concerted effort to be a little less intense.

A little more patient.

That was relatively easy when she was in her own domain, another reason why she didn't favour going out. Celia had let her redecorate, which had probably been a rash suggestion, but elsewhere in the house Nicci's influence had been muted. It was her working space where she had felt the need to make a statement, firstly to inspire confidence in her customers, but secondly to make her feel that she belonged here, doing this job.

She'd begun by painting a sign on the treatment-room door. It was a traditional tattoo design, a swooping bluebird with a scroll above and below. The scrolls were filled with curly letters that read *Nicci's Removals.* It had turned out that customers liked it; for some reason they were pleased to know that she could do the artwork, even though they only came to her when they wanted it taken off.

The treatment room had originally been a neutral shade – calico or oatmeal – one of those ultra-safe shades that only belonged in rental properties. Nicci didn't show Celia until it was finished, then she brought her through to the hallway and made a show of opening the door. Celia's gaze was drawn to the centre of the floor where Nicci had installed an old-style dentist's chair, reupholstered in black and red. Then she slowly panned; the walls were papered dark blue with what was designed to look like a small fleur-de-lys pattern, but on closer inspection proved to be tiny skull and crossbones prints. Photographs hung on three of the walls. Not the wall with the window, but the others.

'They're all Norman Collins designs,' Nicci had told her.

Celia had looked blank.

'The guy that Sailor Jerry's named after. I'll keep a bottle of it in the cabinet over there, just in case anyone needs a shot. I'm sure I'll remove plenty of tattoos that are the result of a drunken night or a drunken weekend. Seems to me, if they come in sober and want it taken off, there's no reason why they need to stay sober while I'm doing it.'

'It hurts then?'

Nicci had trained, had removed tattoos under supervision, but this place had been the start. 'Depends on the person. Like anything, it's all relative.' She'd tried to sound confident, but it had been a step into uncertainty. Now this room was the safest place she knew.

Celia climbed into the old dentist's chair, closed her eyes and imagined the burning of the laser.

Rob and Gemma, Callum and Jack.

She'd seen Gemma. So that left Rob and Callum and Jack.

Celia seemed convinced of Jack's innocence, but Nicci wasn't. Not at all. And if not him, then one of them knew something. Someone had tried to kill her.

Rob and Callum and Jack. How hard would it be to find them all? How hard would she need to push to discover the truth? She needed to be a little less gullible. A little more ruthless.

She fell asleep like that, with the laser burning those three names into her skin. Over and over.

Nicci woke with a start. For a split second she thought she was lying on a lounger with the sun beating down on her. She hadn't had a holiday like that since she'd been to Croatia with her parents in the summer before starting sixth form. Her eyes snapped open as Celia spoke.

'You remind me of an undertaker sleeping in a coffin.'

'Was that an article you wrote, or personal experience?'

'Very funny.' Celia tugged at her arm. 'We need to talk, Nicci.'

Nicci slid from the chair to stand on the floor.

'Rob runs a gym just over the bridge; Jack told me where to find him. And I went there.'

An uneasy feeling crept through Nicci's gut; Celia's seriousness was unsettling her. 'What did he say?'

'I was trying to locate Callum, and Rob raised some concerns about Callum's behaviour. I need to ask you, did Ellie ever mention that she felt intimidated by him?'

'No.'

'Rob says that Callum bothered his sister. Pestered her to the point of harassment.'

'No,' Nicci repeated. 'Rob has always been a bit too precious about his sister. Ellie never said anything like that. She found Callum frustrating at times, but that's all. He really liked Gemma, but she didn't take many prisoners as far as I could see.'

'So she would have knocked him back?'

'Without a doubt. Probably would have taken pleasure in it too. She didn't seem to have any respect for him when I spoke to her, but then again, she's always talked like a bitch. I just never worked out if it was all for show, or only some of it.'

'She could have wound him up then?'

'She wound me up.' Nicci gave a sheepish shrug. 'Then again, I'm not the best barometer.'

'There might be a calibration issue,' Celia replied dryly.

Despite the comment, Celia looked just as serious. If Rob's warning had been the extent of Celia's concern, then her expression would have lightened, and if it had only ever been a case of *Gemma's brother said*, then Celia would have been less perturbed in the first place. 'Tell me the rest then,' Nicci said.

'When Ellie and Callum first moved in, there were two other students, Beth and Stephanie. They'd both gone by Christmas. That happens sometimes, and I certainly didn't read any more into it at the time, but I suddenly thought of it when Rob was talking to me and it made me wonder . . .'

'Can you get hold of either of them?'

'More than that, I've spoken to both of them already. Beth said he hung around her, trying too hard to get close. Items of her underwear went missing, and although she had no proof, she said she felt increasingly paranoid about his presence; her boyfriend wasn't happy at all and she moved in with him in the end. Stephanie woke up with Callum in her bed; he claimed to be drunk. She locked her bedroom door after that, but said that there were two further occasions when she heard someone trying the handle. Neither of them said anything; they just moved out.'

'That figures. But then again, that doesn't sound like enough for the police to pursue. I guess I might have done the same.'

'Exactly. The picture isn't quite the same now. Why did Charlie sit in the front of the car?'

The jump in subject surprised Nicci, and she took a moment to answer. 'Because that's where he always sat. He was in my car more than anyone.'

'Okay. So that left Gemma, Ellie and Callum. If Gemma was avoiding Callum, surely the middle of the back seat was the last place she'd sit?'

'We'd been drinking and arguing; it probably wasn't given a second thought.'

'Okay. Well, let me ask you this: what if Ellie was upset by Callum? Is that possible?'

Although some parts of that day no longer existed in Nicci's memory, the time with Ellie by the river was vivid. She knew the answer at once, but she still ran through the episode, giving it life in her mind's eye. Callum had come over to speak to them; Ellie had been frightened then. Nicci had seen the fear and yet she hadn't questioned it. 'Something scared her, and yes, it's possible that it was Callum. But it doesn't prove anything.'

'No, but it's the right place to start.'

A place to start but, in Nicci's opinion, not *the* place to start.

Chapter 34

Celia no longer worked as a journalist; it was a fact and one which she liked to point out whenever it was advantageous. However, Nicci had noticed how far and wide her contacts stretched.

Anglia Ruskin University had begun in the 1850s as Cambridge School of Art, and had evolved via several changes of name and a move to its East Road campus. The site contained a patchwork of buildings, a complicated warren to newcomers, but Celia navigated a precise route from the back entrance towards the office of Dr Otto Hartmann, lecturer in Paramedic Science.

Nicci followed close behind Celia. In daytime the campus was always busy, and even at night there were still pockets of activity. Nicci had only been a few weeks short of completing her first year when the crash had happened. The campus had been her second home and she had loved being there. Now she walked through with heightened senses and more than a little longing.

Dr Hartmann had a student with him, so they waited in the corridor outside his office. Nicci leant against the wall, Celia stood facing her. 'Is this the first time you've been back?' Celia asked.

'Yes. There's a good shortcut through to the shops in Burleigh Street, but I've always avoided it.' At first she had struggled with being in the home where Ellie had lived; now everything about being back in this building was also shaking loose memories. 'It feels taboo.'

Celia nodded, then they waited in silence until the student emerged and Dr Hartmann invited them in. He was a tall, heavy-set man, with the kind of vigorous energy that filled a room.

Celia introduced them both. He gave Nicci's hand a curt shake, then shook Celia's hand more warmly. He spoke with a strong Dutch accent: 'You are the journalist, no less? I am delighted to meet you. I have heard you interviewed on a number of occasions. Are you working on something for the university?'

He didn't wait for a reply, instead he waved at a couple of barely padded utilitarian chairs. 'Please, come in. Sit down. I have time if you like. How can I help you?'

Celia leant towards him, lowering her voice a little. 'This is in confidence, Dr Hartmann, but I need to locate Callum Shaughnessy.'

The name startled him, then he frowned. 'I am not sure I can help. Have you not looked for him via official routes? Your electoral register, for example . . .'

'He's not on it.'

Hartmann interlaced his fingers, resting chin on knuckles. Celia subtly mirrored him.

'Then perhaps he is no longer in Cambridge?'

'There is no Callum Shaughnessy in the east of England.'

Hartmann shrugged apologetically. 'So he moved away. I have not seen him since he dropped out. And I'm sure you are aware that I cannot share confidential information, even relating to former students. But you know he left at least four years ago and . . .'

Celia cut in smoothly. 'That's how long he's been missing.' The lie was enough for him to drop his guard.

'I knew he was struggling . . . He is alive somewhere, I hope?'

This time Celia shrugged. 'We hope so. We are speaking to the police at the moment.' She glanced at her watch. 'We are due there in twenty minutes.'

He thought for a moment. 'I doubt I could offer them much help, but you can tell them that I am willing to speak with them.'

Celia looked doubtful. 'Is it possible to remember when you last saw someone after this length of time?'

Nicci had watched Hartmann throughout the short exchange. He had shifted gears from polite but reluctant, through to curious and, with a nudge from Celia, had just hit fully engaged.

'Of course it is.' He flung his hands out, palms upwards. 'My memory is excellent. He briefly returned to study after the trial. And it was immediately apparent to me that he still wasn't focused on his work.'

'Still?'

'His work had begun to deteriorate some weeks earlier.'

Celia stroked the desktop with her fingertips. 'I understand if you can't tell me, but was that unexpected?'

He clasped his hands behind his neck and then stretched until his seat sat balanced on its back two legs and his vertebrae gave a little volley of popping sounds. 'You know, when I teach, I can very quickly separate the students by potential, from the ones who will get firsts, through the grades to the thirds. I can see this in the first two or three weeks.' He sat straight again and the chair bumped down onto all four legs. 'And Callum was definitely a student who could have received a first.'

'If he hadn't dropped out?'

'No, if he hadn't become distracted midway through trimester two. That was when his behaviour changed. I hoped he would get back on track, but then of course there was the . . . accident.' He glanced at Nicci as he spoke the word. 'And you can tell the police that I will make a statement to that effect, if that is of any help.' He gathered himself, wiped his palm on his hip then held out his hand to Celia.

Celia took the cue, stood and shook his hand again. 'Thank you for your time, you have been very helpful.'

Nicci stood too and he turned to her.

'You have styled yourself on Bettie Page?' he said.

'A little.'

'Notorious in a different way perhaps?' He beamed then. Pleased with himself. He had probably been working up to that line through the whole meeting.

Nicci glanced at Celia, hoping for solidarity, but Celia was smiling at Hartmann, her eyes lit with what looked like admiration. 'Is there someone who would know what upset him during that second trimester?'

'I know. Of course I do. It was because of Rebecca Lake.'

Nicci felt her skin tingle. It began on the back of her neck and crawled its way up her scalp.

Celia remained unperturbed. 'Rebecca Lake?'

Hartmann nodded. 'Apparently they were friends; they worked together.'

Nicci pulled open the door, managed to catch Celia's eye and give her a nod. Celia held out her hand to the doctor. 'Surprisingly informative. Thank you.'

Chapter 35

The meeting had been very short, but more productive than Celia had expected; Nicci was often reluctant to leave the house, so getting her inside the university grounds had been an achievement, without the added benefit of what they'd just discovered. Celia had no idea what that was, because the name Rebecca Lake meant nothing to her, but it had given Nicci a visible jolt.

She was going to ask as soon as the lift moved, but at the last moment a couple of students slipped through the closing doors. She switched topic. 'So, who is Bettie Page?'

'The world's most photographed pin-up model.'

'But he was having a dig at you?'

'It was nothing. Just his clever way of letting me know he knew what I'd done.' The doors opened and they were left alone again. Nicci raised a perfect eyebrow at her. 'I was more surprised when you flirted with him.'

'I didn't flirt, I deployed research. The man is a talented academic, but personally unpopular; a prime target for a little ego massage. I would have taken the same approach if Dr Hartmann had turned out to be a woman.'

'Because Otto is a popular woman's name?'

'Okay, you've made your point. I thought the whole thing would be a waste of time, until he mentioned Rebecca Lake and your eyes lit up. I'm afraid her name means nothing to me. I was about to ask him . . .'

'Don't worry, I know it well enough to explain. You only need the bare bones, after that you can talk to your friend Briggs.' They stepped out onto the ground floor. 'Perhaps you know her as Becky Lake?'

Celia hesitated. It wasn't a particularly memorable name, but something stirred nevertheless. Local news. A missing woman. A body in the Cam. It had been sometime before the accident, when Celia had still been divorced from local news. 'Drowning?'

'She worked for a promotions company, mostly it was about drinks and gig promotions. Ellie and I had seen her around. She never bothered with us, she always approached the men.'

'Why?'

'Blonde hair, short skirt and I think she liked the attention. Anyhow, we didn't know her name then, we'd just think she was asking for trouble . . .' Nicci shot a quick glance at Celia. 'Yes, I know, I know, women should be able to wear what they want . . .'

'They should, but in my experience, a predator takes the weakest from the pack.'

'Right. If there's going to be a nutter in the room, I don't want him choosing me. That's what you mean?'

'Practically word for word.'

'So on this one night we'd been to a couple of places. Mainly in the St Andrew's Street area: the Regal, the Castle, Revs, then later down to Lola Lo. That night she was doing a gin promotion for a few different venues – the point was to advertise the drink, not the pub. So she was in and out of several of the bars that we were in. It was always the same; bold make-up, hair tied up with something sparkly, and she'd be hanging off the arm of any of the doormen if she could; she always liked men in uniform.'

'Did you speak to her?'

Nicci screwed up her nose. 'No. I always found her embarrassing.

A bit cringeworthy, like when your mum gets up at a wedding and starts attempting sexy moves on the dance floor.'

Celia narrowed her eyes as she tried to picture Nicci's mother.

Nicci glared at her. 'Not my mother. One's mother, or another close-enough-to-be-embarrassing relative. Becky loved the attention, didn't seem to realise that people stared because, more than anything else, she was a joke.' They'd reached the front door of the college building and outside dust was blowing in eddies on the pavement. Nicci's straight black hair had been hanging loose down her back. She stopped to fish a hairband from the front pocket of her jeans, tossed her head back and managed to flick her hair into a smooth and flawless ponytail. 'Of course,' she said as she pressed the exit button, 'we saw it differently when she died. It then seemed as though she'd been insecure and vulnerable rather than cocky.'

There was a crossing right outside Anglia Ruskin. Nicci didn't wait for the lights, but stepped through a narrow gap in the traffic and expected Celia to follow. 'Then the next day she was missing. Ellie and I tried to remember the locations where we'd seen her, and in which order. The times. So we kept going back over it . . . look, we were both studying crime and investigation, we were curious people . . . We reckoned we'd seen her about four times during that evening, but never with anyone in particular.'

'So you were never witnesses?'

'No, we saw the reports, but we had nothing to add. We couldn't even agree on what she'd been wearing; it was usually the kind of thing people wear on hen nights – sex-shop fancy dress – don't I sound like a puritan?'

'A little.' Celia was more distracted by the way Nicci was absorbed in the moment; suddenly energised, her thoughts focused.

'The promotion that night was for pink gin, so we agreed on the colour of her outfit, and that it was short – that went without saying. There was no way we could have described her clothes from scratch, but they were shown in a reconstruction and we both recognised them then. She'd been a main topic of conversation between us; right up to the accident as far as I can remember. She was last seen walking away from the city centre, next seen a month later, miles down the Cam at Waterbeach. A few miles from where we spent that last afternoon.'

Nicci strode out and Celia was practically jogging just to keep up. She knew Waterbeach; she'd briefly dated a soldier who'd lived at the barracks. They'd met up at the Sun or the White Horse, and sometimes wandered around the village. Talking about nothing much. She smiled at the memory, but it was fleeting, replaced with a sudden snapshot of Becky Lake. She pouted at the camera with one of those smiles that included two rows of clenched teeth. 'Cow Hollow Wood,' Celia said. 'Found by a dog walker.'

'As always.'

'Yes, if I remember correctly, it was classed as suspicious.' Celia couldn't recall much beyond that and having a vague awareness of the usual sequence: person missing, appeals for information, body found, identity confirmed.

Nicci reached the junction and stopped abruptly. They were outside the fire station, and the fire station stood next door to the police station. 'According to Dr What's-His-Face, Callum knew Becky well enough to be upset by her death. I don't know how they "worked together", but perhaps he was around on the night she disappeared. I don't think Becky Lake would have given Callum a second glance; he would have been shit on her stiletto. It doesn't add up.'

'You're right, it doesn't. But Callum could have just been relishing the drama.'

Nicci shook her head. 'This is more than that.' The wind was cold and blowing hard enough for Nicci's clothes to flap. She wore only a short-sleeved shirt with her jeans, and she should have been shivering, but, instead, she looked flushed and her blue eyes sparkled. 'Please, Celia, go to see your mate Briggs. He can make sure it's checked out.'

‘Where are you going?’

‘Home. I’ll be fine.’ Nicci took a couple of steps back, moving towards the traffic lights. ‘I’ll give Briggs a miss. But you can tell him who else was there that night. Jack. He was doing a shift at the Regal. I know because we saw him.’

‘Callum, Jack, and half of Cambridge’s under twenty-fives,’ Celia muttered. But Nicci had turned away and was already out of earshot, jaywalking across the junction and weaving past pedestrians.

Logically, the connection to Callum was slim. And to Jack, slimmer still. But the feeling that the link was real had galvanised Nicci. There was no hesitation from Celia as she turned towards Parkside Station.

Chapter 36

'Walk with me,' Briggs had said, and now they were halfway around a loop of the city centre, following the path of the traffic. 'I have two hours spare, and walking clears my head, as long as it isn't in the town centre; too many people to step round.'

'And over?'

'Precisely.' He'd led the way, cutting Parker's at an acute angle and re-joining Gonville Place close to the junction with Lensfield Road. 'Once I've gone past the Catholic Church the pavements are clear.'

'Just the fumes to deal with?'

'It'll all be electric one day, and I'll probably die under the wheels of a silent car I didn't hear coming. That'll kill off loads of people our age. At least we'll die with healthy lungs.' He seemed to find that unjustifiably amusing, then he stifled it. 'I've spent the morning discussing death. Always warps my sense of humour.'

'Well, I'm only going to add to the topic.'

He nudged her with his elbow. 'When are you ever going to turn up just for lunch? Or just for a walk? How about a companionable silence?'

She nudged him back. 'How would that work out? One of us would be telling the other some morbid story or other before we made it through the first five minutes. Do you want to try it now?'

He shook his head. 'Absolutely not. I want to hear what's playing on your mind this time.'

'Becky Lake.'

'Becky Lake?' Briggs repeated the name slowly then tilted his head in her direction and eyed her with interest. 'What's your angle, Celia?'

Celia told him about the connection to Callum.

He looked unimpressed. 'So they were both in the city centre on the night she disappeared, along with literally thousands of other people. And you want me to . . . what exactly?' He was more amused than annoyed. 'You know it's not a case I'm working on?'

'I guessed it wasn't. But I'm interested in Callum. He was upset at this woman's disappearance, and even went as far as claiming to be her friend and colleague. According to Nicci, she probably never gave him a second glance.'

'Celia, you knew Callum. He was academic, but not socially accomplished.'

'That's true.' He'd seemed a misfit, never in a worrying way, but someone who might have struggled to integrate. And then she thought about the two tenants who had moved out, most likely thanks to him. At best, his boundaries were blurred. 'Maybe he made it up. I do have some concerns about him bothering previous students staying at mine.'

'Bothering? How?'

'Missing underwear for one of them. Callum climbed into bed with the other. They both sounded credible, by the way.'

They'd made it to the corner of Northampton Street, and Celia expected Briggs to continue across the junction, but instead he took a right turn into Magdalene Street. The pavements were narrow and busy. 'What happened to the path less travelled?'

'Change of plan. I can't exercise body and brain at the same time. You're buying me a pint.'

'Am I?'

'No, I'll buy. I don't want to be accused of accepting press bribes, do I?'

'I'm not the press.'

He snorted. 'Doesn't matter what your job title is, Celia. Have you ever stopped asking questions at any point in your life?' He pulled open the door of the Pickerel pub, and held it for Celia.

'About as much as you,' she told him. She led the way to the bar and ordered a Guinness and a half of cider, then followed Briggs to a tucked away table nestled against dark panelled walls. Celia watched Briggs sip his pint; there was nothing more that she could say that could convince him that she had a valid reason for wanting to know more about the Rebecca Lake case, because, in truth, she didn't.

It stood like a closed door, and she needed to open it to know what lay on the other side.

'What do you want?' he asked.

'To find Callum. I have questions for him.'

'Including some about Becky Lake?'

'Yes.'

He wove his fingers together and dropped his hands to the table, encircling his glass. He studied the drink with pursed lips. 'At first it wasn't clear how she'd died. With asphyxia it can sometimes be difficult to determine the cause.'

'She didn't drown?'

He shook his head. 'There was no water in the lungs. There were some injuries, but none that would have been fatal.' He cleared his throat. 'Nothing goes further. Okay?'

'Of course.'

'The discovery of her body was reported by the media, and the story ran as if she'd probably gone into the water on the night of her disappearance. She was partially decomposed by the time she was recovered, and sure, she had been in the water for some time . . .'

'But not dead for the whole duration?' It was no surprise that information had been held back. The police always had strategies for what was made public, and when.

'She'd been alive for at least a week. Dead for at least a week. But there was a grey area in between, and somewhere in that time period, she was murdered. The post mortem found deep tissue damage consistent with her being restrained. Of course it was initially categorised as a suspicious death, but if it hadn't been for those injuries and the knowledge that she hadn't died straight away, it could have been written off as an accident.'

'What's the theory?'

'That she knew her killer; that she went willingly and was subjected to a sustained sexual assault.' He continued to hold her gaze after he finished speaking.

Celia waited, knowing there was more.

'One hypothesis is that the killer had a relationship with her, or believed he did, and this attack was personal. The other is that she was the victim of something more random, that he was compelled to abduct and rape and kill, and that she was the victim of circumstance. The second scenario makes it almost a certainty that this will not be a one-off; at some point he will attempt this again.'

'What do you know about him?'

'We recovered a partial DNA profile. It may be from the perpetrator, but might not.'

'Enough to identify a suspect?'

He shook his head. 'No, and definitely not enough to secure a conviction, but a partial match would be enough to give us a person of interest. It's not for you to chase down Callum Shaughnessy.'

'He's either fabricated a connection to Becky Lake or there really is a link.'

'That's not your problem.'

'Maybe, but I can't ignore him either. Don't forget, I'm following this up because I need to know what happened to Nicci in that crash. Do you really think I will just let that drop?'

Briggs had only half emptied the glass, but he now slid it away from him. 'I will speak to my counterpart on the Becky Lake case, and I will find out whether we have any information on Shaughnessy's whereabouts, but I won't be able to share that with you. Any of it.'

'Is that officially?'

'Officially, and unofficially. Leave it all alone now, Celia.'

Chapter 37

Nicci loved the cinema, but she had one favourite, recurring memory from the occasional Saturday afternoon visits of her childhood. And it was the same no matter whether the film had turned out to be brilliant or an utter disappointment. It only took two hours in the auditorium for her to lose track of the day outside; she would often emerge expecting it to be night time and be startled by the daylight. Or forget that it had been raining, or was uncomfortably hot. Stepping back outside had given her a few surreal moments of seeing Cambridge with fresh eyes, of feeling like a returning native.

She felt that now.

Thoughts of the accident had never been far away. She had over-analysed the parts she remembered and been haunted by those she couldn't. That day had become her window on the world. It was a puzzle cube that tilted and rotated, but never opened.

The moment she'd heard Becky Lake's name, all that had changed. She saw now that the puzzle had been the wrong shape, and she'd been holding it in the wrong way . . . looking at it in the wrong way. It was turning out to be her day for metaphors and, on that basis, she had just stepped out of the cinema, and now walked towards home as if experiencing everything afresh.

She walked quickly, mostly because she felt angry.

Celia wouldn't mention Jack to Briggs, Nicci was certain of it. She would ask Celia later and then ask her why not. Although she actually knew the answer; Celia had a fondness for Jack, for all the kids from the street, in fact. It was the kind of maternal loyalty that Nicci had pined for when she'd first been imprisoned, but it was also the kind that made mothers find excuses for misogynistic sons and manipulative daughters. It was a double-edged sword, and in her experience, life was full of them.

Like Celia's loyalty.

Nicci was glad of it, so she could hardly complain when it was shown to someone else. But it was misplaced in Jack.

It was then that her gaze was drawn to the shops ahead; there was a supermarket and a pharmacy. And it wasn't a plan that formed then, just a shopping list: latex gloves, cotton-wool buds and clear plastic bags.

Jack was at his Mac, repositioning internal walls, when someone knocked. He glanced at his watch; 4.35 p.m. and he wasn't expecting anyone or anything to arrive. The interruption didn't matter; he'd barely made progress with the drawing and had already deleted most of the ideas, returning twice to study the original. The floorplan belonged to a house that had, at one time, not been dissimilar to his own, but, through the years, had been modified so many times that it had become a muddle of poorly planned extensions and mismatched design. He felt like advising the owners to give up, but that wasn't much of a business plan for an architect's practice. He continued to stare at the screen as he pushed his chair back from his desk, committing the plan to memory so that his subconscious could work on it while he dealt with whoever was at the door.

He should have checked before he opened it, but instead, there was Nicci and he could feel his expression fix halfway between surprise and anger. 'What do you want?'

'I need to talk to you. Can I come inside?'

'Why?'

'Not on the doorstep, Jack.' She glanced over her shoulder. 'You can come to mine if you prefer.'

He shook his head and sighed. 'No. You'd better come in. Go through.'

He followed her to the sitting room. She knew the way.

This was the first time he'd been close to her since he'd been home. He wondered whether he could have passed her in the street and not recognised her. The last time he'd seen her clearly had been in court and she'd looked scrawny, unkempt and frayed with nerves. Since then everything had changed, her hair was straight, black and glossy instead of blonde and wavy, she was still slim, but in a healthy way now, and, when she looked at him, there was no hint of anxiousness.

'I deserve all the hate you have for me, Jack.' She turned and crossed to the window that looked out on the tiny rear garden. She pressed her hand to the glass. 'Charlie was the best. We grew up together and I thought we'd always be close.'

'Nic, stop. I don't want an apology.'

'That's not why I'm here, Jack.' She turned to him again. 'I struggle with what I did, but there's more to it, and I need some answers.'

'Celia told me about your injuries and I don't know anything. But even if I did, you can't dilute it; nothing takes away from what you did.'

'What if it came out that I was more guilty, not less?' His desk stood close to the window, close enough for her to lean against it as she waited for him to reply. 'Wouldn't you want to know then?'

What more could there be? His dad flashed into his thoughts then, just as he often did. He couldn't imagine anything that would make it worth raking up all those emotions. 'No,' he said at last. 'It's done, we have all had enough.' *More than enough.* 'So tell me then.' He pushed his hands into his pockets and set his jaw. He planned to say nothing more until he knew what she wanted.

'Celia's a fan of yours. She thinks you couldn't possibly have hurt me. Someone did though.'

'Not me,' he said. Her blue eyes shone brightly, she seemed unnaturally restless and Jack wondered whether it was just adrenaline that was keeping her alert.

'You really didn't attack me?'

He knew he should have been angry at the accusation. He shook his head, and watched her as she started to pace. She stopped by the doorway to his kitchen.

She frowned. 'Suppose I believe that? It doesn't mean you don't know anything, does it? Suppose you saw something and just don't remember?' Nicci swayed, shifting her weight from one foot to the other. 'Becky Lake, remember her?'

Jack felt momentarily disorientated by the change in subject.

'You do, I know you do. She was that promotions woman.'

'Yes, of course I know.'

'You were working at the Regal the night she went missing. Did you tell the police you'd seen her?'

'The police knew she'd been in the Regal, we'd had thousands through there that evening; they didn't care about me.'

'Apparently Callum was upset about her disappearance, but he barely knew her. How does that make sense?'

'I barely knew Callum. You're jumping all over the place.'

Nicci was breathing hard and didn't seem able to hold his gaze. She'd begun to pace, back and forth in the tiny space in front of the kitchen door. From wall to desk and back again. 'Nicci, why do you want to connect me to Becky Lake?'

'You were there the night she disappeared. Ellie and I saw you, and then, after you were there that afternoon, she became upset. The rest of us had driven there together and she'd been fine. It was after we arrived.'

'What was?'

'That she became scared. We sat beside the river, and I think she realised that we were not far from the spot they found Becky's body.'

'It's miles.'

'No, it's a direct route.' He stepped forward to block her pacing, but she glared up at him. 'I'm not scared of you. Did you think I would be?'

He grabbed her arm at the elbow. 'Stop, this is mad.'

She became still, then looked down at her arm as if only just realising that he had hold of her. Instead of pulling away she just closed her eyes, and, despite her claim, he could see real fear growing in her expression.

He released her. 'I'm sorry.'

She swayed again, her eyes still closed.

'Nicci, look at me. We can talk this through, get it sorted properly. I don't want you thinking that I did something to Ellie. Or that I was involved with Becky Lake's death. I need you to understand how ridiculous that is.' He also didn't want her turning up at his door again; especially in any kind of inebriated state.

She opened her eyes and seemed both wary and bewildered. Haunted even.

She paused. 'Coffee,' she said.

He filled the kettle and they were both silent as he waited for it to boil. He couldn't begin to fathom what was going on in her head. Part of him didn't want to know, didn't even want to be curious. But the other part couldn't just forget how inseparable she and Charlie had been. This was the girl who'd been Charlie's shadow throughout secondary school. He watched the kettle; he didn't want to look at her more than he needed to, and so he didn't realise she was in the room with him until she spoke.

'I need some fresh air,' she sounded subdued. She leant her shoulder against the back door as she opened it; the action still automatic even after all these years. He took a second mug from the cupboard; he hadn't planned to have a drink himself, but then again, he hadn't planned to offer her one either.

She stood on the rear step. She wasn't restless any more. The garden was small and square with a narrow path leading to the rear gate. There was no view, and yet she stared out as though she was looking at something significant. If she was picturing Charlie, then she was braver than him.

He filled the mugs, and slid hers to the end of the worktop. 'It's beside you,' he said.

She turned and nodded. 'Just so you know, I don't want it to be you.' She touched her scalp. 'I need the whole picture, not just about this, but about everything.'

'I've done nothing.'

She shrugged. 'Thanks, but it doesn't matter what you say, because I need to find out for myself. And if it's not you, then you'll want to know just as much as I do.'

'We're not all the same, Nicci. You've always had a need to know.'

She paused with the mug almost to her lips, but not quite. 'Have I?'

And, despite himself, Jack almost smiled. 'You know you have.'

Chapter 38

Nicci had acquired a few skills in prison. One of the first had been to learn how to hide her emotions. Later she had practised the next step, deception, but she'd never been as comfortable with that.

She'd returned from Jack's and her heart had continued to race for several minutes longer. It had been surreal to be back there after so long; the house had seemed like an anaemic version of the way she'd remembered it; totally recognisable, but faded and tired. Some of that was because of Jack. He didn't fill the room the way he once had. And she needed to know whether that was her fault, or down to something he'd done and the toll it was taking on him.

She closed the front door behind her and then leant heavily against it. She held one key in each hand, her own in her right, and Jack's back-door key in her left. It was only as she stared at his key that she realised that she was trembling. She slipped his key into her pocket, then ran upstairs and pulled on a thick sweatshirt. After that she stood at the front bedroom window, the one with the best view of Jack's house. She'd left everything she needed lined up on a small side table next to the windowsill. She checked through the items again, making sure that she never looked away for more than a few seconds at a time.

She continued to shiver and realised that it was nerves, not cold, that was causing it.

The one thing she knew she wouldn't do was change her mind. It wouldn't prove anything, and the only things she could trust were facts, and not other people's facts, but those she'd witnessed herself.

She stayed a few feet back from the glass. She didn't want there to be any chance of Jack spotting movement at her window, although she doubted he ever spent time looking across. Her decision to do what she was about to had been an impulse, but she also realised that since Jack's return to Mawson Road she'd been watching him with increasing frequency. Keeping tabs on him had quietly become part of her daily routine. So quietly that she'd barely noticed it herself.

He didn't keep to much of a timetable, but he often went out in the mornings, perhaps just to walk; he rarely returned home carrying more than a newspaper or a single item of shopping. The afternoons were more consistent: he would leave home between three and four, and be gone for between thirty minutes and an hour. He usually brought back a few items of shopping in a bag filled just enough for dinner for one, and, on the days when he left for longer, he tended to come back empty handed, and she equated these times to him eating out. Probably in a café where the food was served quickly. Apart from that she had not spotted any pattern or regularity to his activities. Nor had she ever followed him, although she had no doubt that she would if the need arose.

She checked herself. Sometime in the days since first seeing him, she realised that she had let him become the focus of so many of her unanswered questions. And, not for the first time, she wondered whether she was wrong.

'Time to find out,' she muttered.

She slipped the items she needed into her jeans pocket, then waited another twenty minutes until, at 3.22, she saw him leave. He wore a heavy jacket, and thrust his hands into its pockets, his shoulders slightly hunched against the falling temperature.

She watched until he reached the end of the road and turned left towards the city centre.

She discarded the sweatshirt, dropping it onto the bed and pulling on a pair of latex gloves as she rushed out. She had to remain in exactly the same clothes as earlier, no matter how cold she felt.

In less than five minutes she was in the alley at the rear of Jack's house. She had hoped to be able to unbolt the gate when she'd been in Jack's back garden, but he'd never moved out of sight. She'd worked out the easiest way over, though, and hopped the low fence into the neighbour's garden and then into Jack's via next door's apple tree. It had been her and Charlie's favourite route.

The door unlocked easily. She checked her watch again: 3.31 already. She was allowing herself a maximum of twenty-five minutes from the moment Jack had left home; already she was down to barely more than fifteen, but she knew what she wanted and where she planned to look.

Straight in and out.

She hurried through the downstairs without pausing. Apart from a single photo of Jack and his daughter, the place was impersonal, not in a minimalist chic way either, more like an I've-fucked-my-life-up way.

She cast a wishful glance at Jack's MacBook, wondering if he might be one of those people who kept their whole lives digitally. Even the incriminating parts. It was irrelevant: she had neither the skills nor the time.

She avoided touching the banister and ran up the centre of the stairs, across the landing and straight into the bathroom. She pulled the first of two plastic bags from her pocket. She had already placed a couple of cotton buds in each. His toothbrush was a fancy electric one with its own charging station, and somewhere in the house there was probably a supply of new brush heads, because this one didn't look more than a few days old. She held it in one hand and stroked each of the cotton buds through the bristles. Flash toothbrushes still held saliva.

She sealed the bag and returned it to her pocket.

According to her plan, she should be collecting hair samples too. She checked the time again: 3.38. She could leave the hair, the saliva would be enough.

There were three other doors facing onto the landing. Charlie's old room and their parents' rooms both stood open. Both had been emulsioned in cream and the furniture was solid and functional; nothing remained of the décor she remembered. Jack must have moved back into his childhood bedroom. She hesitated outside his closed door. She'd stolen a key and was trespassing in his home, but his bedroom still felt off limits. It would be crossing a different kind of line.

The contents in the rest of the house had been sparse. So sparse that they aligned more to someone who had arrived for a week-end in a hotel. She didn't believe that anyone could move house and bring so little. The door was panelled, with a painted over lock and a round Bakelite handle positioned at chest height. She touched it, then gripped it lightly, feeling for any resistance. There was play in it, and it rattled as she turned it.

This wasn't in her plan.

She stayed like that for several seconds. Undecided. She checked her watch: 3.42. Three minutes had just vanished. But she still had five.

Her heart had begun to hammer again. She took a breath, released the handle and pushed the door open with the tips of her still-gloved fingers. The room was no more personal than the others. Whatever Jack had brought with him, she doubted it included any of this furniture. There were two matching pine wardrobes, and a chest of drawers, all stained in a similar shade of orangey-brown.

Every door and drawer was open, not thrown wide, but a little ajar. The drawers in the chest were staggered like a shallow set of steps. Even the bedside table wasn't closed. It stood nearer to her than the other furniture, so she reached out and opened it further. It was totally empty. She slid it back again.

The first wardrobe was the same, and, apart from some underwear in the top drawer, the chest was empty. 'What the hell?' she muttered. A few clothes hung on the half-dozen hangers occupying the second wardrobe, less than enough to fill a suitcase. She moved the items, checking between them as though she expected something significant to be hanging there. She reached the end and pushed the clothes together to approximately their original position, then stepped back to return the door to half-closed, and, for the first time, glanced into the gap between the side of the wardrobe and the curtain. It was full length, and she could see an irregular shape in the way the fabric fell.

She knelt and pushed the curtain aside. The bottom of it had been obscuring a cardboard box. Nicci checked the time again: 3.49. 'Shit, shit, shit.'

She darted into Charlie's old room and checked in both directions along Mawson Road. There was no sign of Jack. What did that give her? Two minutes, perhaps three. Fear immediately knotted in her stomach; she couldn't afford to be caught. Just the risk of it chilled her. She knew she should head for the stairs, but still she couldn't avoid the pull of the box. She ran back and grabbed it, bringing it back to Charlie's room where she could split her attention between its contents and the window.

It was about the size that might hold a pair of boots, only a little deeper and with flaps folded over, but not sealed. On top was a photograph of Jack holding his little girl. The same as the one downstairs, but unframed. The child was on his hip and she had her hand to his cheek. Nicci put the photo to one side. The rest of the box was three-quarters full with what, at first glance, appeared to be packs of photographs and letters. She kept everything in place, just lifting one item at a time. She flipped open a couple of the wallets at random, finding only more photographs of the little girl.

She checked out of the window again. Clear.

She flipped through layer after layer, until near the bottom, where she felt a slightly rougher texture. It was too far down the box to see more than the edge of a manila envelope. She tugged it and realised that it was at the very bottom of the pile. If this box contained anything important, it could only be in here.

As the envelope slipped free she checked the window again just as Jack turned the corner towards home.

'Fuck,' she breathed. She threw the framed photo back into the box and the manila envelope on top of that. She ran back into Jack's room and returned the box to the gap between the wardrobe and the curtain, then ran for the stairs. She couldn't afford to slow on the stairs and had to take the chance that Jack wasn't quite close enough to hear. She darted through the living room and into the kitchen.

She heard him turn the key in the lock.

She slid the back-door key back in place, turned the handle as slowly as she dared, then pulled the door closed behind her. Hopefully he would find it unlocked later and just write it off as an oversight on his part. She ducked below window height and crawled further round the back of the property, then waited.

She stayed still and silent, squatting with her back against the cold brickwork, and listened until she began to pick out the sounds from inside the house. She heard him fill the kettle. The sound of a whisk against a saucepan. Cutlery in the sink. She waited until she heard the toilet flush, then ran for the back gate.

In the alley behind the house she peeled off the latex gloves. Her hands were wet, her fingers wrinkled. And she still shook. She walked for another twenty minutes, stopping to buy a newspaper and discarding the gloves in the bin outside the shop. It was only then that she felt calm enough to turn for home.

She didn't see or speak to anyone along the way, and was relieved that Celia wasn't keeping watch for her return.

Nicci placed the newspaper on her draining board, slid the manila envelope from between its pages. She tipped the contents onto the kitchen table as the kettle boiled. There were photos, including a duplicate of the one in the frame. Jack's passport. His birth and marriage certificates. And one white envelope addressed to him, originally sent to the Mawson Road address, but forwarded on to London.

It contained a folded page from the *Evening Standard*. On the outside someone had scrawled in blue biro and block capitals: *READ THIS.* She unfolded the sheet, and read the first couple of lines. She drew a sharp breath, and lowered herself slowly into the nearest chair.

Chapter 39

During her childhood, Nicci had heard her father talk about work on many occasions. At most meals it was just her and her mum, and when her father joined them the atmosphere shifted.

On bad days the silence would only be broken by polite enquiries about her school work, or one parent asking the other how their day had been. Then the silence again, the only noise from cutlery on china, or breathing and chewing. She imagined her mother trying sentences in her head, sounding them out to see whether they would be too banal or, at the other extreme, likely to become too contentious. She imagined her father preparing his responses.

And she ate her food, but couldn't remember the taste.

When her mother asked him about work, his usual response was brief, a stock answer, but sometimes a thought or a comment would prompt him to share a story relating to a case he was working on, or one with which he'd previously been involved. The longer stories were the best; they had the potential to stave off the silence until the end of the meal. And it didn't matter to her when the content was designed to shock. Her mum would nervously shake her head and whisper, 'Paul?' with her voice full of urgency, but he would plough on.

Nicci gradually learnt to spot the self-aggrandisement, the name-dropping of notorious cases and the way he was happiest when he had control of the conversation. But she relished the stories, and the glimpses of other lives that existed outside of her suffocating little world.

And so it was that the first thing she'd done with the papers snatched from Jake's house had been to spill them onto the table and immediately try to work out what she'd salvaged, and how important it might be. The envelope and the name Emily Moore had shaken her back into the moment, and she remembered one of her father's favourite tips. 'You catch people as soon as they let down their guard. That's when they stop being careful and leave a shitload of evidence.'

She scooped everything back into the envelope, and then, without any further delay, stripped off in front of the washing machine, removing each layer and throwing it straight inside.

Her kitchen window faced the rear of the house and she doubted anyone would be looking in, but she grabbed a clean towel and draped it around her shoulders before removing her bra and knickers last. She closed the washing-machine door and set it on an eco-wash, the long and slow programme that took a little over three hours to complete. She doubted that it cleaned any more thoroughly than the shorter ones, but she liked the idea that every trace of where she'd just been would be washed and spun and rinsed repeatedly, until the value of any evidence was as close to zero as possible.

She grabbed the envelope, switched off the kitchen and hall lights, and rushed upstairs to the bathroom. The envelope stayed in the room while she showered, and the knowledge that they were locked in there together allowed her to relax for a few minutes.

She closed her eyes and tilted her head back so that the jets of water hit her full in the face and the rushing blocked out any other sounds. She'd stolen Jack's DNA without even knowing whether the police had any means of identifying Becky Lake's attacker. Nicci had rushed to enter Jack's house with no proof that she was grabbing anything of any use. She had to admit that it was the perfect cocktail of reckless and stupid, and yet she had come away with both the swabs and the press clipping.

Emily Moore.

Her name had been in and out of the papers for so long that she had started to develop the kind of tragic fame that makes people discuss her on first name terms: *any news of Emily yet?* She had been twenty-two when she'd disappeared and had just started a part-time job in the beauty-therapy rooms of a small country hotel on the outskirts of Norwich. Several photographs had appeared in the papers in the first days of the hunt for her. Emily at a family wedding wearing high heels and a floaty cream dress; laughing as she held a champagne flute towards the camera. Emily at her graduation, her parents squeezing into the frame with her. Emily on the sofa with her spaniel Ralph beside her, his head on her lap, her fingers buried in his fur. And then the one that the press had settled on: a casual photo, Emily wearing a flowered vest top with spaghetti straps, her light-brown hair twisted into a loose bun. She stood alone, smiling gently towards the camera. She wore little make-up, or perhaps it was the kind that gave her skin a natural, outdoorsy glow. The signature photo for every case such as this always seemed to be the one with metatags of happiness, wholesomeness and potential.

She had vanished somewhere between Norwich city centre and her parents' home about four miles away. The last sighting of her had been in the Castle Quarter shopping centre where she'd been picked up by several CCTV cameras, and her mobile phone was eventually found halfway between there and home.

It had happened at the end of July during Nicci's first full year in prison. Some of the other prisoners had theories, most hadn't shown any interest, but Nicci had read every story available. Her father would have brought his theories to the dinner table.

There were no other sightings, no other clues, and throughout August, the month famous for a dearth of stories, the papers repeatedly returned to Emily, filling the front pages with police appeals and speculation.

On 2 September her body washed up on the beach about forty miles to the east.

Nicci kept her eyes shut and reached for the shampoo.

She knew she needed to be cautious. Instinct told her that the Emily Moore connection was important, but she needed to find a way to raise it without going down the route of 'Look what I found when I broke into Jack's house.'

And handing over the swabs presented another set of problems. She was sure that biological samples wouldn't be considered without a full explanation, and what did she have apart from suspicion towards Jack? She couldn't give them to Celia or Briggs without explaining what she'd done. She couldn't imagine going to anyone else, certainly not her father. But she needed someone to act.

Tread carefully.

She rinsed her hair then switched off the shower. The room was cold and the heating had only just come on. She wrapped herself in a towel and stood with her back against the radiator. The envelope remained on the windowsill; it was both a problem and an opportunity, and it was where her gaze rested as she thought it over.

And, in the end she decided, as she often did, that the correct answer began with Celia.

Nicci knocked on Celia's back door, then let herself in. She found Celia at her desk with half a mug of coffee just within reach of her right hand. Nicci could see the glow of the computer screen, but it stood at an oblique angle and it was impossible for her to see what Celia was working on.

'What did Briggs say?'

'He told us to mind our own business.'

'Us?'

'Me in particular.' One corner of her mouth twitched with a smile. 'He says he will follow up on locating Callum – or make sure that someone does – but that it's time for me to leave all of this alone.'

'Do you think he will?'

'I think Briggs is a man of his word; he will do what he says.' Her index finger tapped the desk, a small and silent action, and Nicci waited for the 'but'. It took about ten seconds. 'But to him this is not an active case. Whereas, for us, it is the only case.'

'So, you're not dropping it?'

'Do I walk out of a restaurant before dessert? I don't think so.'

Nicci hadn't thought that Celia would be giving up, but she still felt a wave of relief when she heard her confirm it. Nicci pulled the spare chair up to the end of the desk. 'What did you find out about Becky Lake?'

Celia filled Nicci in on the key events of the case. 'Her lifestyle has created a level of ambiguity. For example, the police have the hypothesis that she knew her killer because there is no evidence that she was abducted by force. But they are tempering that with the knowledge that it hadn't been uncommon for her to spend the night with a man she had only just met.'

'And, because of her job, she met an unusually large number of men?'

Celia nodded. 'Briggs was tactful; he said it added an overhead to the investigation. It has been impossible to identify several witnesses from the evening she disappeared; CCTV in the various bars show her talking to multiple people, mostly men, and mostly untraceable.'

'You didn't mention Jack, did you?'

'There was nothing to say.'

'He was there that night.'

'And what did I just say? Hundreds, if not thousands of others were too. You can't juggle the facts to fit the picture; you know better than that, Nicci.'

'I went to see him today.'

Celia's attention sharpened. 'Why?'

'I asked him whether he'd attacked me. And whether it was because of him that Ellie was upset. And he denied it, of course.

But what if Ellie had had a realisation about Becky and Jack, and that was what freaked her out.'

'What if?' Celia looked steadily at Nicci. 'You can apply that to anything in the world, Nicci; it doesn't make it a fact.'

Nicci persevered; she needed to. 'What about DNA? Was there any on Becky's body or in her home?'

'The police have two full profiles from her flat which belong to unidentified men, and another, partial profile, recovered from her body.'

'From the killer?'

'A person of interest.'

Nicci nodded.

Celia relaxed back into her chair, a reflective expression on her face. 'I worked with a woman named Val. Every time there was a setback, a missed promotion or a promising story that didn't come my way, there was Val. She was always so smug about it too.' Celia picked up her coffee, she put it to her lips, but then put it back down without drinking. 'It's cold. I thought Val was my nemesis. Then one day, with no warning, she left; just packed up her desk and walked out. I didn't get that promotion or the better jobs.'

Celia liked anecdotes, sometimes she recycled them, but this one was new to Nicci. 'Who did?' she asked.

'It doesn't matter. I bumped into Val a couple of years later, and after an awkward first few minutes, she began to talk to me. It turned out that our boss Tony had singled her out for . . .' she rarely used air quotes, but she did now, '"attention". I wasn't the only one who'd misconstrued things. She'd never been my enemy, or even a rival. She'd been victimised by Tony and we'd all compounded it.'

'This is a different situation.' Nicci had a stubborn streak, and she knew that it didn't always do her any favours.

Celia just shrugged. 'Blinkers can keep you focused, but sometimes they help you fall over your feet.'

Nicci was about to reply, but Celia barely paused. 'So, back to Becky?'

'What else do you know?'

'The way Briggs described it, it sounded pre-planned. There was no sign of her in any trouble on the CCTV cameras, and yet the city centre is quite well covered. She seemed to vanish on that night and her body turned up with no witnesses at that end either.'

'So Becky was targeted?'

'Not necessarily her specifically; there is nothing that points to her being at risk, apart from the obvious poor life choices. I mean pre-planned as a crime. They didn't just go undetected at the time of her abduction and when they disposed of the body, there was a period of at least a week in between when she was alive. You don't pull that off without thinking it through first . . .' Celia tilted her head, 'What?'

Nicci had seen the opportunity as soon as Celia had uttered the words 'at least a week', and her reaction to them had been so spontaneous that she was sure that her next words would sound equally natural. 'Like Emily Moore,' she breathed.

'How?' Celia replied sharply.

'Firstly, the obvious. Both disappeared without trace, then both were found in water. But Emily Moore was also alive for some time before she went in the sea.'

'Are you sure?'

'I read it at the time.' Nicci was stretching the truth now. 'There was a visual identification; they couldn't have managed that if she'd been dead in the water for five weeks.'

'Perhaps her body was stored somewhere else. Doesn't mean she was alive after she disappeared. Besides, if there was a connection, the police would have spotted it. They have a computer system called HOLMES . . .'

Nicci hadn't expected Celia to cast doubt on the idea. 'I know what HOLMES is,' she snapped.

'Sorry, of course.'

'And things are frequently overlooked.' Nicci bristled. 'Mistakes are made, we both know that, and maybe HOLMES did flag it up, but along with other cases.'

Celia looked dubious. She shook her head, then stared past Nicci, her gaze fixed. Her thoughts seemed to drift away from Nicci's words.

'Celia, I need you to believe me. Maybe no one could be bothered to investigate properly and the same person that tried to kill me also killed her.'

'Her?'

'Becky. Emily. Both of them.'

Celia didn't reply at first, and it was all Nicci could do to stop herself storming out. When she'd first met Celia that is exactly what she would have done, but now she concentrated on her breathing, and after a few long breaths she began to feel the tension subside. Meanwhile, Celia had adopted what Nicci thought of as her thinking face; her expression was mostly neutral, but her jaw was set. Her eyelids drooped a little as though she was bored or overtired, but Nicci knew she was neither.

'Celia?'

Celia held up one finger. 'Shush.'

Nicci fidgeted in her chair, then spoke anyway. 'I'm sorry I snapped at you.'

Celia closed her eyes completely then, and held still for a few seconds more. Then she was back in the room with a jolt, slapping her palm down onto her desk. 'It's rarely the "what" that's the issue. It's the "why". You snapped at me and you've apologised. But why did you?'

Nicci opened her mouth. But struggled to thinks of words that would explain without her having to say too much.

Celia seemed oblivious; she had the answer. 'Because it was so important for me to see the connection between Becky and Emily. But why? You had only just seen it. Or perhaps you hadn't. Perhaps you already planned to point me in that direction?'

Nicci exhaled heavily.

'But why? Why couldn't you just say, "Hey, Celia, I have this idea"? Most likely because something has pointed you in this direction and you don't want to say what it is.'

Nicci couldn't unlock herself from Celia's gaze. 'I don't want to keep secrets from you.'

'So don't.'

Nicci had no problem keeping secrets unless she was withholding them from someone she cared about, especially someone she hoped would feel able to confide in her. Conscience pushing against self-preservation; she could feel the pressure now and tried to take the edge off it. 'I did something you wouldn't approve of, but it led to Emily's name.'

Celia looking completely baffled was a rare sight, but there it was. 'What about Emily?'

'It was just a press clipping, it came from the London *Standard*.'

'Can I see it?'

Nicci nodded, then stood up to reach into her back pocket. She pulled out the envelope and then the newspaper page from within it. 'If there were any forensics on this, there aren't now.'

'Did you plan to show me?'

She hadn't, but then why had she brought it with her? 'I don't know.'

Celia held out her hand and took the cutting. She smoothed it out on the desk. 'So this is the day after the body was found?'

'That's right.'

It began with the headline *Body Found in Search for Missing Emily*, then immediately cautioned that the identity was yet to be confirmed. 'They were covering themselves, but they knew it was her.' She stopped further down the column. 'The eye-witness statement is interesting.' She turned the page at an angle that slanted between them and pointed.

Nicci knew the part she meant, but read it again:

I was on the beach when a man ran towards me, he was shouting about a body. A few feet beyond him I saw a woman lying at the water's edge. I recognised her immediately and I could see that she had died. I have lived here all my life and I know how dangerous the currents can be.

'See, she hadn't been in the water for long,' Nicci said.

'Yes. But you didn't know Becky had been kept alive until I told you. Why did this,' Celia tapped the page, 'make you believe the cases might be linked?'

'It makes sense that they are.'

Celia huffed. 'At the risk of sounding repetitive, why?'

Nicci looked long and hard at Celia, and then gave in. 'I went into Jack's house while he was out. I found the envelope.' It was still in Nicci's hand, she unfolded it and showed Celia. 'Maybe it was hand delivered, maybe it came inside another, or maybe,' and the thought occurred to her as she spoke, 'maybe this is Jack's writing and he was planning on sending it to someone else.'

Celia took the envelope and turned it over in her hand. 'What will happen if you are caught?'

Nicci shook her head; she said nothing, but she felt her cheeks flush.

'You wouldn't be given any leeway whatsoever. I'm pretty sure you'd be straight back in prison. Is it really worth it, Nicci?'

'Something happened after that crash and I can't stand not knowing. I know you think that Jack wasn't involved, but that's making it worse. Making me feel as though you want to protect him when, in truth, neither of us really knows.'

'That's true, we don't,' Celia conceded. 'But this isn't the way. What will happen if Jack realises that someone has broken in?'

'I used a key.'

'So he'd guess it was you?'

'Maybe, but I went round to see him first, made sure I left fingerprints, wiped my feet, shed hairs – all that kind of thing – and then went back later wearing exactly the same clothes.'

And despite Celia's obvious anger, she smiled. 'Locard's exchange principle? Well thought out.'

'You're not supposed to congratulate me.'

'I can't undo what's already been done, but I can hope for a good outcome, can't I?' Her smile faded. 'For you at least.'

'What do you mean?'

'If you're right to connect these women, then I wonder whether they will be the only ones.'

Chapter 40

Spoilt. That's what she'd been. She knew it now.

Her old life had been filled with petty moans and minor inconveniences.

The time wasted waiting for a late-running bus or queueing at the checkout. Bad wi-fi, dull lectures, friction with housemates and a list of other, petty problems which had completely filled the little picture of her daily life, so that she hadn't seen the bigger one at all.

Had anyone even missed her yet?

She wasn't sure how many days she'd been in here, but she knew that during every one of them she'd tried to trade, or make deals. Some with herself, some with him, but most with fate, or destiny, or whichever string-pulling malevolent entity shared the nights with her, putting whispers into the complete silence and making shadows dance despite the total blackness.

She tried separating her senses. She had heard that smell is the most closely linked to memory. She tried to conjure up the feelings that came with comfort smells: pizza, laundry, the beach. Oranges, deodorant, toast. Even the singed, oily smell that puffed from the bus as the doors opened. Once or twice she had managed a fleeting moment of something tangible, not quite a memory, more a stirring of familiarity. But then it had passed again.

The tape that covered her mouth never budged. She had tried pushing saliva between her lips, hoping to soften its grip, but the tape moved only when he removed it; when he tugged it slowly away from her mouth, his face close to hers and his warm, hungry breath inhaling her own. Without it she would have spoken to herself; she didn't know poetry, but she could have recited lyrics. When the silence became too oppressive she thought of songs she loved, and sometimes tried to hum the melody.

It was hard to know which hours were day and which were night. Even which hours were hours at all.

There were clues of sorts. He often seemed to pace and that seemed more likely to be in the waking hours. She imagined this might be through guilt or anguish, but, when she saw his face, she knew that he didn't connect with any of those emotions. She guessed she was in a cupboard, maybe a cellar. And if it was a cellar, then there had to be a second room, because there were times when she heard him moving around just beyond the nearest wall. And others when he seemed directly overhead. Snatches of music reached her occasionally, nothing she recognised; the vocals and most of the instrumentation were filtered out by the walls, leaving just reverberation of the bass sounds. Those times felt like evening. The rhythm lulled her enough to snatch some sleep, and sometimes, in the distance, she thought she could hear the sea.

She woke from that now with a lurch of fear and her heart pounding. Her eyes strained pointlessly against the blackness. Her wrists and ankles were, as ever, bound, but that didn't prevent her from bringing her knees closer to her chest, or from curling her hands into clenched balls.

At first there was just silence.

Nothing.

Nothing often woke her.

She held still, panting through her nose, listening for sounds that made it past her ragged breathing and pulsing heart. The click was subtle; the small sound of metal on metal, and was followed with the scrape of a bolt being drawn.

He was here.

There were only two scenarios for her death. One day he wouldn't return and she would die alone, probably of thirst, or by asphyxiating against her gag. She would spend her last hours in delirium, succumbing to the kind of insanity that already played at the edges of her mind.

The second would be when he was done, when she was no longer required. It would be faster that way, she knew that already. And she would eventually wish for it; she knew that too, but not yet. She wasn't ready to give up on her family. Her dad and her brother would look for her once they knew.

She needed to believe it.

She closed her eyes when the light snapped on, then blinked them open as he spoke. 'You need to get ready.' He scraped at the edge of the duct tape until a corner lifted, and then he pulled it slowly from her skin. He unbound her hands and feet next. There was a cloth bag on the ground next to his feet. He reached down to it and passed her a small bottle of water. She emptied it in seconds, using the tilt of her head as cover for taking a glance at the door, even though she knew it would be locked. She had tested it twice in the past. And he seemed to find that amusing.

'You need the toilet?'

She nodded.

'Go on then.'

At first he'd turned away, but now he watched as she used the camping toilet in the corner of the room. 'Did you hold it this time?'

She nodded.

'Sure? I don't want to kneel in your piss again.'

'It's fine.'

He studied the mattress for a few seconds in any case. She looked across, wondering whether she should rush him, wishing she had a weapon. She had nothing; not even the strength to try.

'What?' he asked.

She dropped her gaze. 'Nothing.'

'Clean yourself up.' He threw her a packet of wet wipes and she used them on her hands and face, adding them to the overflowing wastepaper bin that stood next to the portable toilet.

He reached down to the bag again. This time he brought out pre-packed sandwiches, a packet of crisps and a yogurt. Strawberry. He'd never brought yogurt before.

'I don't want to do this,' she said.

He didn't reply beyond a nod at the mattress.

She didn't move.

He sighed and walked across to her. 'As far as I'm concerned I did the hard work on that first night.' He put his first and second fingers to her mouth, running them across her lips. They felt tender from the duct tape. 'You were lucky you only lost a tooth. It could have been your ribs. Or your liver, just here . . .' his fingers moved swiftly and jabbed her lower right abdomen. 'You would be surprised how quickly people die when it is ruptured.' He grabbed her arm and dug his fingers into her flesh. She pressed her mouth shut, stifling a yelp. 'Get it ready.'

She hesitated, then closed her eyes, bracing herself for the blow.

He leant in and whispered in her ear. 'Five, four, three . . .'

And, like a naughty toddler, she turned from him and hurried. She pulled the sheet from the bag and laid it across the mattress, then placed her pillow on the floor beside it. She held out her hands for him to tape them together again.

'And?' he asked.

'This is what I want,' she replied.

Then she lay back on the mattress and watched him undress. Watched him and his drug-induced erection push themselves between her thighs. He wanted her eyes open throughout, and when she tried to close them he growled at her, 'Look at me.'

His hands grabbed briefly at her still-clothed breasts, then moved up to her throat. He gripped her neck as he thrusted harder.

She managed 'No,' in a rasping whisper. His hands released her immediately, and she felt him grope around beside the bed. He found the pillow, and looked down at her looking up at him. He was rougher now. Close to climax.

He pressed the pillow into her face. She tried to suck air. Tried to turn her head. Her lungs strained, her body wanted to twist and buck.

He pressed down harder and then it all turned black.

Chapter 41

'Emily Moore and Becky Lake may be connected?' Briggs pursed his lips. 'I am not involved with either case.'

Celia frowned and pushed her hands even deeper into the pockets of her long cardigan. 'So you don't want to know?'

She had turned up at Parkside and pulled Briggs away from the tedium of crossing every computerised *t* and dotting every digital *i* on one of his current cases. There were many of each. And so Celia's arrival was a mixed blessing, but he hadn't invited her beyond reception; he intended to keep it brief.

'I meant that I'm not an expert on either.'

The first thing she'd done was to pass him a photocopy of a press clipping. He studied it, looking for the red flag that had brought her in today. 'What's the connection? They were different ages, from different places. I realise that both women were missing for some time before their bodies turned up by water, but that's it as far as I can see. If there was a forensic link it would have been found already.'

'On the day she disappeared Emily had been out promoting the health spa, giving out money-off vouchers . . .'

'And they were both wearing pink?'

'Really? Sarcasm? Or do you think I'm that clueless?'

He didn't. 'So what then?'

Celia paused before answering, looking nonplussed. 'Surely she had other aspirations when she took a degree?'

Briggs wobbled his head in a maybe-yes, maybe-no way. 'She scraped a third.'

'Ah.' That seemed to satisfy her. 'She spent the whole day in the shopping centre, crossing paths with hundreds, maybe thousands of people.'

'The CCTV would have been checked.' He could hear his own voice sounding flat and unimpressed.

'They would have been easy women to watch. They didn't need to have contact with anyone to be spotted; they were out to make sure people spotted them. Neither of them would have thought twice about being stared at, or even recognised.'

'And that's your connection?'

'Yes.'

'Just like that?'

'If it's true, it's true.'

'It's tenuous.'

He looked at his watch, knowing that she would spot the signal.

'Damn you, Briggs, can't you just trust me on this? If it's already been checked, then it should be checked again. It's not your case, but can you push that in front of the right person?'

'I'll see what I can do.' He was deliberately non-committal; he thought it might prompt her to say more. It didn't. He knew his answer hadn't pleased her, but she simply thanked him and left.

He grabbed a coffee on the way back to his desk, not because he was thirsty, but to buy himself a few uninterrupted minutes. He ran through the conversation. It was something and nothing. But knowing Celia as he did gave it context. She wouldn't have come down here on a whim. She wouldn't knowingly waste either his time or her own. And she was never clueless. Even on a bad day.

He stopped at the nearest window and glanced along the footpath. Celia would be long gone.

Emily Moore and Becky Lake.

Either there was something else Celia hadn't told him or she had it on good authority that there really was a link.

Chapter 42

As Celia walked towards home, she spotted a familiar figure walking towards her. Jack Bailey. He looked like a man on a mission; his head was down, and he was staring at a spot about six feet in front of him on the pavement. He probably would have missed her if she hadn't blocked his path. He looked up, startled.

'We should talk,' she said.

'I'm on my way to the police station.'

'I guessed you might be,' she replied.

'So you know what she did then?'

Celia looked at him evenly. 'I don't know who *she* is and I don't know what you're talking about, but I think it's time you and I shared the information we do have. Do either of us really want this thing to escalate?'

He hesitated, looking past her into the distance towards Parker's Piece and the police station.

'What are you going to say to them?' she asked.

'That Nicci broke into my house.'

'Did she though?'

He turned then, looked at her with a sharp gaze. 'You know she did, Celia.'

Celia kept her tone even, she didn't want him to think she was mocking him or playing games, but she did want him to think through the logic. 'How do you know there has been a break in, Jack?'

'I'm not getting into it.'

'What was the damage?' she persisted.

He muttered something she didn't catch.

'Okay,' she said, 'what was taken? Or what was broken?'

He glared back at her. 'I don't know that anything was, I just know that somebody was there.'

'So why would you think that was Nicci?'

'Who else, Celia? She came round to see me, stood at my back door and stared into the garden taking deep breaths, making me feel as though she needed to take a minute. I don't know what she was doing, well I didn't then, but I do now. What she was taking was my door key. Then she came in when I went out, and left before I got back. Except that she couldn't lock it again, because she couldn't lock it and leave the key where she'd found it, could she?'

'Nicci's smart, she would have locked the door and climbed out the window.'

'Perhaps she didn't have time?'

Celia shrugged. 'Perhaps you left the door unlocked, Jack?'

'I didn't, I know I didn't.'

'Yes,' Celia smiled kindly, 'but, perhaps you did.'

His glare deepened. 'She was upstairs,' he told her. 'She was in my bedroom. I know because the door was open when I came back, and I always leave it shut.'

'And if the police come round . . .'

'When they come round . . . what about it?'

'Are the police, who are under-resourced, really going to come for a householder who may or may not have left his door unlocked? And who may have been the victim of an unknown person, who may or may not have come into his house and may or may not have taken anything?' She mocked up a thoughtful expression. 'Yes, Jack,' she nodded, 'I can see there's going to be a whole trail of blue lights coming up our street.'

'So you'd defend her no matter what?'

'Nicci? Absolutely not. I expect a certain level of behaviour, but let's just cut across all of that right now, because some things, compared to the big picture, really don't matter that much.'

Jack didn't respond, but he didn't walk away either.

Celia touched his arm. 'We can talk at yours, or talk at mine, or go somewhere neutral.'

He raised and then dropped his hands in an I-give-up gesture. 'Not mine, I've had enough of letting people in. And not yours, not with her just next door and butting her nose into things.'

'Hot Numbers then?'

He gave an exasperated flick of his hands. 'Sure.'

They turned around and walked silently to Gwydir Street. The windows of Hot Numbers were steamed up, but Celia had seen it busier and there were several free tables.

'Choose a seat,' she said.

He picked a table at the back, one with two chairs that faced one another. Celia ordered two coffees and two cakes; she needed to find something to break the ice, but, as she guessed, Jack wasn't really interested in either.

He turned the coffee cup by a few degrees on its saucer and, a minute or two later, a few degrees back again. Her coffee was long gone before he finally took a sip.

'I don't know what you expect from me,' he said. But he was looking at her, weighing her up as though he wanted a proper answer, not just a glib response.

'What I would like,' she said carefully, 'is to know everything you know.'

'Which,' he said ruefully, 'as I keep saying, is absolutely nothing.'

'No, you think it's nothing, Nicci thinks you're hiding something. I don't. I think that if you know anything at all, you're not aware of it.'

'Okay, so how do I tell you what I don't know I know?' he said slowly. 'Because we can't carry on as we are, can we, with suspicion and half stories?'

'I'm always going to be honest with you,' she said.

He looked up quickly, dark eyes under dark lashes. 'It's time someone was,' he said. 'I'm a straightforward person; I get facts and I deal with them. My wife hid the fact that somebody else was my daughter's father, and, as devastating as it was to find out, I needed to know.'

Celia doubted he was ever going to be close to dealing with that one, but she said nothing.

'I'm not actively looking for conspiracies and hidden agendas here. But, on the other hand, once I know that something's not right, it plays on my mind. I don't know anything about Nicci or the crash, but since you stirred this up, I keep thinking, what if there is something? And it's dragging up so many emotions.' He took a breath, and then continued, his words slower and more measured. 'I need to know what happened to my brother in a final, conclusive way. But I also need to keep my distance from Nicci. You need to keep her reined in.' He fixed Celia with a steady gaze. 'I don't want to be around her. She can't carry on like this.'

'Let me ask you this, Jack, what happens when someone's desperate?'

'How do you mean?'

'What do they do to get by?'

'I don't know about everyone else, but I've just done what I've had to.'

'Ah, and there you go. Nicci has worked hard in the last year or so. She doesn't want anything apart from the chance to take responsibility for herself, and come to terms with what she did. But now her part in that is in doubt. Somebody attacked her in that car wreck, and she has it in her head that that person was you.'

She knew immediately that her words had hit home.

'Of course it wasn't me, for fuck's sake.' The last three words were almost a whisper, but were sharper and harder for it.

'I believe you, Jack. But, until she discovers otherwise, what do you think is going to happen?'

'Well, I don't know.'

'She's desperate, so what's going to happen?'

He smiled. He had a good smile, but this time it was full of bitterness. 'She will do what she has to do,' he conceded. 'I see your point, but that doesn't have to be fine by me.'

'No, but help me out here.' Celia reached down and lifted her leather tote bag onto her lap. In a pocket it had a small, zipped space. She always kept a pound coin in there in case she needed it for the shopping trolley, and a sticky plaster and a pen. They were pretty much her emergency resources, but today she had added one more thing, another photocopy of the news clipping that Nicci had found at Jack's house. She unfolded it, turned it Jack's way up, and slid it across to him. 'An unnamed source sent this to me. Said it belonged to you.'

'Really? This is you being honest with me? And I suppose that unnamed source was nothing to do with Nicci?' He leant back in the chair and folded his arms. 'Convenient. Tell me, why would anyone send it to you?'

'I don't know.' Celia tapped the corner of the clipping with her index finger. 'But you're not denying you had it?'

He sighed. 'What difference does it make, Celia?'

'When did it arrive?' she persisted.

Jack gave in.

'I received this sometime after Emily Moore's body was found, I knew nothing about the case until then. I don't know why I was sent a clipping at all, never mind one from when she'd first disappeared. I can't be more accurate about the date than that. What difference does it make?'

'I don't know. I'm just gathering information at this stage.'

'And, before you ask,' he said, 'I don't know who sent it.'

'No idea?'

'No idea.' He thought for a moment, then continued, 'Her body turned up at a place called Scratby. It's east of Norwich, almost straight east I think. You go out there and it's the wild coast. You know, where you can stand and if you could look far enough it would be Denmark or Russia or Norway or somewhere. I don't know without looking on a map, but it's just grey North Sea as far as the horizon. I'd been there once or twice as a kid, and once with Sadie and Maya.'

Celia noticed a tiny hesitation and catch in his voice when he said his daughter's name.

'The fact that we'd been there is what made me wonder,' he said.

'Wonder what?'

'Whether it was supposed to mean something to me.' Then he shook his head. 'But I was sent others too, and there was no connection.'

'What others?' Celia asked sharply. It hadn't even occurred to her to check.

'Clippings about women who had disappeared; the clippings arrived after each had been reported missing, but in each case they turned up again. They weren't murdered. One had committed suicide, and the other two turned up safe. The only difference with Emily Moore was that the newspaper clipping was sent to me after the outcome was known. It seemed pointed, as though there was some subtext that I was supposed to understand. First of all, I thought that perhaps she was somebody that I'd met at some point, you know, the kind of thing where you say "Have you seen this?" and show somebody an article that's relevant to them personally.'

'Didn't you think of going to the police?'

'With what? A series of newspaper clippings, and an anonymous note with each saying "READ THIS"? What crime had been committed?'

'You seem very calm about the whole thing, Jack.'

'Do I? I'm not at all actually.' He leant forward, this time resting his elbows on the table and wrapping his hands around his coffee cup. To the casual observer it would have looked as though he had relaxed a little, but Celia could see that he had just transferred his priorities. A minute ago he'd been leaning back to keep his distance from her, now he was leaning closer to block out the rest of the world. 'When we lost Charlie, the case was in the paper. We received all kinds of crap in the post. More when Mum died.' The thought made him wince. 'You'd think people would have some sympathy for people in distress. It doesn't work that way.' He unlocked his hands from the cup and placed his hand palm down onto the clipping, then he slid it back to her. 'I know not to run to the police every time unwanted post comes through the letterbox. Sometimes it's better to let things play out.'

'Yes,' said Celia, 'but it's important to be on stage while that happens.'

'What do you mean?'

'Well, it seems to me that you've become a bit of a spectator.'

He shot her another dark look.

'I'm not trying to insult you, Jack, it's just an observation. You've lost Charlie, your mum and Maya . . . it's hardly surprising that you've stepped back.'

He didn't react, changing the subject instead. 'So tell me about Nicci.'

'I thought she was a taboo subject?'

'She's an itch right now.'

'What do you want to know?' Celia asked, 'You've known her longer than I have.'

'She's like a different person now. If I had to describe the girl I remember, nobody would match her up with the Nicci that lives with you.' He paused to drink more coffee.

Celia nodded. 'She struggles. With what she did, with moving forward.'

He pressed his lips together and gave a curt nod.

'She has bad days, but fewer now than she did. Maybe that's not what you want to hear?'

'I can't let go of what she did. But, up until then, I always liked her. She was funny and loyal. She and Charlie were inseparable, and it feels good to see your sibling have a close friend. I don't want to look at her now.'

'I understand.'

'So, what did she want in my house?'

Celia looked completely blank.

'Okay. The *person* that entered my house was looking for something.' Jack rephrased it. 'What do you think they wanted?'

'I honestly have no idea. Not the clipping; I would assume they had no way of knowing it was there.'

'No, I don't actually remember keeping any of them. The biggest puzzle was who sent them, and why. And why they stopped.'

'This was the last one?'

'That's right. And, like I said, the location of the body resonated with me, so I guess that's why I held onto it.'

'You were fond of the place?'

'Not at all. It's bleak. I'd forgotten until I went back with Sadie and Maya. I hadn't been anywhere in Norfolk since childhood.' But, as he said it, he visibly stiffened. 'Except once. I'd totally forgotten. I went for an interview in Norwich, back when I was dating Sadie and before I took the London job. And, as a favour to Charlie really, I dropped Callum back at his parents' house.' He stared at her, his eyes wide. 'I can't believe I'd forgotten.'

'Do you know where it was? Can you remember?'

He closed his eyes as he thought. 'It was a big estate, maybe inter-war housing, ex-local authority, mostly semi-detached. Next door had built a garage on the side, a double garage, I noticed because I wondered how they'd got planning for it.' He stopped and gave a small smile. 'I'm better with buildings than I am with people.'

They left Hot Numbers and walked side by side back to Mawson Road.

'Come in to mine,' he said. 'I'll get the street map up on my Mac, see whether I can find it.'

He held open the front door for her, then she stood in the middle of the front room while he switched on the Mac. She wouldn't sit unless invited. The room was warm, but that was where cosiness ended. The décor was a drab leftover of its rental days, but she doubted that Jack was ready to redecorate anything in a palette that couldn't deviate far from cardboard, mushroom or deathbed grey.

He saw her looking around the room. His gaze followed briefly, then he looked back at the blank screen and there were a few seconds of awkward silence. He pulled a dining-room chair towards him. 'Would you like to sit?'

'Thanks,' she said. A pile of folded papers and notebooks were stacked at the back of the table, and its surface was partially covered by a floorplan. Next to them was a picture of Jack and Maya. It was a funny, happy shot. She could see an echo of his younger self in his smile. And Maya was pretty and impish. But nothing like him. It was a joyful photo, but it had to hurt. Celia touched the floorplan as though it was that which held her attention.

'It's a house I'm working on. The people who've bought it, they got it at a good price and now they want to extend it – make the layout look more logical,' Jack said. 'These are the plans from the last time it was extended. I saw them and thought the best thing they could do was demolish the whole thing.' He gave a wry smile. 'Of course, they didn't buy the house just to get a building plot, and I can't go round suggesting knocking buildings down. But it seems to me I need to go back and find the last point that was viable.'

'Hence the old plans?'

'Exactly. I know it's going to cause some disagreement. The easiest decision will be to keep adding on to what they've got.'

'And you don't want to do that?' Celia asked.

'No. What I want to do is give them something that will remain viable for as long as they want to live there. Oh,' he added as he suddenly realised that the Mac was ready for him to sign in.

He brought up Google Maps and narrowed his search to streets on the east and south-east of the city. 'It was over this side somewhere.' He said it as though speaking to himself now. He dropped to street view for several locations and harrumphed at each dead end. 'I can't see it,' he said and pushed the mouse away from him. 'Which means I'm coming with you. I'm going to try to find Callum's parents' house.' His frown returned again. 'It doesn't mean I'm buying into what you are telling me.'

Celia nodded at the floorplan. 'Perhaps you're like the people who own that house?'

'How so?'

'The right solution might not be the one they want to hear.'

He considered that for a moment. 'Because we don't like an answer, it doesn't mean it's not the truth, does it?'

'No,' said Celia quietly, 'it certainly doesn't.'

'And I certainly don't want to be letting my dad know that we are back in the middle of a new investigation or make him relive Charlie's death, or my mum's for that matter. But that injury to Nicci's forehead makes no sense whatsoever and if that's a small chip that's going to split and spread and radiate and eventually crack the whole picture, I need to know about it.' He shut down the Mac and rose from his chair. 'I'll come to Norwich with you, Celia, and I don't want to offend you here, but I'm not getting in that little, shitty bumper-car thing you drive. We'll take mine instead.'

Celia glanced in the direction of the window. There were no garages at the back, so perhaps he rented one somewhere. She couldn't ever remember seeing him getting in or out of the car in the street. 'What car?'

'There's a blue Ford parked about three houses along the road.'

'Yeah, I've noticed it.'

'Well, that's mine.'

'How come I've never seen you get in it then?'

'This is Cambridge, I don't need a car much. I've thought about selling it, it's just, well, there are quite a few things I haven't got round to yet.' He walked through to the kitchen and came back with a bunch of car keys in his hand. 'I'm ready to leave if you are?'

'Absolutely.'

Chapter 43

Those had been the last words that either of them had spoken until they were on the A14 and out of Cambridge. Celia mostly watched the road, but a couple of times she found an excuse to look across at Jack or glance round the car. The exterior was mid-blue, the interior grey. Aside from a streak or two of mud on the driver's side carpet, the car was in pretty good shape. The second time she looked round, she noticed that there was a child's car seat directly behind her. Was this, she wondered, a snapshot of his old life? A practical car, duties as a dad and everything in good working order?

He caught her looking. 'Trust me. There's nothing exciting here. I'm just about as boring as you can get.'

Celia looked at him sharply. 'And whose words are those then? Your wife's, I imagine?'

'I actually loved my life. We both had really good jobs, the careers we wanted, as far as I could work out. And we both wanted to start a family.' He stopped abruptly. 'Never mind.'

That was the end of the conversation for another twenty minutes. They turned onto the A11 and almost immediately the scenery began to change. The countryside was already flat, but now it seemed bleaker; the trees grew in gnarled clumps, bare of branches lower down with the foliage up near the top.

It reminded Celia of photos she had seen of trees growing in Africa, but these were mostly Scots pine trees that thrived on low-quality soil. Between them grew swathes of gorse; dark, green bushes peppered with vibrant, yellow flowers.

'Breckland,' he muttered. 'A lot of the local flint that was used in buildings was mined here. Years ago obviously.' She saw his fingers tighten slightly on the steering wheel. By the time thirty seconds had passed, she was pretty sure he was not about to add to the comment.

'When you look at a building, Jack, what do you see?'

'I'm sorry?'

She repeated the question.

'Same as everyone else, I expect.'

'Jack, really?'

'Okay. You can look at a house and see its history, you can see the history of the people who lived there. When I do alterations to a home, I'm planning changes that reflect the lives of the people who currently live in the house. I find it interesting. I know it's not.'

'I disagree.'

'I become immersed in work. I miss out on what's happening right in front of me. That's helpful right now.'

'So what went wrong with your wife, Jack?'

He kept his attention on the road ahead.

'I saw you with her, with Sadie, a couple of times when you came to visit your dad, you know, when you were first going out. That was a few years ago. I don't think you were married at that point, were you?'

Jack shot her a glance. 'No,' he said. 'But I reckon you already knew that. It's always the foot-in-the-door approach with you people, isn't it? Getting me to answer something simple and then it'll lead onto the next question and the next.'

'As ever, I'm offended by the "you people" line. I'm sure in your profession there are architects, and there are architects. I'm not claiming to be a journalistic paragon, but I do have some level of integrity.'

'So, were you going to ask me more probing questions to follow that one up or not?'

'Well, yes, I was actually. Not with my journalist hat on, with the nosy-woman-that-lives-across-the-road hat actually.'

To her surprise, he chuckled. 'You have more balls than I've got, Celia. There's not much to know, and most of it is dull. Depressingly so.'

'Well, that's not how I remember you. Yes, you had a serious side to your nature, but I've seen you many times coming back up the street with your bike covered in mud or kicking a football when you really shouldn't have been.'

'God, Celia, that wasn't even this century.'

'What does it matter? People change the way they behave because of things that happen to them in life, but, underneath, they have fundamentally the same personality as they had when they were born.'

'I became more serious as a teenager. I don't know why. I mean, you can't stop to enjoy a childhood; the whole point of it is to race forward. But I think mine was good; I have good memories of Charlie, and Mum and Dad. Although, I suppose, I never really appreciated the struggles my mum had with her depression, and if I had . . .' he stopped mid-sentence. The silence dragged on, but Celia wasn't about to interrupt. 'Perhaps it shouldn't have been such a shock to lose her after Charlie's death. I understand why; she just couldn't carry on at that point. I've wished so many times that she could've just hung on a bit longer, waited until something gave her a glimmer of hope.'

Like the birth of Maya. Celia said nothing.

But Jack's thoughts seemed to follow a similar track. 'When my daughter was born, my first words were, "I wish Mum was here." I wished she could meet her; she would've loved her so much. I loved her so much, actually.'

'Of course.'

'Maya,' he said his daughter's name as though it was going to be the start of a sentence, but then no more words came.

This time neither of them made any attempt to continue the conversation.

It was a few more miles down the road before they started picking up signs for the suburbs of Norwich.

'I think I'll go south around the ring road. Callum's house was definitely in that direction.'

He drove to an area where the properties were older with many terraced houses and shops lining the streets. Then, without warning, he pulled over to the side of the road.

'Hang on,' he said. He turned off the engine, but left the keys in the ignition. They were parked almost directly in front of a convenience store, but he got out and walked straight past this, and then Celia realised that he was heading for an estate agent further along the row.

'Smart move,' she muttered.

She didn't follow him inside, just waited. He was gone for the best part of ten minutes, and, when he returned, he had a clutch of brochures in his hand.

'What have you got?' she asked.

'Similar houses. All over this side of Norwich. There are a couple of likely estates, but my money's on this one. This house is the right style and the right coloured brick.' He passed her the pile of brochures and the one on top was in a street called Salthouse Road. 'There's a map on the back,' he added. 'I've looked, and it seems pretty much the same area as I remember.'

He put the address into his satnav, and pulled back out into the traffic, somehow, Celia thought, with more purpose than he'd had before.

In the end the house wasn't so hard to find. Salthouse Road was long, but with good visibility, and they drove the length of it before returning and making a sweep of all the nearby side streets. It was in one of these that Jack spotted the house where he'd dropped off Callum. The next-door neighbour not only had a double garage, like he remembered, but had built a porch on the front of the property that had a double arch and served little purpose apart from a failed attempt at making the house look more ostentatious. 'That,' he said, 'is the result of a 1970s package holiday to Costa Blanca.'

The other half of the semi-detached house was the one in which they were interested. Number 15. It had a low wall at the front, built with a mix of house brick and concrete stone wall inserts. The window frames and front door were made of aluminium. 'Looks like the 1970s was big round here,' Jack whispered as they approached the front door. The man who answered was in his late fifties, maybe early sixties. He wasn't tall, and he was skinny in a similar way to Callum so Celia's immediate thought was that this was his father. His already displeased expression darkened at the mention of Callum.

'It's my fucking stepson,' he said. 'He's a waste of fucking time.'

'You're not close then?' Celia said mildly.

He tilted his head back by a couple of degrees and shouted over his shoulder, 'Doreen? There's some people here asking questions 'bout your boy.'

'Who are they?' They both shared gravelly smokers' voices, but hers sounded less harsh than his.

'I don't know, do I? They say they're looking for 'im, they wanna speak to 'im about somethin'.'

'He was my lodger,' Celia cut in. 'I need to talk to him about the road accident, the one when he was injured. Can I ask your name?'

'Derek Watts. Why d'ya wanna know?'

'I'm Celia Henry and this is my friend, Jack Bailey. We would just like a few minutes if that's possible?'

'Yeah well, I've called 'er once 'aven't I? Doreen!'

There was movement behind him and a short woman with dark and very bouffant hair appeared in the hallway.

'We don't have anything to do with Callum, do we love?'

She shook her head. For the first time, Jack spoke. 'I wondered whether we could come in for a minute?'

'Not a problem with me, but I don't really see the point. Like I say, we don't really have anything to do with 'im. That's right, ain't it, love?'

'I do worry about him though.' Her accent was local, his was estuary.

Callum, as far as Celia remembered, must have fallen somewhere between the two, which, she guessed, meant that this couple had been together for quite a substantial period of Callum's childhood. Derek Watts had an expression that was neither kind nor generous.

'Shall I make drinks then?' Doreen asked.

'What for? You can make me a tea if you want, but nah, not for them, they're not going to be stayin', are they? What have we got to say to them other than nah, don't know where he is, nah, don't know what he's up to?'

She nodded and sidled towards the kitchen. Derek stood between them, clearly not prepared to let them further than the mat on the inside of the front door.

'When did you last see Callum?' Celia asked.

He shrugged. 'Dunno. Doreen, when did we last see 'im? Dunno. She won't know. I'd say years ago, but once in a while he pops up, wants some money, of course. He seems healthy enough, don't he, Dor?'

She glanced towards them from the sink, nodded and then turned back to finish filling the kettle.

Derek looked at Celia and tapped the side of his head. 'The kid is a waste of space, just dosses around all the time, Doreen was all like yeah, let him get an education, make somethin' of 'imself.' He held his hands in fists with his thumbs in his trouser pockets, his elbows jutted out and his chest was puffed out. 'Yeah, he was bright, but bright don't mean people ain't stupid, does it? Once he got into drugs, well, that was it. I've never done drugs in my life, don't see why he should.' The fingers of his right hand strummed the fabric of his jeans. 'Cigarettes yeah, alcohol yeah, drugs no. No sympathy for it whatsoever.'

'But can you tell us where he's likely to be?' Celia persisted.

'Not on this planet.' Derek tried laughing, then he half gagged, half choked for several seconds.

Jack tried, 'It's really important I get hold of him.'

'What's it to you?'

'My brother was in the car with him.'

Doreen was still in the kitchen, but Celia saw her look up sharply, and then turn away to open the kitchen drawer.

'Your brother was one of the ones what died then?'

'Yes, that's right.'

'Bad fucking job that one was.'

'Yes. But something's come to light and I think it's something that Callum would want to know. Can you get a message to him?'

Celia knew at once that this was a good move. Derek was one of those people that didn't want to miss out on a bit of information. She could see that just from the way his eyes suddenly brightened.

'Well, I might be able to. I'd have to see.'

'So,' said Jack, 'you do know where he is?'

'No, I didn't say that, but I'm sure I'm going to see him at some point. What d'ya want me to tell 'im?'

Jack straightened. Celia thought that it was an unconscious move, but suddenly he seemed to tower over the other man, and, whether intentionally or not, his words had an edge to them. 'Tell him that something else happened in that crash, and I'm going to find out what it was. Tell him that he needs to get in touch with me and tell me exactly what he knows. Can you do that?'

'And is Callum gonna know what it's about?'

Jack smiled coldly. 'He needs to get the message, Mr Watts. Do you understand me?'

The words hung in the air.

Jack managed to create the kind of silence that Celia never could, a silence that filled the air with uncomfortable possibilities. She looked down the hallway towards the kitchen, but Doreen Watts was nowhere to be seen.

'Well, whatever it is he's done, it ain't got nothing to do with me. Now give me your phone numbers and I'll pass 'em on. That's more than fair I think, under the circumstances.'

Celia already had her contact details written on a piece of paper. She took them from her pocket and passed them to him. 'Thank you, Mr Watts. We look forward to hearing from you, or Callum.'

They returned to the car and Celia noticed, unless she was mistaken, that there was an energy about Jack that she hadn't seen for a very long time. Neither of them spoke until Jack had started the engine, then he said to her, 'Can you see anything?'

She looked out of the window, the street looked just as it did before. 'No.'

He said nothing else, but drove slowly from the street and only stopped the car when they were round the corner and out of sight of the Watts' family home. He pulled over then, lowered his window and reached round to where a small piece of paper was tucked underneath the windscreen wiper. He brought it into the car. Celia knew at once that this was where Doreen Watts had disappeared. The piece of paper just said, *The Purple House, The Rows, Great Yarmouth.*

Chapter 44

She jolted awake.

There had been other times when she had drifted back to consciousness, but this time it was a shock of cognisance immediately followed by the overwhelming throb of her whole upper body aching. It was momentarily so all-encompassing that her guard dropped and her eyes snapped open. She closed them again immediately; he was still in the room.

'I thought you died,' he said hoarsely.

And she heard something in his voice that hadn't been there before, ever. She couldn't quite identify it, but her instincts told her that it fell somewhere between trepidation and full-blown fear.

'Did you think you'd gone too far?' she asked, surprised at how detached her own voice sounded.

'Maybe,' he said, and then repeated the word a few more times.

And suddenly she did want to see his face. She opened her eyes and gave them a few seconds to adjust.

He was sitting on the concrete with his knees bent in front of him and his arms wrapped round them. His face was pale, the sort of colourless, clammy look that goes with a fever. 'It was harder to bring you round this time. I nearly gave up.'

The words '*why didn't you?*' came to her lips, but she didn't say them. She didn't mean them. Saying something to catch him out was the closest she had to any kind of control. 'How much longer will you keep me here? Is it until you can't revive me again?'

He nodded. 'You've come back more times than any of the others.'

'Who were the others?' she asked.

'It doesn't matter, they don't matter.' He pressed his lips tight for a few seconds, his nostrils flared and she could tell that he was fighting to suppress some kind of emotion. 'I don't want you to go,' he said at last. 'Not yet.'

She had watched films where prisoners forged a relationship with their captors. That wouldn't happen unless she kept talking to him. But she needed to find something that wasn't challenging or threatening to him, something that wouldn't ignite his temper.

'Did it rain today?' she asked.

He looked at her blankly for a moment. 'I didn't notice. I don't care about the weather.'

His tone wasn't designed to invite any further conversation, but a voice in her head said *keep talking.*

She cleared her throat. 'Is there any chance I could have an apple some time, please? Or maybe some raspberries, they're actually my favourite.'

'You're thinner now, it suits you better.'

'My dad grows raspberries in the garden at home, and there's an apple tree at the end, but it only produces the crab apples, or whatever they're called. The ones that you can't really eat. My brother and I used to chop them up really small and add sugar. Dad said they would give us stomach cramps, but they never did.'

He wasn't looking at her now, he muttered something she didn't catch. She didn't ask him to repeat himself. She fell silent. She wanted to speak, to keep talking to him, about home and her childhood, but the words dried in the back of her throat.

Then he turned to face her.

'Don't,' he whispered. 'Don't ask for things or try to tell me about your fucking childhood. It isn't worth trying anything like that with me.' He ran his tongue across his teeth. 'We are not going to have a connection. You are not going to reach me, or whatever it is you think you can do.' He paused, and when he spoke again there was a tremor in his voice. This time it was not because of fear. 'I don't want you to die, but that's because I don't want to have to start again.' He unwrapped his hands and moved quickly, half crawling, half scuttling across the few feet which separated them. The action was reptilian, and in a moment his face was close to hers. 'Every time I take someone it's a risk and every time I have to start again there's a gap, a gap when I can't get what it is I need.' His breath was warm and swallowed the air between them. 'If all I wanted was sex it'd be easy, wouldn't it? I could go out, get somebody. Pay somebody. Who knows?' He moistened his lips by sucking them one at a time behind his teeth. 'Do you have sexual fantasies?'

She didn't answer.

'*Did* you then? Not now, but before, did you?'

She held his stare. 'Doesn't everyone?'

'Well, that's more honest than most,' he said, and one side of his mouth curled into a smile. 'Do you want to share one with me?'

She shook her head. 'No.'

'Why not?'

'It's personal.'

'Yes. They would be very personal and unique to you. Well, perhaps they're not unique. How would you know when you keep them to yourself and so does the next person?' He wiped his mouth with the back of his hand. 'I'll tell you mine.'

'You don't have to.'

'No I don't, but I will because then you'll understand.' His grin spread until the two sides of his mouth were almost in sync. To fresh eyes the smile might have been natural, but she could see a lack of symmetry and the way that joy and cruelty flickered on his lips. 'In my fantasy, I meet a woman, I know she's attractive, but she has no face. Then we have sex, but neither of us really knows the other, so it's just about the sex, nothing else.

'And I start to feel angry.

'I want to have sex with her, but I hate her for who she is, this faceless irrelevance of a woman. The more I'm aroused, the more I hate her. I don't want her, but I do. And so it goes on, growing more intense.

'And, in my fantasy, I climax just as she dies.

'And the hate and the need for sex are both gone, both satisfied at exactly the same moment.

'Just the fantasy was enough for a long time, but then of course, suddenly it wasn't, because that was how I was feeling about women in real life as well.' His voice had become rushed and breathless. 'And there was this one particular woman, I didn't plan to kill her.' His expression was intense, probing, as though he really cared whether or not she believed him. 'I didn't even find her attractive. She was a tease. She led men on and each time I saw her I felt angry.' He stretched his hands, his fingers first straight, then contracting into claws. Like talons. 'I ended up with her, having sex with her and it blurred, you know, the fantasy and reality. And suddenly I had my hands on her throat and she liked it, she really liked it at first. And that made it worse because to her it was a joke, the whole thing was a joke. A game. A turn on.'

He lilted his head and blinked. 'The pillow was never part of my fantasy, it just happened. I grabbed it, and I used it, and she passed out. It was surprisingly quick.' As he said it, a glint of excitement flashed in his eyes. 'I had no idea. I thought three minutes, that's what they say, you can manage without oxygen for three minutes, but it was less than that.'

'Was she dead?' she breathed.

'No, not then. I brought her round, but as soon as I did, I regretted it. I had sex with her again, and then I killed her. And don't get me wrong, I had guilt, but I tell you what, guilt is overrated. I felt euphoria as well and that certainly isn't.'

'So you did it again?'

'Yes.'

'So there are three of us?'

'Oh no.' He didn't elaborate further. 'It's good to talk things through. It makes it clearer in my head.' He was calm and self-assured. 'One day I'm going to have a wife, children probably. I'm going to live a normal life, but I'm not going to stop this.'

She locked her fingers tightly trying to stop her hands from shaking. It was the inevitability and calmness in everything he said that rattled her. But she knew that she felt unreasonably calm, as though they were talking about a plot, or something theoretical, not the risk to her own life.

'I will kill you,' he said.

And she nodded. 'It's my birthday next week.' She hadn't planned to say that, her thoughts had jumped several times in the millisecond, and the words had just formed themselves.

'Which day?' he asked.

'The fifteenth.'

He smiled. 'That was yesterday. I think we'll do it once or twice more.'

He reached across and picked up the roll of duct tape. She held out her wrists, like she had done before, but this time he shook his head.

'No. I'm changing things up now.' Instead he bound her wrists to the pipework on the wall.

She knew at once they weren't the flimsy kind of pipes that would pull away from mountings. They were thicker, solid, industrial even. Her hands were above her head. He ripped off another strip, about eight inches long.

'Please leave my mouth.'

He shook his head. He taped it shut without another word.

'I will leave your legs today, but consider if you flail around too much, you will fall off the mattress and that will be painful. Your arms are not going anywhere. I can't have you calling out.'

He felt around in the canvas bag and produced a large pair of scissors, the kind that tailors or dressmakers might use. He began snipping at her clothes.

'I'll burn them this afternoon,' he pressed his hands between her legs, 'but I will think of you. I can't help the fact that this is the most exciting part.'

He finished with the clothes and bundled them up, holding them in a small roll just inside his jacket. She stared up at him, her arms above her head, her eyes wild and her body naked in front of him for the very first time. He stopped and turned back to look at her with the door half open.

'I'll bring you raspberries though,' he said, then turned out the lights and closed the door behind him.

She shut her eyes and tried to block out the silence, repeating over and over in her head, 'My name is Louise Allum and I'm going to be okay. My name is Louise Allum and I'm going to be okay. My name is Louise Allum and I'm going to be okay.'

And the tears stung as they trickled from her eyes, through her hair and onto the dirty pillow.

Chapter 45

The Rows.

The name was immediately familiar to Celia. One of her early assignments had been to write an article on the rejuvenation of Great Yarmouth after the bombing in the Second World War. The Rows had originally been a series of narrow, parallel streets. The law of the day had dictated that all the houses must be built within the boundaries of the town and so, over a few hundred years, the houses had been crammed in back to back and facing each other with only a narrow walkway in between. Many had been lost in the war and more had been replaced since, but the last time she had visited Yarmouth, perhaps ten years ago, she had noticed that many of the buildings still retained the white and black row numbers painted on their brickwork. Less than half of the original Rows still existed, but it was enough for them to realise that pinpointing the purple house could be quite daunting.

They parked up and began at one end, working methodically along each of the surviving streets. The first likely house they came upon was what Celia would have described as a dusky pink, but Jack insisted that it depended on your eyesight, so they knocked upon the door. After a couple of minutes they decided to move on. They didn't really know what they were looking for, but this particular house had a quaint almost cottagey feel to it, and somehow Celia doubted that it was the one.

The second house was closer to a shade of maroon. They shrugged at each other and knocked on the door. A young woman answered. She had curly hair, masses of it, scraped back in a bandanna. She wore a T-shirt and jogging bottoms and looked as though she'd just woken up. Behind her a toddler in a high chair was banging his plate and yelling, 'Mum, Mum, Mum, Mum', with impressive consistency.

'Is this the purple house?' Celia asked.

The woman frowned. 'Is that its name, or its colour?'

'Well, I don't actually know.'

'Well, it's not this one. Who are you looking for?'

'Callum Shaughnessy?'

She shook her head and the curls jiggled. 'No, I've never heard of him. I tell you what though, about three roads up,' she pointed behind them, 'there's one . . . well, it's the only one I can think of that I'd call any shade of purple. It's sort of a lilac colour, but they haven't done a good job of it. You'll see. That's the only thing I can think of. Try there.' She screwed up her nose, making a deliberately pained face. 'Hold on to your handbag though.'

She closed the door before they'd had a chance to move away from it, and they glanced at each other.

'Okay,' said Jack, 'we don't have anything else to go on.'

'And, luckily, I don't have a handbag,' said Celia.

The curly-haired woman made it sound an easy place to find, but it took them another fifteen minutes. They counted across three alleys, but inadvertently missed a couple and had to go back again.

Celia was certain that these narrow alleys had seen poverty and misfortune time and again, and she found it impossible to walk between these houses without imagining the squalor that must have existed before the days of mains drainage and decent plumbing.

Jack saw the house first and nudged her elbow, but even then, in the gloomy walkway, she didn't spot the purple. To her the house looked more like a sombre grey, but then, as they moved closer, she saw what the curly-haired woman had meant. The purple had been painted on top of another much darker shade, and the result left the walls looking like they were uneven, or even melting. The house was also narrower than those around it and looked as though it had been built to fill a gap, perhaps to replace something that had collapsed or burned down at some point in the town's history.

The purple house was only about three times as wide as its front door, with just a painted frontage and one small window. It wasn't possible to see anything through the small panes in the door and all that was visible through the window was a net curtain, black with mould for its bottom eight or ten inches.

Jack rang the bell, but neither of them heard it create any sound within the house. They waited for a few seconds and then he knocked. Again they heard nothing, but some way back behind the dirty window, Celia saw a glimmer of yellow light.

'There's someone home.' She reached forward and banged again, harder this time.

The door was opened by a man possibly in his early thirties, maybe older. He wore black drainpipe jeans and Doc Martens boots; he stood with his lower leg filling the gap between the door and the frame, with the door itself pushed up tight against his foot. It seemed to be his plan to stop anybody else getting their foot in the door first. 'What?' he grunted.

Cheerful men seemed to be the theme of the day. 'We're looking for Callum, we heard he lives here.'

'Callum who?'

Celia fixed him with a dead stare. 'How many have you got? We have some questions for him.'

'And?'

'Look, can you tell us where he is? Is he in there? We'd like to see him.'

Jack cut in then. 'I'm Jack, and this is Celia. What's your name?'

'Bob.'

He didn't look like a Bob.

'So what's it really about? Are you police?'

'No, I'm his old landlady actually.'

'And he and my brother were in an accident a few years ago. Something's come up.'

It wasn't that Bob relaxed, it was more that the answer was unexpected and he was taking a moment to reassess the situation. 'He's been gone a while. He's always been a bit edgy, but he got really agitated, more than normal. Said I'll be back when I'm back, and he cleared off. He will be back though 'cause he told me not to do anything with his room.'

'This is your place then?' Jack asked.

'Yeah, kinda.'

'He's your lodger?'

'Yeah, if you like.'

'Bob?' Celia waited until he looked at her. 'Where do you think he might have gone?'

'I don't know.' Bob shrugged his shoulders in a way which looked as though something had dropped down the neck of his shirt. 'I don't usually know where he goes and it don't matter, but this is quite a long time for him.'

'We want to make sure that Callum's all right, and we do need to speak to him.' Celia smiled, hoping her expression conjured up the right mix of warmth and maternal concern. 'Is there any possibility that we could look round his room? I'd like to see whether there are any clues that could tell us where he might have gone.'

Bob looked uncertain, half suspicious, half worried. His gaze jumped from her to Jack, and back again. A moment later she saw his expression clear and a moment after that saw the little bundle of notes that Jack was holding in his hand.

'Perhaps I can help him keep up with his rent. Is that any good to you?'

Bob took his foot out of the gap and let them inside.

Chapter 46

The whole house reeked of damp and marijuana and old cigarettes and spilt beer or worse. The carpet was sticky under foot, thin and stretched with age, which created ripples across the floor. Bob led them up a narrow and steep staircase with the wood creaking under their feet. There were three rooms leading from the landing; two doors immediately obvious as they reached the top of the flight, and then a little gap and a step down to what must have been a tiny extension put on the back of the house many years before.

That was Callum's room and although it was no more than seven feet square, it was immediately obvious to Celia that it looked as though two people resided there. 'Does he have a girlfriend?' she asked.

Bob just snorted. 'He's never had a girlfriend for as long as I've known him. Talks about women from time to time. But I talk about owning a Porsche, if you know what I mean.' He nodded with a rapid bobbing of his head. 'I'm going to leave you to it now, I've got things to do. But I'm only going to be in the next room mind, so no funny business. No taking anything, all right?'

He left then. As soon as he'd gone Celia used her phone to snap pictures of the room before they began to touch anything. There was only a single bed, but it was everything else that pointed to more than one person. The furniture consisted of a narrow chest of four drawers, a small bookcase and a bedside table. The strip of carpet that ran between the bed on one wall and the furniture on the opposite wall was strewn with carrier bags. She nudged one with her foot and it tipped over. It looked as though it contained nothing but empty chip wrappers.

It smelt that way too.

The bed was unmade and the curtains hung limp at the windows. But for the bookcase and the surface of the chest of drawers, the story was quite different; they were both clean and dust free. The bookcase, although narrow, had enough space for larger books at the bottom and then two shelves of paperbacks above. She scanned the titles: several books on anatomy, a couple on psychology, plus several study guides and a selection of true-crime titles. The shelves above were filled with novels, mostly crime, and a sprinkling of self-help books: everything from overcoming shyness and building confidence, to guides on successful relationships and understanding the opposite sex. There were more true-crime books here too – the inside-the-head-of-a-killer exposé type that looked like trashy novels. Books written for entertainment, sensationalising notorious crimes which, to Celia's mind at least, were still too raw and too recent.

'Wow,' said Jack.

Celia photographed the spines. 'Give me your first thoughts.'

He kept his hands in his pockets as though he didn't want to risk contaminating them, and turned slowly to take in the whole room.

'This is not living, just existing and barely that. I can see why you asked whether he had a girlfriend though; it's definitely a two-personality room. But I would look at it a different way. When everything went wrong between me and Sadie, I was a complete mess for weeks. Still am. But, the point is, there were still things I hung on to. A small selection of items that I kept safe because they meant so much, and they gave me hope, and they represented something important. I think that side of the room is him functioning on a day-to-day basis, and these bits over here are the ones that matter.'

She had no idea whether he was correct, but she liked his thinking. 'Okay then,' Celia replied, 'I'll start with the drawers.'

'What are we looking for?'

'Who knows? Something to tell us where he's gone? Something to tell us more about his mindset?'

'Perhaps we should look through these bags of rubbish.'

Celia winked at him. 'Well done, Jack; I thought you would never volunteer.'

She reached in her pocket and fished out a pair of latex gloves. 'And in case you're wondering, no, I don't spend my life planning to do this sort of thing. I tint my hair, you know. They stop my fingers getting stained.' She smoothed the hair from her temple to behind her ear. 'It's the same as my natural colour, but I do like to cover the little flecks of grey.'

Jack raised an eyebrow. 'I suppose you just have the one pair?'

'Sorry. Can you take photos as you go? Things that may seem like nothing now could prove useful later.'

He nodded and they both began searching the confined space. The drawers didn't take long at all as most were half empty. Callum seemed to own a very small selection of clothes: one pair of jeans, a couple of pairs of jogging bottoms, two hoodies and a bundle of T-shirts. None of them folded, none of them clean. The drawer that contained underwear was split between pants and socks, cigarette papers and a stash of chocolate.

'I am so hungry,' said Celia.

'Really? You can think of eating among all of this?' Every bag seemed to contain fast-food packaging: wrappers, kebab boxes and KFC bags. 'I don't think I'm going to eat fried food ever again.'

'Oh come off it, Jack, we'll go for chips as soon as we leave here.'

He knelt on the floor, surrounded by bags that he had already checked. 'He's going to know that somebody has looked through his stuff.' His eye level was a couple of feet lower than Celia's and, as he glanced round the room, his gaze fell upon something. He ducked a little lower. He was looking at the bottom shelf of the bookcase. He reached forward and tugged at a copy of *Macleod's Clinical Examination*, a four-hundred-plus-page book that was wedged between two other anatomy volumes.

'There's something in it,' he said and, as soon as it was free from the other books, Celia could see that its covers were springing open with the force of the extra sheets of paper rammed inside. She could also see that they were newspaper cutting. Her first thought was how unusual it was to find people taking cuttings from newspapers these days when they could just bookmark them on the internet. But then she immediately realised that there was no sign of any technology, no phone charger, not even a TV, never mind a computer.

She made a mental note to ask Bob but, in the meantime, they both moved to sit on the bed. Jack opened the book on his lap and Celia reached out to stop the pages sliding onto the floor. There were more of them than she had first thought.

'Oh, wow,' Jack breathed.

'That's the second time you've said that,' she commented. But he wasn't wrong; they'd hit on something here. He picked up the top page from the pile, and she picked up the next.

'This is the same one that was sent to me; about Emily Moore.'

'Becky Lake,' Celia replied.

He turned to the next.

Jack read the first few lines. 'I haven't heard this name before. Debbie Lagoudi.'

'Oh, I have.' Celia reached forward and they both read at the same time. 'I remember her. She disappeared from north London. That was last year. Autumn I think, yes, the nights had got darker.' She traced her finger down the column until she found the details. 'Yes, here it is, look, she disappeared with her passport and they wondered whether she'd gone abroad. Then later on decided she hadn't. No money has ever been taken from either of her bank accounts. She had no cash on her at the time and no change of clothes. No sightings and no activity on her credit card ever since.' Celia stared at the photograph and Debbie Lagoudi, a young woman with ebony eyes and black hair that cascaded over her shoulder, stared back. 'Yes, I remember that one.'

'And what do you have there?' Jack asked.

They turned their attention to the paper that Celia held. Again, it was a different name. Sam Morgan.

'What date?' Jack asked.

'Spring last year.'

'Okay,' he said, 'Let's get them in date order, that'll give us some idea of what we're looking at.'

In some cases there were several newspaper clippings related to the same disappearance. They sorted them through and ended up with five names, beginning with Becky Lake, then Emily Moore, Sam Morgan, Debbie Lagoudi and, finally, Louise Allum.

Louise had been missing for three weeks and six days.

She had been studying at Bournemouth University. She'd been out in the evening with a group of friends, celebrating one of their twenty-first birthdays. They'd all been dressed up in the theme, quite simply, of twenty-one. The photograph that appeared in the paper had been taken on that evening. She'd been wearing a 1960s-style minidress. At first glance it looked as though the pattern was psychedelic, but on closer inspection it was the number '21' repeated and interlinked, all in shades of Jaffa orange and Barbara Cartland pink.

There had been nine in the party at the start of the evening, all female, but, by the end of the night and after quite a lot of alcohol, three of the women had been separated from the rest.

Nothing had been thought of it until the next day when only eight of them could be contacted. Louise had gone missing somewhere between Smoking Aces and Sixty Million Postcards. There had been a couple of possible sightings at Bar So, a restaurant and club close to the shore. The coastguard helicopter had spent two days searching the coastline, looking for a body washed up on the beach, but there never was one.

'We need to call the police,' said Jack.

'Yes, I'll phone Briggs and he can liaise with the local police.' She looked around the room. Apart from the bed, there was no corner of it that they hadn't touched or disturbed in some way. 'He is not going to be a happy man,' she said.

Chapter 47

Celia banged on the adjacent bedroom doors until one of them opened. Bob looked bleary eyed. 'Does Callum have a laptop?'

He shook his head. 'He sold it when he ran out of cash.'

'What about a mobile?'

'Yeah, well, he got rid of his iPhone too. I think he ended up with some sort of burner, and before you ask, no, I don't have the number. Have you finished because I need to lock up? And if he does come back, I doubt it mind you, but if he does come back and finds you trawling through his stuff, he's going to go mental at me.'

'We're nearly done, just a couple of quick questions. When he talked about girls, did he mention any names?' Celia asked.

'Nah, there aren't any, are there? It's all just a figment of his imagination.'

'There is just one more thing if you can cast your mind back. You said Callum's been gone for a while, could you be more specific?'

'Do you think I know what day it is today? Or any other day for that matter?'

She glared at him.

'Hang on, I'll try.' He sighed, but seemed to make a genuine effort to remember. 'It wasn't this month 'cause Fran gave me her rent, so I knew that Callum's was due as well.' He paused to think some more. 'See, Fran's on time, she's got a job and all that stuff. She's on time, and when she pays me I know it's time to ask Callum. Except he wasn't here by then.' He looked mildly triumphant in a stoned kind of way. 'So before the start of the month then.'

Just then the second door was opened by a surprisingly wholesome-looking young woman. 'It's all right, Mason, I'll take it from here.'

She directed Celia into her room with a jerk of her head. She wore jeans and a hand-knitted jersey made of squares of different jewel colours. Her hair was a light brunette, a natural tone Celia guessed. It was short, in a pixie cut.

'You're Fran, I take it?'

The young woman nodded. 'Yes, and that's Mason, not Bob. I was trying to keep out of it, that's what I normally do, but you seem fairly sound, and I guess something important is going on?'

'Yes.'

Fran's room was on a par with Callum's well-ordered bookcase. The furniture was basic, but everything was clean and tidy. She had hazel eyes, a jumble of freckles and a very direct tone. 'What do you want from Callum then?'

Celia indicated towards the single bed. 'May I?'

'Sure.'

Celia perched on the edge, her hands folded on her lap. 'Okay, I was Callum's landlady when he was studying in Cambridge. This is going back several years now. He was injured in quite a serious road accident, and I need to ask him some questions.' She chose her words carefully, sensing that Fran would be most likely to respond to a straightforward but serious request for help. 'It may be that he witnessed more than he told anybody at the time. It is very important that we speak with him.'

Fran nodded. 'He told me about that crash, not much actually, but there was a whole lot more written on his face than the details he gave me, and I wondered whether that's why he's, you know . . .'

'You know?' queried Celia. 'Always on edge?'

'Yeah. I think he has nightmares. He wakes up in the night and he's agitated. I hear him pacing and talking to himself. When he has an episode, he's usually out of it, well I guess he takes . . . uses whatever works to calm himself back down. I don't know where he's gone, by the way, I'll say that before you ask, and no, he's never tried it on with me.'

Celia smiled. 'So you were listening then?'

'I always listen in this house. Callum's not my type and he clocked that right away. In the first couple of weeks I was here, and I've been here probably almost as long as he has, I thought maybe we were going to be mates, but then, just as soon as we seemed to be making a connection, he backed right off. I've never seen him speak to anybody apart from us two here.' As she'd spoken she'd moved closer to the window. Celia couldn't see the view from where she sat, but she couldn't imagine that it consisted of anything apart from rooftops and patches of sky. Fran glanced out, then pointed. 'He seems to like the water. I've seen him sitting down on the front with a bag of chips just staring out at the sea. I know you're looking for him. I reckon you'll find him by the coast; he seemed happiest there. And I do remember the last time we saw him. I'm training as a physiotherapist and I work part-time in a craft shop.'

She tugged at her jumper as if to prove the point. Celia glanced round the tiny room, wondering how this bright and articulate woman hadn't found somewhere better to live.

Fran smiled. 'Cheaper than living at home. I'm saving up for my own place and it's an incentive-filled way of doing it, because I'm not going to stay here any longer than necessary, I tell you. Anyhow, I work at a craft shop on a Saturday and that was the last time I saw him. I came home and I think it was a couple of days later when I paid the rent, but Callum was gone by then. That Saturday was the last time I saw him for certain.'

'That's the twenty-fifth,' Celia said slowly.

'Yeah, I guess that's right.'

It was the day the newspaper had come out, the one that showed a picture of Louise Allum and the first concerns for her safety.

'How did he seem that last time? Do you remember?'

Fran nodded slowly. 'Oh yes, very clearly. Like I said, I'd just finished work and I came upstairs and I could hear sobbing, more than sobbing, he was almost hysterical. His door was open and I tapped. He was sitting on the floor next to his bed, in the middle of all those carrier bags of rubbish. He was on something, his eyes were completely blank, jumping all over the room. I don't know if he could even see me. He knew somebody was there, but he was far from coherent. He just kept saying that it was his fault, it was all his fault. I knelt down beside him and I asked him what he was talking about, and then he started raving about the world in general, saying that everything was wrong. I suggested he find somebody to talk to.

'He became angry then. He didn't want to be branded as some kind of weirdo. And in the space of just a few seconds he switched.' She clicked her fingers. 'Like that. And the empty look changed to something else.' She paled at the memory, not by much, but it was still noticeable. 'I wasn't scared, I mean, it was just Callum, so why should I be afraid? It was unnerving though.'

'And how would you describe this look?'

She looked past Celia then, her eyes focusing far beyond the wall behind her. After what felt like a full minute she dragged her attention back to Celia. 'It was a different kind of empty. Like staring into a void. One that was swallowing him from the inside out.' She shuddered as if someone had walked over her grave. 'I hadn't connected it to him leaving. In fact I think I had stopped myself thinking about it until now.'

Chapter 48

Nicci paced. She could have gone with them, of course, but it certainly didn't need three of them, and it was only Jack who could possibly, maybe, but not definitely, remember where Callum's family lived. Nicci really wasn't needed, and she had no doubt that Celia would use the journey as some kind of bonding exercise with Jack. Well, Nicci wasn't needed for that either.

She paced some more.

It was just over two hours since she'd had a text, *Going to Great Yarmouth.* She immediately knew that would have something to do with Callum. Perhaps, she'd thought, they had found him. She and Celia had already exchanged a flurry of texts before Celia had updated her with the news that they were driving on to Great Yarmouth, but there had been nothing since.

She still had her phone with her and every couple of minutes she looked at the screen again just in case she'd missed another message or a phone call. She was looking at the phone's blank face when she saw an email arrive.

Dear Miss Waldock,

We are pleased to tell you that we have successfully extracted a full DNA profile of *a sample you have sent. The information is in the attached letter.*

She sent a copy to the printer and then grabbed the paper.

Paying for this had taken every penny of her savings; she'd paid for a laboratory with an excellent reputation and paid for the result to be expedited. She hadn't been able to risk just handing over the swabs to the police for them to be put aside, or lost, or to never know whether they had been good enough to produce any results.

Using a third-party testing facility had been the only answer. She could hand the findings over to Briggs now without losing the information herself. And, if they lost it, she would still have it to hand.

Jack's involvement looked far less likely than it had at the time. She paused, reassessed the thought, and then corrected herself; she was far less suspicious of Jack than she had been. But gut feelings and intuition were never going to be as trustworthy as genuine evidence. She was halfway to the police station before it occurred to her that she had just left the house without any of the usual trepidation and, more than that, she was now heading to the police station without many qualms either.

Into the lion's den itself.

She had folded the printed sheet into thirds and slid it into an envelope. She had written 'FAO D.I. BRIGGS' on the front even though she had no intention of handing it to anybody but him.

She asked for him at the front desk.

The man behind the counter remained unsmiling; he made a quick call then invited her to take a seat. She tried, but there had only been so many minutes of calm left in her. Within a few seconds she was up on her feet, moving her weight from one to the other, moving from information poster to information poster.

But Briggs was quick and appeared within a couple of minutes. 'I hear you've roped Jack Bailey into this now,' he said.

'They went to Norwich, and then on to Yarmouth.'

'I know where they've been,' Briggs said, 'because it feels as though every time they turn up somewhere our resources have to follow.' He spotted the envelope. 'What do you have there?'

'It's a DNA profile. Celia said that you have a partial for Becky Lake's abductor.' Nicci had already taken the swabs when she'd discovered that. Her original motivation to enter Jack's house had been more speculative, and driven in part by the idea that the police would be able to use the profile to prove that it was he who had attacked her.

'We have a partial for somebody who *might* be Becky Lake's abductor,' he corrected.

'Well,' said Nicci, 'there's a DNA profile in here, a full one.'

'Whose?'

She shook her head. 'Come back to me if it's a match, and I'll tell you.'

'You can't do that,' he said.

She bristled instantly. 'I'm protecting myself and the information. You'll have to excuse me if I'm not a hundred per cent trusting of the police.'

Briggs sighed. 'I mean, you can't just go around sampling people's DNA,' he said. 'For one thing, it's not going to be admissible.'

Nicci held out the envelope, waggling it in his direction. 'Do you want it or not? It might not be admissible in court but, if there's a match between this and your partial profile, then come back to me and I'll tell you where to look. Surely that has to count as a lead?'

It was cold outside but Briggs was just in shirtsleeves. At first he made no move to take the envelope, and instead folded his arms and frowned at it. 'Where did you get this?'

'Somebody visited my house and I swabbed a glass,' she lied.

'Do you have CCTV of everybody going in and coming out of your place?'

'Why?'

'So you could prove it came from your property, and not, for example, from somewhere you shouldn't have been?'

They spent the next few seconds with each weighing up the other. Finally she folded the envelope in half, then took a step backwards towards the door. It was intended as a hint that she might just put it in her pocket and walk away.

He unfolded his arms. 'Okay,' he said. 'I'll take it.'

Chapter 49

Jack had stayed in Callum's room in order to make a call to Briggs while Celia had gone to speak to Bob. Her reasoning had been simple; she would occupy Bob, and stop him from causing any problems before the police arrived. She had been sure that he would either clear off, lose his temper, or be somehow disruptive or obstructive.

Jack photographed the room and the newspaper clippings, and then he checked through his phone, making sure he was happy with all of the shots. He could read everything clearly, but leant over the originals to view them again. Of course, it was only Becky Lake's murder that had occurred before Charlie's death, but knowing that Callum had collected all of these, and that Callum had also been there when Charlie died, meant that the clippings and everything else in the room was linked to Charlie.

He called Briggs, who answered on the second ring.

'Hi, it's Jack Bailey here.'

'Oh,' he said, 'is everything all right?'

'I'm with Celia.'

There wasn't a groan, but Jack imagined that there might have been.

'We're in Great Yarmouth, and we've found something.'

'Is there any sign of Callum?'

'No, he's long gone. Celia's trying to find out more, but there's a press clipping here from the start of last month, so, assuming that no one else has left it in his room, he was certainly here then. It's about the disappearance of Louise Allum—'

He heard Briggs draw a breath.

Jack explained the newspaper clippings to Briggs, and described Callum's room. Briggs listened, and didn't speak until a couple of seconds after Jack had finished.

'Don't touch anything,' Briggs instructed.

Jack stood on the small square of carpet in the very centre of the room in a patch he'd cleared of carrier bags. He shifted uneasily, making a rough inventory of the few items that they might not have touched.

Briggs read the silence easily. 'Right,' he said, sounding resigned, 'just don't touch anything else.' Briggs told him to wait, and Jack could hear him on his desk phone, giving instructions and passing on the skeleton of the information.

It left Jack in limbo for a few long minutes. He was conscious of the stale air he was breathing and the grubbiness underfoot. The dirt in the room felt old, as though it had built up layer upon layer over the years, probably starting way before Callum had arrived. Jack's room, when he had first been to university, had been a similar size, and there had been times when it was dirty and times when it had been messy – nothing on this scale, but he related to it somehow. There were always students that had taken on too many shifts, fell victim to each flu bug that went round campus, whose grades had dipped a point or two here and there and then suddenly started to slide; they went from flying high to wheeling off towards the earth, smoke trailing from their engines. It hadn't happened to him, not at college, his burnout had come later, but as far as he could see, each year the university had at least one Callum.

'Jack, are you still there?'

'Yes, of course.'

'What you have provided,' he said, 'is a very interesting set of names. Becky Lake and Emily Moore had already been linked by the major investigations team. We know that Becky Lake and Emily Moore were kept alive for quite a considerable time after their abductions, both were from the East Anglia region and both bodies had been dumped in water. But those links are circumstantial. And I'm not telling you anything here that hasn't already been reported, but . . .' there was a pause and Jack imagined the phone being switched from one ear to the other, 'the bodies of Debbie Lagoudi and Sam Morgan have never been found; evidence linking those cases to the two others would be a major step forward. Do you have any information on his whereabouts, Jack?'

'Do you think we know and we're not saying?'

'I'm just checking. You've come this far; is there anything you haven't told me?'

'You know everything.' It felt wrong to Jack that they'd been able to jump ahead of the police. Callum's mum didn't have the same surname as Callum, but he guessed the police wouldn't have found it particularly difficult to track her down. 'Only we gave it a higher priority than you, didn't we?'

'There's some truth in that, Jack,' Briggs conceded. 'But we are working to find Callum now.'

'Good,' Jack replied, and fought back the urge to snap at Briggs. He reminded himself that the police never had more than the say so of him and Celia about the imperative of locating Callum. 'Do you mind if I ask you a question?' he said.

'No, fire away.'

'How do you think all this relates to the car crash? Could Callum have caused it somehow?'

'I don't know, I really don't. We're reviewing the forensics now. I'll talk to you when I know.'

The call finished, and a snapshot flashed through his head; Nicci semi-conscious and Callum grabbing hold of her and slamming her head against the steering wheel. His recurring snapshot had, for years, been Charlie transfixed in an endless moment of fear, meeting certain death. His expression frozen in horror. He still saw Charlie's face in his nightmares at least once every week.

Jack had often thought back to the day of the accident; everyone's life was filled with pivotal moments, seemingly inconsequential days that turned into dates burnt into their memory for life. The loss of Charlie, of his mother, his father's deteriorating health, the abandonment of the Cambridge home, his own marriage, its subsequent collapse, the birth and then loss of his precious Maya. They were a chain of events that were inextricably linked to that day by the river.

His world had been a tunnel ever since; a shaft where the destruction lay behind him, where he had experienced light and sound as nothing more than reflections and echoes.

He had ended the call to DI Briggs and had known beyond any doubt whatsoever that today was another similarly pivotal day in his life. He didn't immediately abandon the room; instead he took it in, in all its squalor. Black, velvety fungi had spread fanlike from the corners of the walls nearest the window. The window itself was the sash style layered with so much paint that Jack doubted that it could ever do more than scrape and ease its way up two or three inches. In the chips and dents of the woodwork, he could see four or five different colours of ancient paint, dark brown and purple, navy blue, then, older still, yellow, pale green. He wondered if the wallpaper was the same, whether somewhere under the Anaglypta might be the primary shades of the 1980s, the mustards and browns of the 1970s and so on, back to a time when this room had been part of a proper home.

Somewhere along the way it had become the last stop for the desperate, so it seemed rather ironic that this was also the place and the moment when Jack felt his hopes and future reunite.

It was raining outside. He couldn't remember whether it had been during their journey, but now rainwater was dripping heavily from the outside guttering, hitting tiling with a heavy rhythmic plink, plink, plink, and, further away, there was the sound of gulls. Of panting traffic. Of a man running, his feet slapping the wet pavement. Jack had been in that grey, thick-walled and almost endless tunnel for such a long time, and now suddenly he'd hit the fresh air. And he could smell, and see, and hear without the layers of grief and pain and solitude smothering everything to crushing insignificance.

'Jack.'

He looked around and saw Celia in the doorway.

She had a bemused expression. 'You spoke to Briggs?'

'Yes.'

With perfect timing, sirens pushed away the sound of rain.

'What's happened?' Celia asked. 'To you, I mean?'

He didn't know whether she was just very perceptive or whether the change in him was written that clearly.

'I believe her,' he said. 'Nicci, I believe her. I believe she was driving, but I also believe that Callum caused the crash. That's not so hard to imagine, is it? That he somehow reached forward and grabbed Charlie or Nicci. That he did it because someone had worked something out. And now he's hiding with this Louise Allum girl. He has her prisoner or he's already killed her, I don't know. But we need to get out of here, because, between us, we can work out where he is.'

Celia shook her head. 'Hey, Jack, you're getting ahead of yourself. We don't know the first thing about finding Callum.'

'But we do. We can speak to Gemma, she must know something, or ask Nicci. There must be some clue, Nicci was close friends with Ellie; there must be something.'

'They'll want a statement from us first, Jack, and they'll have better resources than we'll have. They'll find Callum.'

'They won't, or at least they might not. Look, things were missed the night of the crash, that can't happen again. You see what we've got here.' He waved his arm towards the newspapers still spread on the bed. 'Becky Lake was the first, he snatched her from the street and he killed her and Ellie knew, that's why Ellie was hysterical, she worked it out. There must be more, there must be some way of knowing how he caused the crash. The police didn't find it because they weren't looking for it. They were just looking at a bunch of teenagers who'd drunk too much, who'd driven too fast, who'd driven off the road and hit a tree. That's all they looked for; but had they looked at what was behind it, they would have discovered a serial killer.'

Celia just looked at him, her brown eyes assessing him and reassessing him with every word he spoke.

He guessed Bob had let the police into the building because two uniformed officers appeared behind Celia. She tilted her head a little and cast her gaze sharply to the right. It was a clear let's-get-out-of-here signal.

'We'll need you to stay and answer some questions,' the first officer explained.

But Celia shook her head. 'We're not making a statement today,' she told him. 'Get your car keys, Jack,' she said, 'we're leaving.'

And then as soon as they stood on the pavement outside, she turned to him and smiled. 'Welcome back to the land of the living, Jack.'

Chapter 50

Nicci had two clients that afternoon so it wasn't as though she could have gone with Celia and Jack, well, not without cancelling, but she still felt strange thinking of Jack and Celia together, and being at home not really knowing what was going on. As soon as her four o'clock appointment left she called Celia.

'We'll be going back to the car soon,' Celia told her, 'so we'll be a while yet, but there's nothing to worry about.'

'Did you find Callum?' Nicci asked.

'No, not exactly. But things have developed,' and, at the very end of Celia's words, Nicci caught a sudden reluctance in her tone.

'Developed how?' Nicci asked sharply.

'Can I talk to you when we get back?' Celia added.

Nicci felt an immediate tingle. 'What's happened, Celia?'

'We're going back to see Briggs next. I'm guessing you won't want to join us.'

'Should I? Is there a reason that I need to be there? Something's happened, hasn't it?'

'Nicci,' Celia sounded firm, 'Listen. We tracked Callum as far as Great Yarmouth, but he hasn't been seen for several weeks. Beyond that, we have no idea where he is.' Celia gave a long audible sigh, one that could only be heard by Nicci, one that was no doubt meant to say, *Just drop it will you? Wait till I'm back.* Nicci gripped the phone more tightly. She knew if the call ended now that she would be plagued by restlessness or even fear until Celia made it back home and explained properly.

'Can't you tell me anything?'

'All you need to know is that they are looking for him now. We're making progress.' And then she hung up.

Nicci couldn't blame her, but then spent the next ten minutes moving restlessly from room to room. They'd gone to Norwich and ended up in Great Yarmouth, so Callum had left Cambridge, gone east and had then kept going east until he hit the sea. Was that to get as far away from here as possible? She reached the kitchen and stopped by the breadbin. She took two slices of seeded bread and dropped them into the toaster. She stood at the counter with her elbows resting on it, looking into the top of the toaster and waiting. She knew she would jump when the toast popped up, she always did, but she liked the deep, orange glow of the elements and watching the toast slowly darken.

The kitchen looked different to when Callum and Ellie lived here. Celia had repainted the walls and changed just enough so that neither of them were reminded too much or too often, but there had been many occasions when Nicci and Ellie had sat at the kitchen table and just talked well into the night. They had bonded so quickly that it hadn't felt like only two trimesters that they'd known each other.

She picked up the toast, a jar of Nutella, and grabbed butter from the fridge, then took them over to the table.

There had been two other housemates for a while, but Ellie hadn't mixed with them much, and then there'd been Callum. She spread the butter thinly, and then tried to remember whether Ellie and Callum had hung out grudgingly at first, or whether they'd genuinely got along, but she could no longer remember the order of things, just that at some point Rob and Gemma had had a party, Callum and Ellie had been invited and then she and Charlie had ended up tagging along.

They were an odd bunch, but for a while it had certainly worked. Now she looked back on it, the dynamic was weird, they were people who didn't naturally fit together, yet somehow they had for those few months been almost inseparable. She took a teaspoon and used it to spread the Nutella. Nutella and butter on toast, it was comfort food. Maybe that's what made her think, made her remember that, when she'd caught a bug, and she'd been headachy and running a temperature, she'd stayed at home while the others had gone away for the weekend.

Where had they gone?

It had been somewhere on the coast, not Great Yarmouth though, somewhere less built up, somewhere . . . she hesitated, could it have been . . . She dropped the toast back on to the plate, brushed the crumbs from her hands, then grabbed her house keys and hurried up the road to her mum's.

She couldn't let herself in there any more, but it was a good bet that her mum would be home, she usually was, and sure enough her mum opened the door with a question on her lips, but no words. Nicci hurried past, muttering something, telling her enough just to make her leave her alone.

She ran up to her old bedroom and began searching through what was left of her things.

There was nothing there now for her apart from half-a-dozen boxes that had been loaded into an overhead cupboard. It wasn't long before she became aware of her mum standing against the doorframe, arms crossed and watching silently.

'I'm looking for a photo,' Nicci said. 'I was ill and the others, Charlie, Callum, Ellie and Gemma, they all went to the coast somewhere. Do you remember?'

'No.'

'I was ill, I was on the sofa, Mum. Charlie gave me a picture. It used to be on my pinboard.'

'And?'

'I need to find it. Or work out where they stayed.'

'Run up the road and ask your friend Gemma.'

'Ugh.' Nicci turned back to the boxes. 'Where is it?' she muttered, sorry she'd even tried to ask her mum who probably wouldn't have remembered even if it had been last week.

In her mind's eye she could see Charlie clearly, but not the background.

One of the group had snapped a photo of Charlie standing by the side of the road with some kind of scenery in the background, she couldn't remember what; she just remembered sand and tufts of grass where he stood. It had been taken with his phone and he'd then gone to a photo booth, printed it off, and sent it to her with 'Wish you were here' scrawled upon it. He thought it was funny, and she found it amusing because it was a toss-up whether or not he'd written the words sarcastically, and it definitely didn't look like the most glamorous holiday destination.

She pushed the first box aside and began on the next. 'Where is the fucking thing?' she muttered. The shadow disappeared from the doorway then and she knew she was alone. She carried on quietly looking through every piece of paper and in every envelope.

She found it at the bottom of the third box.

It was just the size of a normal photograph, but it had been printed on heavier stock. She held the photo as she studied it, aware of Charlie's ghost. He looked straight at the camera as the wind ruffled his hair over to one side, he stood on the path beside a straight road that disappeared into the distance behind him. He wasn't standing on sand after all, but there were drifts of it across the path and across the road, and there were tufts of grass protruding from the verge. In the background were houses, little bungalows; they'd probably once been decent-sized holiday chalets, but in the photo they looked as though they were tiny and dilapidated and probably abandoned.

The closest was yellow with a flat roof and walls that looked slightly at an angle to one another; the next property was maybe fifty yards further along. There was nobody else in the picture, no cars either. The place seemed like a ghost town and she wouldn't have been surprised to see a tumbleweed somewhere in the background. She photographed the image with her phone, then slipped it into her pocket and left.

Chapter 51

She knew why he'd left her legs unbound. She'd seen it on his face. He'd reached the doorway and turned back to look at her before extinguishing the light. He had liked the sight of her flailing nakedness. And he'd taken that away with him.

He'd never stripped her before; throughout she'd worn the same clothes that she'd been wearing when he'd taken her. That bloody pink and orange dress, a black push-up bra and matching knickers. They were clothes that she'd picked to boost herself; so that she could find an alter ego to inhabit and the chance to keep up with her more confident friends. They'd talked of lip fillers and contouring. On special occasions and job interviews she ran to gloss and blusher. They understood the references when they talked of Kim and Khloé, Paris and NeNe. She barely recognised the names. The sandals she'd worn had black straps that had criss-crossed her feet, and heavy wedge heels. They lay broken in the corner now, with the knickers he'd torn away that first time.

She thought the dress would bring her confidence, instead she'd felt uncomfortable and insecure. Its fabric had been cheap, and the cut poor enough for her to have to tug frequently at her hemline and reposition her shoulder straps. She'd wanted to go home.

Are you Louise? They had been the simplest of words; enough for her to drop her guard for a moment. To hesitate. To end up like this.

She corrected herself. Not *end up*, not yet. Because, in his keenness to strip her body ready for disposal, and to leave her posed to fuel his anticipation, he had changed the way he'd left her tied. She lay supine on the mattress. Her arms were stretched above her head and her wrists taped to a pipe running horizontally about six inches from the floor. When she turned her face to one side however, the corner of her mouth could brush the inside of her bicep. She was persistent, and after several hours of small movements, the tape at the corner of his lips was finally curling back. At first the opening was tiny and she was careful to only exhale through it; she couldn't risk sucking the tape back into place. But gradually, the tape peeled free, taking with it much of the skin from her lips and leaving them stinging and seeping blood.

She didn't care.

Her head pounded and her arms were alternating between heavy aching, numbness and waves of cramp by the time the tape finally came away. She stretched her mouth wide and drew breath as though she was yawning. The air was stale and dirty, but she sucked it in as though it was rolling in from the ocean.

She had thought that she might be able to manoeuvre herself closer to the pipe, but hadn't dared to try it until her mouth was free in case a change of position would make removing that tape an impossibility.

She paused to think. The easiest way would be to shuffle up the mattress towards the wall, but, if only her head and shoulders made it into the gap between the mattress and the wall, she wasn't sure that she wouldn't become wedged with her chin to her chest and constrict her breathing. Safer then to roll to one side and onto the floor.

Despite the total darkness, she still closed her eyes to picture the room, and to double-check that she wasn't about to impale or trap herself, then she took a breath and rolled left, off the mattress and onto the bare concrete. The drop was only six or eight inches, but enough to wrench her tethered right arm. She pressed her lips tight against the pain.

She waited until it subsided, and then, inch by inch, she wriggled closer until her mouth was about six inches from her left wrist. Her right arm was stretched too far in the opposite direction for her to move further. She slumped back for a second or two, panting as she caught her breath. The duct tape was in full contact with the pipe; she doubted that there was any way to slide either hand closer to the other. She began to rock gently, testing the tape on each wrist in turn.

Perhaps she had time to fight this. She didn't know where he was, but she could sense him: thinking, visualising, anticipating. Perhaps she had time, but perhaps she had none at all.

Chapter 52

The road ran in a straight line, the land either side completely flat until it reached the dunes. The skies were huge above him and, unless there was driving rain, the weather never seemed to close in, so visibility was good here. It should have been a terrible place to hide and yet it wasn't, but then again he was careful, he chose his times for venturing out and did so infrequently. He liked dusk, but, then again, he also made sure that there was no pattern to his movements. That way, when crossing paths with people was a necessity, it was rarely the same people.

He was frugal, never purchasing more than he needed and sticking to bread, milk and cereals; all items that no one would remember. He was aware too, although less acutely than he would once have been, of his own decline.

He had one change of clothes, though he couldn't remember the last time he had used them. He was careful to wash his face and hands, and occasionally his hair, but he was conscious that he must have deteriorated because when he did cross paths with another person, they glanced and then glanced away, a two-to-one mixture of discomfort and pity. After he'd spotted the expression a couple of times, he'd looked into the mirror on his return to the little house, trying to see what they had seen.

He had swiped his sleeve across the dusty glass; he could see that he was unkempt, his hair had grown too shaggy, his ability to shave had become erratic, but the thing that struck him more than anything was that he couldn't spot the person he used to be. Yes, he was recognisable, but in the way that somebody might recognise the character printed on one of those paper Halloween masks. However lifelike, it was still a flat, two-dimensional representation; flat and emotionless, dark, sunken eyes.

He spoke rarely, even less frequently to himself. He didn't have anything to say apart from the same one sentence: 'They're not gonna find you. They're not gonna find you. They're not gonna find you.'

He was walking back to the little house now. The air was cold and there was a slight breeze, enough to whip occasional threads of sand to head height. He walked with his eyelids lowered, his gaze cast towards the ground. He barely needed to glance up to know where he was going, everything about his life was just one automatic action after another. He'd passed the point of questioning, or planning, or hoping even.

Louise Allum would die, just like the others, and thinking or saying that he didn't want it to happen made little difference. One day it would come to an end. He knew he was either going to die or suffer the consequences of everything he'd done, but changing his fate wasn't in his grasp, any more than changing the fate of Louise and all the women who had gone before her.

He drew a breath as he reached the gate. It was tired and sagged on its rusted hinges. He needed simultaneously to lift it and drag it across the uneven pathway that led to the front door. He closed it behind him. The action was futile; he had opened and closed this gate every time he passed through it; no one else used it. Or cared. Every time he'd reminded himself to leave it open. Next time, leave it open. But he seemed unable to change his way of behaving, even with the small things.

He took the door key from his pocket and slid it into the lock;

he paused then, gripping the head of the key, ready to turn it, but not quite ready to go inside.

He turned back to the gate, pulled it open again, and tore it from its rotting post. He dragged it from the path and onto the nearest patch of weeds.

'Enough now,' Callum told himself, then he twisted the key and stepped inside the dark and crumbling house.

Chapter 53

Jack drove into the car park at Parkside Station. The only available bays said reserved on them, but he parked up anyway, figuring that that was the least of their problems. He hurried across the car park, aware that Celia was walking at double time just to keep up. Her phone bleeped as they went up the steps, and he held the door for her as she fished it out of her bag. There was a young woman on the reception desk. Jack was sure he could remember the time when it was uniformed police that greeted visitors, but this particular woman was definitely a civilian. Her hair was tied back and she had unnaturally tanned skin. He thought she would be more at home at a reception desk in a beauty salon.

'We need to speak to DI Briggs,' Celia said.

The girl looked unimpressed.

'Can you let him know we're here? It's Celia Henry and Jack Bailey, and it is urgent.'

She told them to take a seat and it was then that Celia turned away and unlocked her phone, but Jack caught sight of the photograph.

'What's that?'

'Nicci just sent me a text message. It's a photo of Charlie.'

'I can see that,' he said. 'Why?'

'She says Charlie and the others went away for a weekend and this is the photo of . . . IDK, somewhere by the sea. She says, "Ask Jack. Tell Briggs this could be where Callum is."'

Jack had taken Celia's phone from her. He hadn't meant to be rude; it was the photo of Charlie he'd grabbed at, one he'd never seen before.

'What makes her say that?' he muttered.

'I don't know.'

The picture rang no bells with him apart from a very vague memory of Charlie visiting the coast, and Jack thinking it strange that Nicci hadn't gone too. The door to the reception opened and Briggs stepped through to greet them. Jack took out his phone.

'I don't have Nicci's number, I'm going to ring her now,' he said and started copying the digits across.

Celia moved towards Briggs. Jack followed, but with only one eye on the detective.

'So you both walked away from the scene?' Briggs was stony faced.

'Only once the police were there,' Celia told him. 'We can tell them what we have to at a later point. What's more urgent is seeing you now.'

'You know this isn't my investigation, right?'

Celia shrugged. 'Invite us through anyway, will you?'

'Well of course I will. Just because Norfolk can't hold on to you doesn't mean that I won't.'

He led them through to a bland corridor, Jack had his phone to his ear, but Nicci's number was just ringing out.

'Come on, pick it up,' he muttered, willing her to answer.

It went to voicemail, but he didn't bother leaving a message. Did anyone even listen to them any more? He sent her a text instead, *This is Jack, ring me urgently*, then another, *We're at Parkside, ring me*, then, *It's urgent*. He kept on like this until they were seated with Briggs in an interview room. He wanted Nicci to know that he was going to keep bugging her until she replied.

Briggs sat opposite them and looked expectant. 'What's going on?' he asked.

'We were looking for Callum. The same as you.' Celia sat very upright in her chair with a proud, almost indignant expression on her face. 'We should not have been able to get ahead of you lot, Briggs, but there we were. What do you know about him?'

'Me?' Briggs said. 'What do you know about him? You're the ones who have delved into all of this.'

'You put on this mild-mannered, not-my-problem facade, but you . . . you,' she pointed with her finger, making a little twitching motion in the air, 'you are tenacious and stubborn and hmm,' she paused and looked for the last word, 'you are the proverbial dog with the proverbial bone, Briggs, and it might not be any of your business, but it doesn't stop you hopping over the fence and going down somebody else's rabbit hole. I've seen it before and I know how you work, so, share with us because it might be that we have next to no knowledge, but there might be one fragment of our knowledge that matches up with all the bits of yours and pulls this picture together.'

Jack expected Briggs to look increasingly angry, but instead the intense stare he'd held just a few minutes before first softened, then evaporated. 'Norwich contacted me, said you'd cleared off . . .'

'We weren't under arrest.'

'I know, I know. And part of me expected you just to hotfoot it back here. You are, after all, pretty expert at hopping over the fence and ripping through the neighbour's tidy lawn.'

Celia smiled benignly. 'Touché. So,' she said, drawing her chair a little closer, 'what do we have?'

Briggs returned her smile, and Jack saw a conspiratorial look pass between them. 'Okay.'

'Okay.'

'Maitland's on his way over now, and there . . .' He waved his finger towards a side table that was laden with a pile of folders. Jack hadn't noticed it before, he'd been too preoccupied with his phone. 'In among that lot are the post-mortem results. I want him to talk me through them, I want him to find if something's been missed and I want you two to fill me in on how the hell you ended up in Norfolk.'

Chapter 54

It was Gemma who opened the front door. She wore jogging bottoms and a pale-blue V-necked T-shirt which might or might not have been a pyjama top. Her eyes were pink at the corners as though she had just woken up. She muttered something that Nicci didn't catch, and then walked back down the hallway towards her room at the rear of the house. Nicci pushed the front door shut and followed.

Gemma sat in the same place as last time and pointed Nicci towards the chair opposite. She was in a visibly different mood to the one during Nicci's last visit; the hardness hadn't totally gone, but it had softened. Nicci could still see the tension in Gemma's expression, and, from the way she held herself, it was clear that the physical discomfort hadn't gone. It was, Nicci concluded, the anger that had subsided.

'You're persistent, aren't you?' Gemma said.

'It's that or give up. I don't know of any other options,' Nicci replied. 'I'm not really one for ignoring things and pretending they're not happening, so that leaves this.'

'Which is what? A social?'

Nicci shook her head and slipped the photo from her jacket. When she leant forward and held it at arm's length, it was just within Gemma's grasp, but she didn't reach for it, didn't take it.

She didn't look surprised at seeing it either, but Nicci found it very hard to gauge what her actual expression was. Valium perhaps.

'Where was this taken? Do you remember?'

Gemma shook her head. 'No.' She had given the photo a single, fleeting glance, and now fixed her gaze on Nicci as she spoke.

'Do you recognise it?'

'Why do you want to know?'

'You went away together, all of you.' Nicci stood up, stepped forward and dropped the photo on to Gemma's lap. 'You know what? Have another think.' Then she sat back on the chair, making a pretence of being relaxed, trying to look as though she had all the time in the world. Gemma's eyes searched her face, but Nicci was pretty sure that she was damn good at giving away nothing.

After a few seconds, Gemma's gaze dropped on to the photo. Nicci glanced down at her phone. Celia still hadn't replied to her text message, but she guessed they were driving and, knowing Celia, her phone would be set to locked. She looked back at Gemma.

'I was ill and the rest of you went, you and Ellie, Callum and Charlie, but the thing is, Gemma, I know you know where it is.'

Gemma's chin jutted just a fraction and her expression tightened.

'The reason I know is because Charlie told me that you'd been there a lot as a kid, and if I'd been there as a kid, I would not be looking at that picture and thinking, "I haven't got a clue where it is." No, I'd be looking at it thinking, "I walked down that road, I stood on that sand dune, and the shop is over there, or the main road's back there."'

Gemma blinked slowly.

Nicci pressed her again. 'All those things that you would know because you've been there. You've spent time there and you have it locked in your head,' Nicci tapped her skull, 'as a childhood memory. So where is it, Gemma?'

She shook her head. 'What difference does it make? That was years ago.'

'I need to find out.'

'Why? Our family used to have a holiday home there years ago. They rented it out for holidays, but that's gone. They didn't use it any more, so they sold it. It's gone,' she repeated.

'So tell me where it is.'

'Why?' At the last visit Gemma would have made the word a demand, a confrontational question. This time it was plaintive.

Nicci softened her own voice in reply. 'I think you know why.'

Gemma shook her head, but too late, it came after a pause of half a second, three-quarters maybe. A pause that seemed far longer than it was, that gave her enough time to look towards the door or window and search for a way out of the conversation.

'I think it might be where Callum is hiding.'

'Callum?' She tried to sound surprised, but her voice was hollow.

Gemma didn't move, didn't twitch, but she couldn't stop the colour draining from her face and then rising again at the top of her chest where the bare skin showed at the V of her T-shirt. Her fingers tightened, locking into each other, but a new tremor in her hands was still visible.

'You know he's there, don't you? Or nearby.'

She shook her head. 'No. Why would I? Why would I have anything to do with him?'

Nicci glanced round the room, the room that had once been part of the family home, but now existed like a cave where Gemma had burrowed herself away. Nicci knew what it was like to avoid the outside world. She looked sharply at Gemma.

'I've lived like this, for different reasons of course, but I was scared to go out of the house, didn't want to face people, didn't want to risk anything more. You're scared of him, aren't you?'

'I'm scared of Callum?' Gemma said the words slowly, tentatively and gave a half nod. 'Yeah, I'm terrified of him. He's not normal. I've kept him away from here.'

'That doesn't add up. If you're scared of him, why would he listen to you?'

'He's always had a thing for me. He's very single-minded. He said he's had girlfriends, but they won't do, they won't do.'

'So why would he listen to you, Gemma?'

She chewed on her lip for a second, a few seconds, almost a minute, time dragged out.

'Because there's one thing he cares about more than me. The drugs. He needs the drugs. I supply him as long as he stays away from me.'

She leant forward and put her hand into a little pouch that hung from the side of her coffee table. It was the sort of bag that should have contained crochet hooks, knitting needles and bags of wool. Instead she pulled out a handful of blister packs. Drugs. All unboxed.

'It's the opiates, he can't get enough of them. He stays away because I send him the drugs.'

It was at that moment when Nicci felt her phone begin to vibrate, a number she didn't recognise was trying to ring her. She slid the phone under her thigh.

'I need the address,' she told Gemma.

Gemma nodded and then, without warning, a tear slid down her cheek.

Chapter 55

Celia sat on the plastic chair, the type that looked like a large version of a primary-school dining-hall chair. She felt too big for it and it creaked and bowed as she moved. But she was more distracted by Briggs and by Jack. Each of them was preoccupied; Jack fiddling with his phone and Briggs staring at the pile of folders that he'd brought. She wondered whether there was one in particular that he was itching to open.

She was certain that he knew something, but he wasn't in a hurry to share it. Probably because he shouldn't.

She passed her phone across to him.

'See that photograph?' she said.

'Charlie Bailey?' Briggs muttered.

'Yes, on holiday. A bunch of them. The ones from the accident, but not Nicci, she was the only one not there. They went away for the weekend just a few months before Charlie died. They were somewhere in Norfolk, but we're not sure where. But if you could find out the location of this photo . . .'

Briggs studied the image, his full attention on it. 'Photos these days hold digital information, including which type of camera took the photo, the exposure settings and even the location. Could she send the file?'

She shook her head. 'No, no, Nicci took this from a physical copy; there's none of that information available.'

He passed the phone back to Celia. 'So, what makes you think Callum might be there?'

'I don't know,' she said. 'Nicci texted it to us. She sounded sure, but I don't know what triggered the thought. Jack's trying to get hold of her now.'

They both looked at Jack, and, in reply, he shook his head. 'Maybe because we went as far as Great Yarmouth. Perhaps it put that part of the countryside in the forefront of her mind.' Jack shrugged. 'That's just a guess.'

'But,' Celia cut in, 'it's worth checking out, isn't it?'

Briggs nodded. 'Forward it to me, can you?'

She did, and Briggs's own phone gave a muted ping. He opened it, tapped at the screen for a few seconds, and then made a phone call.

'Jenkins. Hi, Briggs here. I've just sent you a photograph. See if any of your guys can locate where it was taken. Definitely Norfolk, so I'm told. Hang on . . .' He covered the mouthpiece and spoke to Celia. 'What sort of property are they looking for?'

She shrugged. 'Apparently they might have stayed in a caravan.'

'Jack?' She nudged his arm and he looked up from his mobile. He seemed to replay the conversation in his head before replying, 'I can't remember, but it was some kind of holiday let.' As soon as he had spoken he frowned down at the phone again, simultaneously rising from the creaky chair. 'I'm going to go over there,' he said. 'You don't need me here.'

'Go where?' Celia asked.

'To find Nicci. This is ridiculous. She should be answering.' He reached the door. 'Text me. If she calls you, text me. Maybe she didn't recognise my number. Maybe she just hasn't picked up the messages. I'll find out what else she knows about this place, and I'll call you straight away.'

And without further conversation, he left, the door swinging shut behind him.

'Well,' said Briggs, 'he's fired up.'

Celia nodded. 'Yes, there's been a bit of a turn of events there. Seems that he's shaken off a few things in the last couple of hours.' Her thoughts went straight back to Callum. 'Wherever Callum is, he's not nearby. It might be worth canvassing local shops along the coast.'

'With which manpower budget, Celia?' Briggs gave her a wonky smile. 'Besides, some places have plenty of strangers. They don't always stand out.'

'I know,' said Celia, 'but isn't it worth a shot?'

Briggs raised one brow. 'I've shared the photo. The digital forensics team will have it, and they have the power of the internet, Celia, and of location software that may well work even without geotagging. We're not in the dark ages.'

'But still short of having all the lights on with this case? Although,' she said, moving on before he had a chance to respond, 'I can tell there's something that's drawing you to those files.'

'Well,' he leant from his chair and reached the top two folders with his fingertips, pulling across the other table, then scooping them up and dropping them heavily on the desk in front of him. 'I probably wouldn't have shown you in front of Jack. I mean, it's not like I can open up these things to the world, but,' he gave her a warning look which she recognised as *this goes no further*, 'but, as it's you . . .'

She nodded in both agreement and understanding.

Briggs continued, 'I went through the files again. So much emphasis is given to looking at cause of death and the injuries of people who didn't survive an accident like that. Less attention is given to those who did, like Nicci.'

Celia wiggled forward in the seat, ready to see whatever it was that the file would reveal.

Briggs reached inside the folder. It was maybe a quarter of an inch thick, but he seemed to be able to locate the item without looking. He pulled his hand back out and, with it, a ten by eight photo. It was Nicci.

'She's unconscious in this shot, but the police photographer managed to get a couple of photographs of her injuries, and, as you can see from this one, heavy blood loss.'

Nicci's hair had been blonde then. The kind of slightly yellowy blonde that came with over-the-counter hair dye and lack of experience. It was heavy with clotted blood, mostly to the front of her head, but more streaks of it running through some of the longer strands of her hair. Somehow, the shot reminded Celia of a doll she'd owned as a child, one whose hair had been nylon and had stuck out in unnatural shiny curls.

Nicci's hair was glued like that, stained rust-red and deep crimson with various thicknesses of the clotted blood.

'When the CSIs attend a crime scene, they don't go round swabbing everything or fingerprinting everything. We don't have those kind of budgets or resources. The CSI has to look at the scene and decide which items of potential evidence are most likely to yield results. But luckily, in this case, the CSI was new, inexperienced, they didn't want to miss anything, so they went round merrily swabbing bloodstains from all angles of the car. Most of them weren't tested for anything. Most of them were put into storage, others were sent to the lab. That's normal practice.'

'Because testing costs money, right?'

Briggs nodded. 'Of course. And in this case we had a potential drunk driver, plus youth, lack of experience, late night, dark road, all of those things. We deal with them all the time. Obviously most of them aren't fatal, but we still collect the evidence, we still try to build a case for what might or might not go to court. The samples should have been destroyed; the case is closed and Nicci's conviction is spent. But, luckily for us,' he reached in the folder again and this time pulled out another sheet of paper, 'turns out not all the blood in her hair was hers. Some of this,' he pointed to the bloodstains further down her hair shaft, 'this dark staining here, it's not her blood.'

Celia's eyes narrowed and she looked from the photo up to Briggs and he stared back.

'It's Ellie's blood. But Ellie's blood doesn't appear anywhere else in the front of that car and that can only mean one thing.'

'That somebody touched Ellie and then Nicci?' Celia asked.

Briggs nodded.

'In an accident like that, there's going to be a lot of blood, but mostly in logical places, so, for example, someone with an open wound is going to leave bloodstains in the vicinity of that wound.

'In Ellie's case, she'd suffered serious injuries to her torso and there would have been substantial blood loss, some of that under pressure. However, blood was found on the front of Nicci's headrest and in Nicci's hair, but it's absent from elsewhere in the front of the vehicle.

'The most likely explanation is that somebody with, quite literally, blood on their hands interfered with Nicci in the front of the car, and that implies two things: firstly, that they had had substantial physical contact with Ellie and, secondly, that they were the person who tried to kill Nicci.'

Celia thought back to a previous theory. 'But surely it's possible that they tried to help Ellie and when that failed turned on Nicci in anger.'

'Of course,' Briggs agreed, 'but it's also possible, and in my mind more likely, that *both* Nicci and Ellie were subjected to something violent and intentional. And that's why I'm sitting here waiting for Harry Maitland. I've requested that he review the injury reports on all five people in that car. He needs to tell me the likely chain of events, tell me why somebody would have had Ellie's blood on their hands when they grabbed hold of Nicci and tried to kill her.'

Briggs chased Maitland, who replied that he was ten minutes away. Celia and Briggs spent the minutes alternating between silence and small talk. 'So,' Celia asked at last, 'what else is in the files?'

Briggs had brought the pile of folders across to his desk, and he now placed his hand on top of them. The motion looked casual, but she had no doubt that he was ready to stop her touching anything.

'Let's just wait,' he said. 'Maitland. He won't be long.'

She nodded.

'And what's with Jack,' he said, 'rushing off like that?'

'He's being careful. He hasn't heard from Nicci,' she said.

'And that's a worry because . . . ?'

'I think it's a worry because that's Jack. He's suddenly become engaged with this case.'

Briggs nodded. 'Yes, I think we all have. We've passed the tipping point now and we need to get to the end. How is Nicci doing, by the way?'

But there was something in his tone that told her that it wasn't just a casual question. It would have been easy to give him a spontaneous reply, *instinctive*, or *reckless*, or *determined.* Instead she chose 'Clever.' She said, 'She's really clever.'

'Do you know she came to me with a DNA profile? She said somebody had been in her house. How does that work?'

Celia shifted uneasily. 'I don't actually know anything about that.'

'She said someone had been in her house. Someone she thought might be of interest.'

Celia sighed. 'She's had a bee in her bonnet. Or a feeling. Or something between the two.'

'You're hedging, Celia.'

'I am. She has an idea, somewhere between a hunch and a wild flight of fancy, that Jack is somehow involved in all of this.'

'In his brother's death?'

'No, no,' she said quickly. 'No, that he might have come across the scene. That he found Charlie dead and attacked her.'

Briggs looked down at the closed folder, imagining, she guessed, that he could see the picture of Nicci's injuries through the cardboard cover. 'And what do you think about that?'

He studied Celia as she replied.

'You know, I would say that's incredibly far removed from what I know of Jack's personality. But on the other hand, he loved Charlie deeply and in that moment of grief, who knows?'

'And if it was Jack?'

'I wouldn't doubt that he's regretted it ever since.'

'But that wouldn't make him innocent of it.'

'God no, I know he would have to pay. But my feeling is, no, not Jack. So, you think the DNA sample might be his?'

'It's possible and Jack would have gone to her house, had a drink with her.'

Celia shrugged. 'You need to talk to Nicci.'

'Or Jack,' he added.

'The point is,' Celia went on, 'either that profile she's given you corresponds with the partial profile you have from the Becky Lake case or it doesn't.'

'Well,' he said, 'I did check the DNA profile she gave me against the partial we had from Becky Lake's disappearance. It wasn't a match. Obviously . . .'

She finished the thought for him, 'That doesn't put Jack in the clear.'

'Or Nicci.'

'I'm sorry?'

'I happen to know that Jack reported activity in his house, not quite a break-in, but somebody had been there. We all know how things are these days. We weren't going to fingerprint that, nothing was taken; but he also reported that he'd had a strange visit from your Miss Waldock, and I would imagine that if we had been fingerprinting we would have found plenty of hers around the place, and we wouldn't have been able to do the first thing about it since she'd legitimately been there earlier in the day.

'Has it occurred to you that you're seeing everybody through rose-tinted glasses? Just because they grew up in your street doesn't mean that they wouldn't have done anything bad.'

'Well of course I know that.'

'Celia, step back a minute. You were acquainted with everybody who was in that vehicle, but what do you actually know about them? You're not the expert here. That's why we have science, that's why we have forensics, that's why we have good police work. So, please, I'm happy for you to stay in the room, but don't think you can be sure of who is innocent when some of the people you're talking about could be pretty damn guilty.'

His voice softened. 'I know you, Celia, and you want to believe these kids, these kids that you've watched since they were growing up, but I'll tell you something: Nicci might have been a victim of something, but she's definitely guilty too. She drove that car and now she's pointing the finger at Jack. He hasn't jumped to the top of our suspect list . . .' there was a knock at the door, 'but I don't believe they're both in the clear,' he added as the door opened.

Harry Maitland was shown inside by an incredibly young-looking police officer. Maitland shook hands with both Briggs and Celia, and then joined them, pulling up another one of the plastic chairs.

Briggs reached across and brought the rest of the files on to the table. Maitland signalled a 'no' with two fingers and pulled a laptop from his bag. 'I have everything on here.' He looked at Celia and then looked at Briggs questioningly.

Briggs confirmed, 'It's fine. I'm happy for Celia to see any of this. If there is anything.'

'Oh yes,' said Maitland. 'I think you'll find it very interesting.'

And nothing was said then for the next thirty seconds or so while the computer powered up. Maitland signed in with his password and then clicked on a series of files. Briggs seemed relaxed, but Celia felt tense; it had been a rare outburst from her friend.

'What we have here,' Maitland said, 'is most interesting. Eleanor Daniels died of cardiac arrest due to hypovolemia, resulting from an arterial bleed. In layman's terms . . .'

'Yes,' said Briggs, 'I know. She bled out.'

'Exactly. She had several injuries. Crush injuries to her lower legs – serious, but not life threatening; broken ribs and skin abrasions of the chest, neck and abdomen; classic seatbelt trauma. The most serious injury, however, was the puncture wound to her left upper chest area. At the moment of impact, Gemma Hayward would have extended her arms.' And as if to demonstrate, he stretched both of his arms out beyond his laptop. 'Miss Hayward's arms impacted the back of the seats in front of her. It's not an uncommon injury and we all know in any chain it's the weakest link that breaks.'

'Being her arm bones?' Celia queried.

'Precisely. The ulna and radius snapped in each arm. And you imagine,' he held up his right forearm and pointed to the approximate point at which the bones would have broken, 'what would have happened.'

He dropped his wrist.

'She lost control of the lower part of the arm on each side. The bones broke through the skin and then she recoiled, and, as she was flung backwards,' and again he made the motion with his right arm vertical, fist aloft as if he was giving a salute, 'her arm flung back and one of the bones, probably the radius, punctured Miss Daniels's chest. Clearly this wasn't deliberate, and it might not have been fatal, but for two things. Firstly, as Gemma flailed around the bone pulled back out of Miss Daniels's chest, and, secondly, the now open wound was further disturbed.'

Celia expected Maitland to continue unprompted, and Briggs clearly expected the same, so there was a long pause before Briggs spoke. 'By?' he asked.

'Well, here's the thing. In the initial examination it was concluded that the shape and size of the wound was consistent with the broken radius puncturing the flesh, the artery and the blood vessel. But, on closer examination, and there is some room for interpretation here . . .' He hesitated and ran a hand through his hair. He picked up a ballpoint and clicked it on and off a couple of times. Then he regrouped. 'There will be a need for second opinions, and these may dispute my findings. That's my word of caution. But, having said that, I am confident about this.'

Celia wanted to tell him to spit it out, but she knew, from experience, that cautious people were likely to slow rather than speed up under pressure. She pressed her lips together and waited.

'Well, you have to use science to prove or disprove a theory. You have to use science to decide whether or not something is more or less likely and, in my opinion, what is most likely is that somebody deliberately tore that wound. They aggravated the blood loss.'

'How do you know?' Briggs gasped.

'When Gemma Hayward's arm bone came out of the wound, it would have pulled in that direction; that is laterally towards the centre of the vehicle. Gemma Hayward was in the rear, centre seat, and there's a definite tug mark on that side of Miss Daniels's wound, and it is clear how far her bone impacted Miss Daniels's chest cavity. So far, so consistent.'

Both Celia and Briggs nodded. Neither spoke.

'However, what I then discovered was that another unknown object, but possibly a finger, was poked into the wound, and then the wound was dragged in the opposite direction, away from the centre of the car. The open wound was disturbed, it was ripped.' He nodded too, as though agreeing with himself. 'That's the best way to describe it; ripped, making the wound wider and deeper, and making her bleed out more quickly than she might otherwise have done.

'At that point, the responsible party would have had a considerable amount of blood about their person and it is totally conceivable that they would have then transferred this on to Nicci Waldock when they subsequently attacked her.'

'So the verdict for Ellie's death?'

Briggs read Celia's thoughts. 'Yes,' he said, 'it was murder.'

Chapter 56

The air in her room was stale and hot. It had been breathed too many times and Gemma was sure it was depleted of oxygen. She was sweating. She could feel the dampness between her shoulder blades and between her breasts, but she shivered.

Or maybe she was shaking because she was trying so hard to keep herself still. Her hands were clenched together, palm to palm and clamped between her knees. One foot began to jiggle. She repositioned it so she wasn't resting on the nerve, but then she could feel her lips begin to tremble.

She didn't realised that they weren't alone until he appeared at the doorway. Nicci half turned but he grabbed her, and, with what looked like a single, fluid movement, slammed her against the door frame and hit her again. She staggered, and then crumpled to the hallway floor. There were a few ragged breaths, then silence.

Then he turned to Gemma, standing over her, close enough for her to know that there was only her and him.

'It wasn't what you think,' she managed to say.

He looked at her, but didn't seem to be in a hurry to reply.

'I thought giving her the address of the beach house was a good idea, I really did.'

'So why tell Nicci?'

'She knew. She had the photo of Charlie standing on the road just around the corner. I wasn't telling her anything she didn't already know.'

He paced. Her room was small and it was just a couple of steps in each direction. Then, when he'd done that a couple of times, he stood squarely in front of her, looking down on her, raising himself onto the balls of his feet and then back down again.

'You've never asked what I do with them, have you?'

She shook her head.

'D'you want to know?'

She shook it again. 'No,' she breathed.

'You do know I keep them alive though, don't you?'

She nodded.

'And what else?' he said.

She didn't reply at first. She stared at him. Shivering, waiting for him to move on from the question. But the silence stretched out until it filled her ears, becoming a single strained note, the sound of a nail scraping a taut wire. She held on until she could no longer stand it. 'There's only one, I think. One at a time.' She nodded. 'They don't overlap do they?'

He slow clapped.

'Nicci is next and, on this occasion, there will, briefly, be two of them alive at the same time. And I'm thinking, maybe it's the way forward.'

Gemma held herself tighter. She needed to pee. Or she needed to throw up. Either one would be fine.

She didn't know what was next, but she guessed she was going to lose.

His eyes were dark, the pupils dilated. There wasn't much emotion there, but she knew that already. She'd closed herself off to the idea that it might be possible to reason with him. She didn't believe it was, although she could see why others fell for the fake way he behaved.

He'd practised it. He was very good at it.

'Where will this end?'

'For me, or for you? I'm nowhere near done,' he said.

He caught her by surprise then when he ducked down, squatting in front of her, putting his face close to hers. There was a cold, hard smile.

'I take my time, Gemma. You've worked that out, haven't you? It's why I'm so good at it. It's why it is lasting so well. You have to think, and then act. Don't rush.' He sniffed. 'I don't rush.'

Gemma listened, hoping to hear some noise from the hall. Not a noise that would be enough to alert him. She hoped for the click of the door, a quick movement of air as Nicci escaped.

But there was nothing.

'What did you think you were doing?' he asked.

She closed her eyes and shook her head. It didn't matter what she answered now.

'And I'd asked you, hadn't I? It's not like I hadn't. And you'd said, "I really don't know."'

He shook his head slowly and tutted, mocking her with his fake disapproval.

Then he sighed and reached into the pocket where she kept her medication. He took out three blister packs, all Tramadol, and there was more of it than there should have been because some days she managed without.

Chapter 57

Jack was relieved. His car was neither clamped nor was there a ticket flapping from under the windscreen wipers.

He jumped into the driver's seat and drove quickly towards home. He parked the car a few houses along from his own, lucky to find a free parking space at this time of day, even though they were all reserved for residents.

He went straight to Nicci's. He knocked, but there was no reply. If she hadn't found the photograph at her house, it must have been her mum's. He walked quickly towards the corner, but by the time he turned and the house of Nicci's mother was in sight, he was jogging. He didn't know why he felt the urgency now, but there it was, propelling him forward.

He knocked at the door, and he knocked a second time before she answered.

'Jack,' she said, a languid statement of fact.

'Is Nicci here?'

'No,' she said. She glared at him. 'Why do you want her?'

'Was she here earlier?'

'Yes,' she said. 'She wanted your brother's photo. Just saw her rummaging around in her stuff. I didn't see it. She wouldn't have told me what it was about anyway.'

'Do you know where she went?'

Nicci's mum had one of those expressions that said that she was not going to help, even before he'd asked the question. He almost didn't bother and he almost turned away before giving her a chance to answer.

'Well,' she said, 'if she listened to me, she would have gone up the road. But if she listened to me, she wouldn't have done half the things she has.'

'Mrs Waldock, please, what do you mean by up the road?'

Mrs Waldock shrugged.

'I told her to see that girl. The one she hates.'

Jack frowned. 'Gemma?'

'Yes, the only woman in the street that goes out less than I do.' She laughed, it was shrill and rang in his ears even after she'd closed the door behind him.

Chapter 58

It wasn't like Briggs to snap at her and Celia didn't doubt the situation was difficult for everybody, but she still felt stung and had fallen silent as the other two continued to talk. Maitland and Briggs were concentrating on the pathology reports on the laptop.

She didn't ask permission to look at the files, she just opened the top one and started reading, flicking from page to page, her eyes being drawn to paragraphs that jumped out at her, but more to the pictures that she occasionally passed.

Celia had a few theories about life and one was that when somebody said something that felt like a bigger insult than it actually was, there was probably some truth in it.

She considered what she knew of Mawson Road and of the children she'd known as they were growing up there.

She didn't know that Nicci wasn't too reckless to have driven that car. She didn't know that Jack wasn't so angry in that moment that he hadn't attacked Nicci, but she knew that Jack wouldn't have attacked Ellie. The idea of somebody putting their finger into a wound and ripping it open; that was a different kind of rage. That was an insight to the sort of personality that she couldn't begin to understand.

She sat back in the chair for a moment wondering how often she'd ever seen that kind of fury.

She didn't have an answer, well not at first.

She leant forward again and continued to leaf through the pages. She shot a glance at Briggs and Maitland. They seemed to be having their own moments of soul searching. The pathologist was wondering how things might have been different, how he might have spotted Ellie's injury. She knew Briggs and knew how he would be cursing himself about the oversight regarding Nicci's head injury.

Celia opened the next folder. She was sure that everything was computerised these days, but Briggs was pretty old school, so she wasn't surprised that he had hard copies too.

She didn't understand the next documents when she first glanced at them. They were older, and they dated back to before the crash, to before Becky Lake.

She read the details. There'd been an assault on Parker's Piece in the early evening. Gianna Moretti, a classics student from one of the colleges, had been crossing after finishing an afternoon shift at one of the restaurants. She'd said that a man had come from nowhere. It'd been January, so dark already. And she'd barely caught sight of his face as he had been bundled up; a thick coat, a balaclava.

Celia couldn't remember the last time she'd seen anybody wear a balaclava, never mind a young man, but that was the description Gianna Moretti had given. A young man, tall and slim, who'd grabbed hold of her, knocked her to the ground, and felt his way up her skirt. He'd briefly pulled at her knickers in what she thought was about to be a sexual attack. But then he had pushed away to arm's length, and had punched her three or four times, breaking two teeth and fracturing her cheekbone. It had been over in less than a minute, after which he jumped on a bike and cycled away.

But it was the ferocity that she kept mentioning. Her statement was dappled with words such as 'furious', 'intense', 'crazed', and three times she said, 'I thought he'd never stop.'

This, then, was the man whose DNA profile was a partial match to that of the man who may have taken Becky Lake. Celia had no memory of the attack being reported in the local paper. Perhaps it had been sanitised by the press, made to look less significant; perhaps *Woman assaulted on Parker's Piece* might not have caught her attention and a headline like that would have gone nowhere close to showing the full horror of the attack.

Celia glanced back at the date, wondering if perhaps she'd been out of town when it had happened, but then she saw it and she knew she had been in Cambridge, on that day in fact. And she suddenly knew why that date was important. And what she'd seen, and what it meant.

Just then there was a sharp knock on the door, and the same overly young officer leant into the room. 'They've identified the house, sir, it's in a Norfolk village called Hemsby. Officers are attending.'

But Celia barely heard, she was still processing what she'd just seen. Double-checking herself.

Briggs excused himself to Maitland and rose from his chair. But then Celia uttered, 'Oh my Lord,' and Briggs turned to look at her.

'What's wrong?' he said.

'I know who killed Becky Lake,' she replied.

Chapter 59

The little house had been built in the 1930s, two rooms and a kitchen and an outside toilet. It had gradually fallen into disrepair before being bought and refurbished in the 1980s, but the crumbling cliffs and the encroaching sea had left it open to the elements, and it had been left to fend for itself. Several neighbouring properties had succumbed to the waves, going from being over a hundred feet from the shore to toppling onto the beach within a few short months. This little cottage, with its cracked grey walls and flaking yellow window frames, had hung on so far, but its days were numbered.

The police cars pulled up outside, four of them in convoy, sirens off but lights flashing; a precautionary ambulance trailed a minute behind. The police disembarked from their vehicles and spread out around the property. They broke through the front door while other officers waited at the back.

The lead officer, Sergeant Mukherjee, shouted out a warning and when no reply came he nodded for the battering ram. It took out the front door in two swift blows.

The inside was unlit with virtually no daylight making it through the rain-stained windows and filthy net curtains. There was a short hallway with a glow of light at the end where previous owners had added a kitchen with large windows. To either side of

Mukherjee was a closed door; he pointed PC Craven towards the room on the left and took the room on the right himself; they went in simultaneously.

PC Craven shouted, 'Empty,' just as Mukherjee spotted the outline of a figure and shouted, 'In here.'

He ran forward. There was only one person in the room. Lifeless, pale and slumped in a chair.

'I need the paramedics,' he shouted. 'Keep checking the rest of the house, check the loft. Check around the back.'

He knew they would do all those things anyway, but he wasn't going to take any chances. Besides, shouting out the rooms made a clear inventory in his head, and stopped everyone piling in here.

He dropped to one knee, reached out, grabbed the wrist and felt for a pulse. It was faint, but it was there. 'Can you hear me?' he said. 'Talk to me. What's your name? Talk to me.'

There was no response.

He shouted for the paramedics again.

He put his hand out and lifted the young man's face. 'Can you hear me? Talk to me.'

He didn't think his words would get through; he'd been to scenes like this plenty of times in the past. Sometimes they'd been as much as a couple of weeks late, alerted by neighbours complaining of flies at the window or unidentified smells. Occasionally, like now, they arrived in time to see the victim's last breaths.

He tried again. 'Callum, I need you to wake up.' It didn't matter what he said, he doubted there would be a reply, but he thought the sound of another voice might be enough to keep the lad hanging on.

He turned his head and shouted over his shoulder, 'In here,' and then a moment later two green-suited paramedics were beside him. He stepped back. And, as he did so, he thought he saw movement in the young man's mouth, just a twitch, an attempt at maybe a single word.

'What did he say?' Mukherjee asked.

The closest paramedic shook his head. 'I don't know. I don't think he said anything. Give us some space?'

He stepped back and then looked around the room properly for the first time. There were bowls and a kettle, packets of soup and a duvet. Perhaps the kitchen appliances didn't work, but more likely, the guy had holed himself up in here and barely left the room.

His gaze stopped when it reached the second chair and there he saw an envelope. It was used, but the original address had been scrawled out and instead the words *READ THIS* were written across the front.

He took a pair of latex gloves from his pocket and stretched them over his hands, then he unfolded the paper.

Chapter 60

Briggs looked at Celia sharply.

'What do you mean?' he said. She had been looking at the file for the original assault, the one on Parker's Piece. He looked down at the pages in front of her, scanning the document.

After her outburst, Celia had immediately regained her composure, and now she spoke with her usual patience. 'Have you had that experience when something jars with you, somebody says something and it's off in some way but you can't work it out?'

Briggs shrugged, then nodded. 'Of course, it happens in interviews all the time.'

'Yes, and it's exactly the same thing in journalism. You're interviewing somebody and sometimes it's a bare-faced lie and other times,' she tapped the page, 'somebody will say something that should seem completely reasonable but only your subconscious knows why it isn't. I find that moments like that always stick in your mind. Why should a little inconsequential sentence stay as a memory unless it's important?'

'Celia,' Briggs practically growled her name, 'who killed Becky Lake? And how does it connect to this attack?'

Celia shot him a warning glance. 'Trust me, if I explain it my way it will be quicker because you will only need to hear it once.'

Briggs held his breath and nodded.

'I was outside at the front of my house when I saw Rob pushing his bike along our street. He was coming from the Mill Road end and walking towards me. Heading for home, I imagine. As far as I was concerned Rob had always been polite, he would say hello if he passed me, but there was never any conversation. Never had been, not once.'

Briggs's hand twitched with an involuntary *hurry up* gesture.

'But, on this particular occasion, I glanced towards him and he saw me look; when he was a little closer I happened to look again, and I noticed that he was already staring at me, as if he'd been waiting for me to look a second time. I found that odd. There was something expectant about the way he was watching me. I remember glancing down to see if there was something strange about my appearance, and he was almost at my house by the time I looked up. And he said, 'I fell off my bike." I glanced at it, it was the automatic thing to do, but there was no sign of any damage. I caught sight of a couple of scratches on him, nothing on the bike, though, and he was looking at me with an expression that seemed to say he was waiting to see whether I believed him, and it stuck in my mind. It didn't make sense.'

'And that's it?' Briggs shook his head. 'And, from that, you think he was the one who attacked Gianna Moretti on Parker's Piece?'

Celia remained unflustered. '"Isn't today your sister's birthday?" I asked him. He nodded and I told him, "Wish her a happy one from me."' Celia ran her finger down the page, stopping at the date of the attack. 'This is Gemma's fifteenth birthday, and that's how I know the date of our conversation. The scratches on him weren't from any bike, maybe if he'd gone through a hedge, but no, they were scratches from somebody who'd been trying to defend themselves.'

Chapter 61

'For fuck's sake Rob, what have you done? Is she . . . ?'

'No, she's not dead. Not yet. That's one thing I've learnt.'

Gemma was still in her chair. Rob moved quickly across the room. He bent at the hip, leaning forward with his hands on his knees, his face inches from hers.

'I'll tell you what I've learnt. You take your time. You don't rush these things. I rushed with that Becky Lake woman and that's the one that nearly tripped me up. I messed it up with Emily Moore, but less so. And what I got wrong was again because I rushed it. No, I will kill her in my time. Right now, she's going nowhere. But you?'

He shook his head very slowly, but kept his eyes pinned on her the whole time.

'You knew where Callum was. How many times have I asked you?'

She didn't reply.

'Gemma, how many times have I asked you?'

'I don't know.' Her voice was hesitant. Timid.

He took a breath, then screamed the question again.

She held still. She didn't recoil, but closed her eyes against the sound.

'Lots of times,' she replied before opening them again. 'You asked me lots of times. I was trying . . .' she began.

'You were trying what, Gemma? What were you trying to do?'

'To protect you,' she said quietly. 'Protect all of us.'

'Do I look like somebody that needs fucking protection? And how on earth were you protecting me by keeping Callum safe? Hmm?'

'I didn't want him to go to the police.'

He snorted. 'That's not protecting me, that's protecting you.'

'If you'd found him, you would have killed him, wouldn't you?'

'Well, I wasn't going to make friends with him, was I?'

'And how does it help you to kill him? It's just more blood on your hands.'

'How does it help to keep him alive? It's simple. He knows what happened, you know what happened. You won't talk, but he might.'

There was a flash, a millisecond, when she suddenly visualised herself as brave, as fearless.

'I might,' she breathed and he slapped her hard across the face before she'd even had time to register his hand moving.

'What the fuck, Gemma?'

Gemma sat low in her chair, her scarred arms wrapping her knees.

She split her gaze, staring first up into his face and then from time to time, when that became too difficult, at the carpet in front of her.

It was strange how arguments could start off in any direction, but always ended up following the particular pattern of the particular two people involved. She already knew that this argument would not be one she had any chance of winning.

The conversation had returned to Callum. Now he knew the truth, it would keep coming back to different versions of the same questions.

'I kept him out of the way,' she said. 'I kept him safe. He wasn't going to go to anybody. Not when he was down there, not with the drugs. And if he had gone to somebody, then so what? Who's going to believe him? You should see him. He's like a drowning rat or a . . . I don't know . . . there's desperation written all over him.'

'How many times have I asked if you've heard from him? I asked if you knew where he was, and what have you said to me?'

She shook her head and didn't reply.

'Gemma, what have you said to me? What did you tell me?'

'I know what I said.'

'Tell me now. What did you say to me?'

'That I didn't know.'

'So, you lied?'

'Rob, we've been over this.' An unattractive whine had crept into her voice. 'Did I want his blood on my hands? Not after everything else. Look, we've come this far, and neither of us has told anybody. We won't. I will never back up his story, and who's going to believe him? Nobody.'

'You are missing the point. You lied to me, Gemma.' And there it was, the real reason that this argument would keep running in circles and coming back to the same point; she had deceived him.

'Haven't I sacrificed enough for you? You know I've always protected you.' She looked at her arms and held them up, forearms facing him.

'Yeah, yeah, I know. I've seen your arms enough times, Gemma. I didn't know that would happen, did I?'

She snorted then, a dry humourless laugh. 'We both know what you planned, what you thought the outcome would be. Didn't I get off lightly?'

'When did he come to you?'

She shrugged and suddenly he dropped to his knees right in front of her, bringing his face close to hers so there was nowhere to look apart from directly into his eyes.

'When did Callum come to you?'

And again, they were back to Callum and her betrayal of Rob. 'I don't know,' she said miserably.

'Gemma, you do know. Come on. When?'

'He spoke to me in court. He asked me about that Becky woman.'

Rob snorted. 'Then what?'

'It was a while after I read about one of the others. Debbie Lagoudi. He phoned me up and asked me . . . well, he started to ask me. Then he hung up. Next thing I knew, he came here. Dad was away, luckily. Same as now, off on one of his business trips, and Callum came in. Sobbing, he was, because of you.'

'What did you tell him?'

'That he was wrong. That I didn't believe him.'

'And was that the truth?'

'No. I wanted it to be, of course, but we both knew you'd killed her.' She met his gaze. 'I want you to stop. I need you to stop, Rob. I can't keep protecting you.'

'You're not doing it for me. You're doing it for Mum and Dad, aren't you? You saw how they were in court. Devastation. And you're protecting them. You don't give a shit about me.'

'If I didn't give a shit about you, Rob, I'd have gone to the police, wouldn't I? Ages ago.'

'No, you wouldn't. You're self-absorbed and then the part of you that's not selfish is not going to risk damaging our family again. You lied to me, Gemma. I can't trust you any more.'

She laughed without humour. 'I didn't know you trusted me anyway.'

His expression hardened.

'Funny is it? I see. The thing is, you were supposed to be, above everything else, on my side. And now look.' He sighed. 'I'm not ready to give all of this up.'

Gemma looked past him to the doorway that led to the hall.

'What about her?'

'Nicci? She's not exactly a problem is she? When she comes round, she'll be tucked away like the others. I'll keep her there for a few weeks, like the others and then . . .' He shrugged. 'Comes back to not rushing things, you see.'

'I need to deal with Callum.'

'You don't,' he told her.

He interlinked his fingers as if in a gesture of prayer.

'Because this can't go on, Gemma. Not now.'

In the pit of her stomach she knew what he meant.

'What do you mean?' she still heard herself ask.

'You have a bottle of water. Look, just there beside you. Take your pills out of that bag and swallow. It's not so hard. I'll watch you.'

'You want to kill me?'

'Gemma, I've always wanted to kill you,' he laughed, and she genuinely couldn't tell whether he was joking or not.

She didn't move, so he reached into the bag and pulled out more blister packs.

'There's plenty here and I can wait because, like I say, I don't like to hurry. Please let me tell you what I do to them. I don't know why you've never asked.'

She shook her head. 'I don't want to know.'

'You see, it started because of you. I think I was jealous. Boys fawning round you. I didn't have women fawning round me.'

'Of course you did. At the gym there were always women hanging round you. Anyone who does . . .'

He tipped his head back and rolled his head first clockwise, then back again. His neck made a cracking sound. When he'd finished he spoke again. 'Take the tablets, Gemma.'

She shook her head, but she held the blister pack in her fingers. She didn't drop it or even try to stand up.

That was the thing. When you had a history with somebody you knew how they might behave and, in anticipation of it, you behave differently to the way you might otherwise. In her head, she was pushing him aside and running for the door. He'd always been stronger and faster and now he was the hunter and she was the prey. That was just in her head. In reality she didn't move.

She shook her head again.

'Swallow the tablets, Gemma.'

He picked up the bottle of water and pushed it into her free hand.

'I'm going to count, okay? It's childish and immature, but, look, let's do it this way. I will count to ten and before I get to ten, I want you to drink the water and take the first tablets.'

He reached forward and unscrewed the bottle top. She still held the bottle in her hand, and he put his underneath and raised it so that the neck moved towards her mouth. Her wrist became rigid as she resisted him, and she could see the rapid speed at which his eyes were darkening. It was the first warning sign. It always was.

She couldn't look away.

Watching him was the same as hearing the tick, tick, tick of a bomb.

Then he pounced, grabbing the tablets with one hand and the bottle of water with the other.

He pushed her backwards and sideways. She slumped in the chair, trapped over the arm, his full bodyweight on her.

He splashed the water into her face. Some of it landed in her mouth and then with the other hand he began to pop the pills out of the blister pack. The first couple flew onto the floor, but in no time he had two or three in his hand.

He tried to poke them between her teeth, but she was clenching her mouth tightly shut.

He pinned her down tighter and then with the other hand, pushed his forefinger and thumb into the side of her jaw, forcing a gap between her teeth. He pushed the tablets in and then gripped her by the neck, holding her mouth shut, forcing her to swallow.

She felt tablets go down. Two, maybe three, she wasn't sure. She gasped for air.

'I'll have bruising. They will know.'

'They won't know it's me.'

'They'll find traces of you around the house.'

'What, around our own family home? You're fucking mad if

you think they're going to catch me, not now. They never have before. I've been right under their nose and nobody's seen it.'

'Ellie did.'

'Yeah, and I dealt with her.'

Gemma tried to stand.

Rob knocked her feet out of the way and she tumbled back onto the sofa. He grabbed more of the blister packs from her stash, popping more and more of them out into his palm until there were at least twenty. He closed his hand around them, gripping them tightly. For a few seconds she fought to get away, but again he was on top of her. He twisted her arm and she yelped in pain.

'No! Please stop!'

He was close to her, breathing into her face. The air around him had always been toxic, but she'd been the only one who could taste it until the day of the crash. Then Ellie knew, and Gemma knew, and Callum knew, and they were all going to die.

He twisted her arm harder and she cried out in pain. In a flash he rammed the tablets into her mouth. Then with both hands, gripped her face again, holding on, pinching her nose and covering her mouth until all she could do was swallow.

'Now lie down,' he said, 'and stay there. I'm going to watch. Can't have you throwing up. Can't have you doing anything any more, Gemma.' And he sat like that, watching her, ready to pounce on her if she tried to put her fingers down her throat. She felt sick, but not sick enough to vomit.

She glanced towards the door, praying that Nicci would stir, wondering if Nicci was even alive. Another ten minutes passed and then she heard movement. A shuffling, scraping sound. Someone struggling. Nicci struggling to gain purchase on the cold, hard floor.

Rob darted from the room. She heard a blow and a sob and in those seconds she managed to get to her feet, managed to reach the window. But that was as far as she got.

'Oh fuck,' she heard him snap, his voice half anger, half something else that she would never identify. And then he was next to her and she thought she'd been punched. It was only when she looked down and saw the blood that she knew that it had been a knife.

Chapter 62

Jack knocked twice on Gemma's front door, the second time more insistent than the first. He thought he heard movement from inside the house, but wondered whether he'd mistaken sounds coming from the neighbouring property.

He was tempted to walk away, but knocked again, and as he waited, he tried Nicci's phone one more time. It went straight to voicemail. He dropped his phone back in his jacket and pushed his hands into the pockets of his jeans.

He had no reason to think Nicci was here, but he remembered what Nicci's mum had said about Gemma being a hermit. He guessed that Gemma was in there and just ignoring him. The thought irritated him, and he wanted to find some other way to grab her attention.

He took a couple of steps back from the house and looked up at the first-floor windows, then along the terrace. All these houses had alleys running behind them, and he walked along the row and then through the gap between this terrace and the next.

He'd done this plenty of times when they were kids, when he and Rob had knocked for each other, when they'd gone out for the afternoon and come back muddy or tired and used the back gate rather than treading mess up Rob's mum's hallway. Despite himself, he smiled at the memory; it was a shame their friendship hadn't lasted. He'd been to this house often enough in the past to know which back gate was theirs.

It turned out that it had been replaced since the last time he'd been here, but he still recognised the back of the house that peered over it.

He tried the gate, but it didn't budge. He didn't know whether it was locked or just latched from the inside. This was one of the only houses with a garage; he tried the door of that too and was surprised to find it swing open. He hesitated for a moment. It was far removed from the days when he'd been able to walk in uninvited. 'What the hell,' he breathed. The door from the garage to the garden was also unlocked, just as it had always been.

The room facing onto the garden had once been a smart and airy dining room, but the first thing he saw were piles of books and papers up against the patio door. He took his right hand out of his pocket, unsure whether to knock on the kitchen door or the patio door next to it. He was halfway across the short lawn when he saw the unmistakable shape of an arm and a hand, its fingers outstretched.

He darted forward close to the glass, cupped his hands and peered inside. Gemma was sprawled on the floor, lying on one side. One arm under her, the other outstretched. Her legs at odd angles as if they'd just collapsed from under her.

He banged on the glass, then rattled the handle. He went to the kitchen door and pulled on that too.

'Shit,' he breathed.

He pulled out his phone and dialled 999, but he had smashed a small pane of glass through the back door before he even had time to say 'Ambulance.' He let himself in, rushing through the kitchen and towards Gemma.

'Ambulance,' he shouted.

He gave them the address.

'There's a woman, she's injured.' He saw the blood. 'I'm not sure what's happened. She's bleeding on the floor.' He knelt down.

'I don't think she's breathing.' He put his hand to her mouth. 'She isn't breathing, no, she's not breathing. And there's blood.'

He felt her neck and then her wrist for a pulse and put his hand in front of her nose and mouth again. 'There's nothing, nothing, what should I do? Do I try chest compressions?'

The call handler remained calm, but behind that he could hear tension in her voice. 'Is she in the recovery position?'

'No, I told you, she's not breathing.'

'Okay, first of all, go and open the front door so the paramedics can come in, then come back to her and tell me if she's moved.'

He rushed to the door, opened it wide. He came back and shouted down the phone, 'No, she's just the same.'

'Okay, do you know what to do to give chest compressions?'

He nodded and then said, 'Yes, yes I do.'

And he turned her onto her back and as he did so a heavy slick of blood slid onto the floor, pooling around his knees. He put his hand to her sternum. 'She's been stabbed in the chest, I'm sure, there's what looks like a puncture wound, her clothes are damaged. I don't think I can.'

But he tried, and he was still trying when the paramedics arrived and pulled him gently away.

'She's gone, mate,' the paramedic said.

Jack stumbled on to his feet and staggered backwards. He stood in the doorway between the room and the hall for a minute, not wanting to abandon Gemma, but needing to put some space between him and the chaos that was unfolding. When he saw the paramedics agree that there was no sign of life he turned away and took a few breaths of air that wasn't fresh, but wasn't from that room either. Just then his phone rang, he saw Celia's number and answered.

'Gemma's dead.' He mumbled the words. 'Gemma's dead, I found her.'

Celia replied, 'Jack, listen to me, it's Rob. Rob's done it all.'

Chapter 63

Nicci regained consciousness just in time to see the light disappear as the car boot closed.

She moved as much as she could within the confined space, but only managed to flex her ankles and her wrists. She was sure nothing was broken, but that didn't stop the pain. Her ribs hurt, her face throbbed and her head pounded. The car pulled away, bouncing slightly as it travelled down the uneven track behind Gemma's house.

Nicci felt the rear-light casing with her hands. It was solid. She tried to kick out the lights with her feet but failed – so much for the YouTube videos that said to knock out the rear lights and wave at following vehicles.

She had no idea of the make or model of the car, or even the colour. She now knew that it wasn't designed to be dismantled from the inside though. But it had given her a couple of minutes of distraction and a few minutes of not thinking specifically about Rob.

It was obvious now.

He had a temper; she'd seen a glimmer of it once when she was a kid. He hadn't done anything violent, she'd just seen it on his face, the frustration, the flash of the eyes, the ability to strike out even though he hadn't used it.

That didn't make him a killer; but she now knew that was what he had become.

She wasn't going to second guess where he was taking her. She made a sudden, futile search about her person just in case her phone was there. Of course it wasn't. He would have disposed of it, and wouldn't be so stupid as to let himself get tracked by GPS.

She was in the car for three minutes, four at the most. Then he came to a stop, and she heard the ratchet as he pulled the handbrake. He stepped from the vehicle, slamming the door and then, from further away, she heard him open some kind of roller door.

'Shit.' Where were they?

The answer arrived almost as fast as the question itself.

His gym.

She thought it would be open now, that there should be people around, but also she knew that couldn't be the case, not when he'd just unlocked it. He returned to the car and she felt it reverse. That meant they were about to be alone together in a deserted building.

Up to that point she hadn't noticed any of the normal panic signs, no racing pulse or sweating, and no change in her breathing. But now her heart began to beat loudly, thumping heavily in her chest. Enough to wonder whether other sounds could be masked or distorted by the sound of her own fear.

She wanted to be out of this confined space, but she didn't want him opening the boot, she didn't want to see him. She wasn't scared of him exactly, but she feared what she would see when she looked into his face.

She never heard him approach the car, so she jumped when the boot sprang open. Her vision was flooded with the white unforgiving light of the gym. She blinked a couple of times. He had a strange expression; midway between satisfaction and determination, but behind it she could clearly see the fury lurking.

He told her to get up. The space was awkward and it took her a few seconds to twist over onto her front and raise herself to a kneeling position. It was too slow for him and he hauled her roughly onto the floor, her shins banging on the lip of the boot and then again on the back bumper as she fell to the ground. He immediately hauled her onto her feet and pushed her towards a single doorway in the wall. It looked like an office. She stumbled forwards.

'Keep moving,' he told her.

She realised then that she hadn't spoken at all. She wondered if that was natural; wasn't she supposed to be pleading for him to stop? To let her go? But her instincts told her that would be wrong and she had no urge to enrage him right then.

He shut the door behind them, turned the key in the lock and removed it. The door had a glass pane looking out into the gym. She glanced through it hoping that against all odds there would be someone coming for her. He shoved past her, knocking her into the desk.

'Wait,' he said.

He kept one eye on her as he fiddled with part of the plasterboard wall. Nicci scanned the space, urgently trying to find something, anything, that she could grab. The wall moved a little, and she realised with cold fear that there must be a room behind it. Some kind of extra compartment.

That was one place she didn't need to go.

She backed away.

The office was, at most, ten feet by six. The wall he had just opened was in the narrow side, and she backed away as far as she could. He took a couple of steps towards her. He reached out, missed, and then bellowed as he jumped at her. She flung herself towards him, catching him by surprise. The two of them collapsed to the floor. She was tiny compared to him, shorter, but mostly thinner, lighter, not a match for any part of him attacking any part of her.

His hand grabbed at her throat. 'You're not supposed to die like this,' he growled when he was on top of her, his full weight down on her, his body crushing the air from her. His hand moved from her neck up into her hair, his fingers gripping it close to the scalp.

It had been him at the crash, she had realised it a few minutes before, but now she felt it. It was exactly the same way as he had held her then. Her hands flailed by her side, there was nothing for her to grab, nothing for them to reach, her legs were trapped under him.

He was trying to subdue her, though, not kill her; he still wanted her alive. She relaxed a little. 'Okay, I won't fight,' she told him.

She needed him to release her a little if there was going to be any chance of her fighting back. He might as well have read her mind. The rage suddenly bloomed, full and ferocious in his eyes. He banged her head against the floor and the force sent a ripple right through her. Her vision momentarily blurred and then cleared again.

Whatever plans he had made for her had been replaced by blood lust. He'd just killed his sister, as far as she was aware. He banged her head against the floor, harder this time and the sound seemed to come from further away, an echoing, his voice distanced too.

She knew she couldn't fight him. That it was as good as over, but then, from nowhere, a woman, naked and wild eyed, jumped onto his back and grabbed him. The two of them fell away from Nicci, writhing in the confined space.

Nicci struggled up, and it was instinct more than decision to grab at them, to try to find his neck and hold onto it. She briefly found his throat, clasping as tightly as she could. The other figure, bloodied, and flimsy, was thrown aside as if she was nothing.

Rob spun towards Nicci and threw a punch at her face with such force that, if she hadn't managed to move and catch just a deflecting blow, he might have killed her. And there he stood between her and the door. The other woman lay lifeless, and Nicci herself felt as good as dead, when behind him the glass pane of the door smashed and she saw the unstoppable kick of a fury-driven shoe.

As the glass flew, she heard the sound of sirens and then the same boot kicked the shards of glass aside. She heard Jack's voice. 'Leave her,' he commanded. 'Leave her alone, Rob.'

And then finally it was all over.

Chapter 64

Callum was at Addenbrooke's hospital in a small private room that overlooked Hills Road. Briggs noticed when he sat down that the actual view from Callum's bed was little more than sky and clouds. Perhaps seeing normal life in its full flow would be too much right now, and, as he looked at Callum, he could see that there was such a long way to go.

Briggs had everything he needed to take notes with him, but he had brought a voice recorder too. 'We can do this at any speed you like,' he said, 'you can take your time.'

Callum nodded. 'I think I know what to say. I mean, I have the words.'

'Well,' said Briggs, 'if I press record we can start there, and then I can ask you questions. You can review it all before it becomes a final statement to make sure that I have everything down. What do you reckon?'

'Sure.'

It took a couple of attempts before Callum found his voice, he moved up the bed a little, sitting slightly straighter. He still looked incredibly frail; his skin so pale that it almost had a blueish tinge.

'Can I just talk, and you can interrupt if I get stuck, or if I don't make sense?'

'Absolutely,' said Briggs.

'My name is Callum Shaughnessy, and I was in a serious car accident four years ago, on 28 March. I was in the car with four other people, Nicci Waldock, Charlie Bailey, Ellie Daniels and Gemma Hayward. We'd been at the Five Miles from Anywhere pub.

'I'd got to know them all because I was lodging at Celia Henry's property, and so was Ellie. And I was on the same course as Gemma. Gemma and I were studying to become paramedics,' his voice wavered for the first time, 'well, that was the idea. Turns out I'm not cut out for it, but I didn't know that then. My science had always been good, biology in particular. Anyhow, I liked Gemma, really liked her. I kidded myself that something might happen between us. I can see that was ridiculous now, but she did flirt with me. She made me feel like it was a possibility. So we were at this pub, the five of us plus Gemma's brother Rob; we'd all come there together.

'It was Charlie's idea. He'd found out about this music festival that was on over the weekend. I'd completely forgotten that Jack worked there, but I don't think Gemma had. Jack was Gemma's ex, by quite a long time I think, but still, there was some kind of tension between them.

'And then Nicci and Ellie went off, and they were down by the river. Gemma sent me to get them and as soon as I was within ear-shot I could tell that Ellie was upset. I had no idea what it was about.

'And the rest of the day . . . it never gelled.

'There was friction and, even when we were sitting together, it was like we were pockets of people, not one group.

'It went quiet for a while, with Ellie I mean, and then, we'd all had a few to drink. We'd brought our own alcohol, and I don't think that helped because we lost track of how much we'd had.

'I was pissed. I think everybody was.

'Then this row breaks out. I really didn't get what was going on, to be honest. But Rob storms off and the next thing I know, Nicci's saying, "Right, we're leaving."'

Callum had closed his eyes. He was back there, in the moment. And Briggs noticed that he had begun to slip into the present tense.

'We go out to the car park and we all get in the car. I don't know if we are chasing after Rob, or what the deal is. So, we are in the car and Ellie's hysterical by then. She's ranting on about something to do with a hairband. It just, it seemed so . . . meaningless. I just kind of followed along after everybody else. The others were leaving, and I couldn't stay there with no transport.

'So, we are sitting in the back of the car, me behind Charlie with Nicci driving, Gemma is in the middle and Ellie's behind the driver's seat. I'm vaguely aware that Gemma was on the phone just before we got in the car, but I didn't question it at the time. Ellie wouldn't stop crying and screaming, and I remember shouting at her and asking what the fuck was happening. And Charlie turned round and told us all to shut up. Said they were dealing with it. And Nicci kept driving. Anyway, we hadn't gone that far up the road when . . .'

For the last minute or so he'd been speaking quite fluently, but he stumbled over the last few words and then stopped. He closed his eyes more tightly, frowning and looking pained. Briggs wasn't sure whether Callum was picturing those last moments or trying to block them out.

Callum drew a couple of deep breaths, and, as pale as he was, Briggs was certain that Callum's skin grew a couple of shades whiter. Sweat broke out on his forehead and across the tops of his cheeks.

Briggs left the recording running and just waited, eventually asking him, 'Can you go on?'

Callum opened his eyes halfway, stared at the pale sky outside the window and then nodded.

'From nowhere . . . and I mean from nowhere, there was a car coming towards us. I think it had been driving with its lights out, and then it suddenly switched them on, right at the very end.

'I don't think anybody screamed at that moment apart from

Ellie, who was already screaming. There was the endless split second. If we could have been snatched out of the way just then, we would have been unscathed, but, at the same time, our fates were sealed. At that second we were totally whole and healthy, but as good as dead. Do you understand?' He opened his eyes and stared at Briggs.

'I do,' Briggs nodded gently, 'I do understand.'

'Then Charlie shouted "NO!" and yanked the steering wheel in the moment before impact. And he changed everything. That's why we missed going head on with that other car. Charlie pulled the wheel and we spun off into a tree. We went from, I don't know, fifty to zero in . . .'

He held his hands about a metre apart.

'I mean, mathematically, that's better than hitting another car straight on. But it doesn't feel like it. Trees don't budge.

'There was no sound from those two in the front. Gemma's arms broke. I heard them snap. It was a little volley of cracks, a different frequency to everything else that was smashing around me. And then there's this moment of silence and she starts screaming.

'And then Ellie is screaming because she is bleeding . . . and I don't know . . . I didn't know until much later that it was Gemma's broken arm that had impaled her.'

He screwed his eyes shut again and breathed heavily through his mouth.

Briggs glanced round the bed, found a cardboard bowl and put it in Callum's hands, just in case he threw up. Callum nodded his gratitude and carried on breathing deeply until the nausea subsided.

'Rob was driving the other car. I didn't know until he yanked open the door. And he was in this rage. You know, people say about the red mist. He was terrifying. He'd wanted to kill us all . . . and himself as far as I could work out.

'So he yanks open the door and he stops dead when he sees Gemma's arms like that. And it's not like he cares about her, it's like he's enraged to find her still alive. He looks in the car and he doesn't know what to do.

'And then Ellie starts screaming "You killed Becky! It was her hairband! It was hers!"' For the first time Callum's gaze steadied and it fell on Briggs. 'She wouldn't stop screaming about this woman. This woman I'd never heard of. I didn't understand what was happening. Rob looked her over. He knew a bit about anatomy. They learn about it in sports science. But you wouldn't have to be a genius in any case. She's there, bleeding out of the hole in her chest, made by Gemma's arm bone.

'And he just reaches forward and he pushes his fingers into it and then pulls, ripping the skin, ripping the flesh. And she's screaming. Writhing. And he just hangs on.' Callum's voice was barely audible, and he stared at Briggs with wide eyes and utter horror etched on his face. 'The blood was gushing. It was hitting her lap . . . it was spreading down her legs. I could just see it, even though there was barely any light, it was just the interior bulb. But I could still see everything. And he hung onto her like that until she stopped.

'Then he rushes straight to the front, and he looks at Charlie, but he's clearly dead. Then he grabs Nicci . . . he grabs her head and he is slamming her against the steering wheel. She was already unconscious but he keeps hitting her, and then Gemma starts shouting "Stop it Rob! You can't kill us all!"

'She kept using his name, and she said . . . and I don't know why . . . she said "We'll protect you" . . . like me and her . . . like somehow I was different to the other people in the car. And I never knew why she did that. I asked her, but she never told me, and I can only think that she didn't want to be left alone right then.

'Not the way she was injured.

'She needed me, needed me to phone for help.

'And then he looked at me and looked at her. He didn't need to say anything. And he ran. He ran back to his car and drove away. I rang for an ambulance then. And I was going to take Gemma's phone and call Jack, but she was already doing it. She spoke to him . . . I was going to tell him what had happened, but she just shouted, told him to get down there. And before we knew it there were paramedics everywhere and there was only me and Gemma. And the police came. They thought that Nicci had crashed the car because she was going too fast and over the limit. She was going fast. And yes, she'd drunk. We all had.

'Turned out she wasn't over the limit. She'd had a couple, maybe it made some kind of difference, but I don't think so. We never would have crashed if he hadn't tried to kill us.

'Then Gemma and I made a pact. She convinced me . . . it sounds so stupid now, she convinced me that Rob would have been frightened. That he'd done nothing wrong and that he was attempting to stop when we crashed. That he'd made a terrible mistake, and that it was out of character, all of those things. Charlie and Ellie were dead; no one thought Nicci would survive either.

'I didn't believe the excuses. How could I? But I couldn't process what I'd just seen either. I took the route of pretending it hadn't happened like that. And Gemma told me that she would deny it all. She would make out that I'd been the one who'd attacked Ellie, that I'd been sexually harassing her.

'And I'd had . . . we'd had lodgers at the house before, other lodgers, and they left because of me. I'm not . . . I wasn't good, I did things that I thought were humour, horseplay, that they took the wrong way. But with all that stacked against me . . . Right then, for the next twenty-four hours, I convinced myself that it would be okay, that we could put it behind us, that the people who were dead, we couldn't help them. By the time I'd made my statement, it was too late. Too late to change it.'

'Had it begun to play on your mind?' Briggs stood a little closer. 'Callum, were you struggling?'

'Of course I was struggling. The worst of it hit me when I went to court; we were all there giving statements and I was lying and Nicci was going to prison. She didn't deserve that. And I didn't have the balls to intervene, and I didn't know what I could say.

If there'd been evidence against Rob it would've come up, her defence would have brought it up.

'So, it would've been my word against . . . not just Gemma . . . but against the findings of the police. So, I sat there quiet, said nothing and watched Nicci go down.' Callum nodded to himself. 'I did that,' he murmured.

There was a long silence and Briggs had to prompt him to speak again.

'The name Becky played on my mind. Rebecca. That's how she appeared in the papers. I knew who she was too. I'd seen her often when I was working. She was this weird woman, middle-aged, liked to dress up as if she was twenty-something, always flirting with the doormen. I didn't know her particularly. I'd spoken to her, I didn't care about her particularly, but suddenly we were connected. I'd go on her Facebook profile and look at her pictures. I read all the press reports, the newspaper clippings.

'And then I couldn't deal with it . . . it was still a live case, and it was in the Cambridge news all the time. I couldn't take it, so I tried moving back home. Everything caught up with me. More than that, it caught up and ran me over. I don't have a good relationship with my stepfather. Living at home was never going to last. In his eyes I was a big balls-up, I'd failed, I'd dropped out and left university.

'I wasn't working. I wasn't badly hurt in that crash, but I started off on painkillers and I liked the spaced-out way they made me feel. And one thing led to another and sometimes when I was taking drugs I had this super clarity. Other times it blanked things out, but sometimes I could see . . . and I saw other women. And I started looking every day.

'Not on the internet but in the papers. Because when I saw . . . I saw somebody who'd disappeared, I thought maybe it was Rob . . . I thought maybe he'd done it again. And then most times they turned up again, but sometimes they didn't, and in my head it was Rob . . . Rob was responsible for all of them.

'Sometimes he would let them go, and sometimes he would keep them. And when they turned up, they didn't turn up in the same place, there was nothing to link them. But in my head they were all . . . all his . . . he'd taken them all.

'I tried to talk to Gemma. I told her. I said, "We have to go to the police, we have to stop it," and do you know what she did? She hid me. In that old beach house that they used to use. It's going to fall into the sea, so no one goes there any more. She gave me the key and money for drugs and sometimes more in the post. Prescription drugs that she didn't use. Opiates like Tramadol, or whatever she could get at the time.

'Until, in the end, all my life has been is *hide there where he won't find me, grab a newspaper, read about all the missing women, hide, hide, hide.*

'And I just couldn't do it any more. So, I managed to stack just enough to finish it.

'Because Rob's done so much, and so have I.

'And I couldn't live with it any more.'

Chapter 65

Three weeks later

Nicci picked up two items of post from the front doormat, went to the back of the house and climbed over the fence, before knocking on Celia's back door. Celia had just boiled the kettle and the two of them sat at the kitchen table with the two envelopes between them.

'Two of them on the same day?' Celia commented. 'I reckon that's a good omen.'

'Don't,' Nicci whispered. 'You'll jinx it – one, or both. I don't know, just don't.'

'Which one are you opening first?'

Nicci looked from one envelope to the other. The first from Anglia Ruskin University, and the other from Holden Laboratories. 'You choose,' she said.

Celia pointed to the one from Anglia Ruskin. 'If you open the other one first, you won't wait to open this.'

Nicci nodded. She picked it up and gently pulled at the gummed lip, wanting to keep it as neat as she could. She slid out the paper inside, and paused long enough to cross her fingers.

Celia rested her hand on Nicci's. 'It will be okay,' she said, 'you'll see.'

And she was right.

Nicci unfolded the page and read: *We are delighted to offer you a place on our Crime and Investigative Studies BSc (Hons) course, commencing this September.* Nicci stared at the words, a lump in her throat. At the bottom of the page someone had added a hand-written note in blue pen: *We are pleased to welcome you back.*

Nicci closed her eyes, and tears spilled on to her cheeks.

'I told you,' Celia said.

It was several minutes before Nicci trusted herself to speak. 'Can I still live here?' she asked. Nicci couldn't imagine being anywhere else. She couldn't imagine Celia saying no either, but she needed to check.

'Of course, but just you, I don't want other students this time. I'm done with that.'

Nicci nodded. 'And can I carry on removing tattoos here?'

'Of course,' Celia said again. 'It's your home, Nicci.'

Nicci grinned. 'I need to pay my way, and that'll be the best thing for me.'

Celia squeezed her hand. 'It's going to be good, Nicci.'

'It's already good, isn't it?' Nicci said, looking at the second envelope. 'I hope I'm right.'

This time Celia crossed her fingers. And then Nicci tore it open.

Jack had finally completed the drawings for the impossible house extension. He'd had to choose between one which looked good and one which was functional. He'd found a compromise that was 90 per cent functional and 70 per cent good looking, and he reckoned that was the best he was going to do.

He had just pressed send on the email to Frank Bennett when there was a knock at the front door.

If there was one thing he'd learned over the last few weeks, it was to check out of the window before opening the door. Nicci was on his doorstep.

Each time he saw her he had a rush of mixed feelings. She'd still been the driver of the car, but Charlie had been the one who had pulled at the wheel. Was either more responsible than the other?

He didn't think so. Especially as none of it would have happened without Rob.

And that was something far bigger that he still had to face. There would be a trial; Charlie's death would be a much smaller part of the picture than it had been before. The case would primarily be about the other murders.

Nicci had done everything she could, he knew that, but he had a little way to go before he was comfortable around her. He hoped that would come.

He opened the front door and let her in. And he immediately noticed a brightness to her, an energy that he hadn't seen for such a long time. The old Nicci was there, that was certain.

She held an envelope in her hand and he could tell, from the position of her fingers, that she was gripping it tightly. She took a breath, and then seemed to take another on top of that one. 'Okay, first of all, Briggs is about to drop by. He's going to give us an update, and I thought you might want to be there. Hear it from the horse's mouth.'

'I wasn't involved as much as you two were.'

'Yeah, but you were in there. He knows that. He'll speak to all three of us. Anyhow, the whole thing's off the record, so, if he's going to speak out of turn to Celia, he may as well get into three times as much trouble.'

Jack nodded, not sure how to respond.

Nicci didn't wait for an answer. 'But first,' she continued, and took the envelope in both hands. Without warning tears welled in her eyes. 'It's like this, Jack, you saved me and I'm not really very good at owing people anything . . .' She took a breath. 'Yes, I know I owe Celia the world, and I will find a way to pay her back one day. But I was trying to think of what I could do to make things even with us.'

'We don't need things to be even.'

'I need things to be even. So I sat and I looked at the photo of Charlie on the beach.' She took a moment to gather herself. 'I guess you already know, but I broke into your house?'

'I worked that out.'

'I grabbed a bundle of things and that's where I found the press clipping. And I found this inside.'

He hadn't noticed it before, but there was a photograph tucked behind the envelope. It was a picture of him and Maya. *The picture.* His favourite photo; the two of them cheek to cheek. He took it from her, and studied it for five, six, seven seconds.

Until it stung too much, and he had to fight not to look away.

'The thing is, Jack, when I was thinking about what I could do to make things even, I looked at this picture and the photo of Charlie . . . There are things I'm good at, and things I'm not. And I'm good at detail, and I saw something . . . it's your ears. She is the spitting image of her mother, but you, Charlie and Maya have the same ears.'

He stared harder at the photo.

'Ear shapes can run in families,' Nicci told him.

Maya looked back at him, and although he knew what Nicci might be about to say, he held himself still, not daring to hope.

Nicci kept talking, the words flooding out of her. 'When I broke in here, I swabbed your toothbrush, just in case . . . just in case it was you who was responsible. Of course it was Rob, but I didn't know that, and I didn't trust Briggs to take the swab and not just dispose of it. So I sent it off myself. That way I could give him the profile and still have a copy. And it meant that I had one to match to.' She took a breath. 'I ran a DNA test on Maya.'

'How?' he mumbled.

'I found out where they lived. I waited until they were out . . .' She gave him an apologetic smile. 'On second thought, you really don't want to know.'

'You broke in their house too? Seriously?'

'It was important. And it won't happen again.' Nicci shrugged. 'And I'll be honest, I only met Sadie a couple of times, but I never liked her. Women's intuition, I guess.' She handed him the envelope then.

He looked into Nicci's face, searching for reassurance that he hadn't made some terrible mistake in interpreting what she was telling him.

She nodded. 'Jack. You're Maya's dad,' she whispered.

He took the paper from the envelope and stared at it.

He barely heard Nicci then. 'I think she either had a friend with a child pose as her and Maya for the test, or borrowed somebody else's child to fake the results. She lied, just to shut you out of your daughter's life.'

'Oh God.' It was just sinking in and he could barely breathe.

Nicci kept talking. She was ahead of him. 'You need to report it to the police,' Nicci said. 'Sadie lied in legal documents, Jack, she committed a crime. And you have time to catch up with Maya.'

He looked up from the page, from the wonderfully incomprehensible detail which culminated in the statistic that the chance of him not being Maya's father was less than one in 13 billion. 'I'll give the Briggs thing a miss.' He took his car keys from the table. 'I need to go.'

She nodded.

He reached out and took her hand; he squeezed it softly. 'Thank you, Nicci.'

Celia opened the door for Briggs. She'd been undecided whether to invite him into the kitchen or into the office. In the end she decided on the latter. She knew he was coming and had the coffees ready, biscuits too. Homemade ones just for the sake of manners, although she guessed that no one would touch them.

'So,' she said.

'Well,' he smiled warmly, 'it's been a journey, and I thought you deserved to hear it from me, rather than see it in the papers.'

She led him through to the kitchen. Nicci was already there. Briggs smiled just as warmly at Nicci.

'No Jack?' he asked.

She shook her head. 'He's a bit busy. I'll speak to him afterwards, if that's okay.'

'Yes, of course,' he said. 'But I'd like confidentiality beyond that.'

'That's no problem.'

'You've probably seen the news.'

'The police are not giving much away,' she replied.

There had been non-stop coverage. They had ripped apart the gym, but the press had been kept firmly behind a very wide cordon, and what they had shown on the television and in the papers had been little more than long shots of police vehicles moving around, people wearing protective clothing, and occasionally a senior officer speaking to camera. He seemed to like the word 'ongoing' and used it frequently.

'The gym used to be a workshop years ago. Vehicle maintenance, that kind of thing. It had an inspection pit.'

Celia prided herself on staying calm, keeping her poise. She dug one thumbnail into her index finger. It was a trick she'd learnt to stop the pressure showing anywhere else. She tilted her head, just by a couple of degrees, and looked him straight in the eye. It was important to remain professional, but she found the phrase *inspection pit* rather unnerving.

'It was deep originally, enough for a man to stand up and work under a vehicle. And it was long too. We've, literally, got to the bottom of it and we found six women down there. Sam Morgan and Debbie Lagoudi, just as we suspected. And then four more women.

'We need to cross-reference them with the missing-person lists from around the country, but we're not sure at this point how quickly we'll identify them all.'

Nicci spoke for the first time. 'So, he buried them in the inspection pit?'

Briggs nodded. 'One at a time. And each time he filled it up a little more.'

Celia felt a chill. Nicci remained indecipherable, a trait she seemed to deploy at the toughest moments. 'Ellie,' she said at last, 'how did she know?'

'Well, we have Callum's account, and there's no reason to doubt it. He and Ellie had been to Gemma's. There'd been some flirting between Ellie and Rob, and he thought she liked the idea that something might develop. The next day Gemma gave Callum a hairband – she thought it had to be Ellie's. Callum passed it on to Ellie and thought no more about it . . .'

Nicci nodded slowly. 'But it was Becky Lake's?'

'Quite so. And Ellie worked it out. She fretted about it, but it seemed to be at the pub when she suddenly realised the implication; that there wasn't a viable innocent explanation. On top of that, Gemma realised and Callum thinks she told Rob.'

'And we were all drinking and oblivious. Ellie said she didn't know if she had what it takes to get involved. She was trying to, wasn't she?'

'Things could have been very different for all of you.'

They each gave the statement a moment.

Celia broke the silence. 'How is Louise?'

Briggs smiled softly. 'Struggling, but glad to be alive. She uses those words. It makes a big difference that she's fighting for it. She had no idea where she was. Nothing at all. She thought she could hear the sea, but it was the sound of a rowing machine. She's out of hospital. She wanted to be home but she's got a long road ahead of her.'

'Could I visit her?' Nicci asked. 'Obviously, only if she'd like me to.'

'I'll ask. And I'm truly sorry for everything you went through.'

Nicci brushed it aside. 'I'm here because of Celia. And Jack. I'm lucky.'

'I am sorry.'

Nicci nodded. 'I don't blame you.'

The three of them fell into a brief, but comfortable silence. Broken when Briggs tried one of Celia's biscuits. 'So have I heard the last of you for a while?' he asked.

'Well,' Celia raised an eyebrow, 'we will have to see.'

Acknowledgements

I find that it's both a pleasure and a challenge to write the acknowledgements. I don't want to miss anybody out, and if I have, I'm very sorry. On the other hand, this is the point where I can stop and reflect on the journey that I've been on with this particular book.

The Moment Before Impact has, for a variety of reasons, taken me longer to complete than some of my previous books.

This has been my ninth book working with wonderful Krystyna Green, and never has her support and insight been more appreciated. On top of that, Krystyna, you gave me the best night out I've had in a very long time.

Thank you to all at Little, Brown who have worked on this book, including Amanda Keats and Rachel Cross, with a special mention to Sean Garrehy. Sometimes you can't judge a book by its cover, but I can't help thinking that that's precisely what the cover is supposed to do. Sean designed this one based on the synopsis, and before I had written a word. I thought it was stunning – I still do – so I put the image above my desk and set out to write a book that would do it justice.

One of my favourite stages with a book is the editing process; it's exciting when it falls into someone else's hands and they point out tweaks that are needed or notice the things I've missed – characters with changing eye colour, sudden weight gain and so on, and then it comes out the other end polished and ready to be launched. Rebecca Sheppard and Howard Watson, thank you both; I always enjoy your input.

I had written a good proportion of this one when I reached a bit of a plot dead end. I was discussing this with my daughter Lana; she thought over what I had said, and then, in a single sentence, made me see why I needed to throw most of it away and start again. Although the revelation stung (throwing away thousands of words does hurt), I could see that it was the best thing for the book, and I am genuinely thrilled with the difference it made. So, thank you, Lana, for letting me bend your ear and for all the support you have given me.

I am definitely a plotter, and during the planning of this book I had to spend a lot of time weighing up options and limitations, particularly in relation to body trauma. Dr William Holstein has been incredibly generous with his time, and I love our (often dark) conversations, especially the ones where I'm left thinking *what if . . . ?*

On a personal note, special mentions to both my sister Stella and to Liz Bradbury, who went far above and way beyond in their support. Thanks too to those who have read, and listened, and let me ramble on about all kinds of bizarre topics: Lynn Fraser, Genevieve Pease, Martin and Sam Jerram, Jane Martin and Lisa Sanford. And, as always, love to Claire Tombs and Christine Bartram.

Some characters have been named after real people. In 2018, Tom and Naomi Roy bid in a charity auction and won the chance to name a character. After discussion with the family, they decided that the name Roy Maitland should appear. I have also named characters after some of my university friends: Lewis Allum, Emily Moore, Despina Lagoudi, Sam Morgan and Francisca Matos . . . some of their characters didn't fare so well, but we were studying Crime and Investigation, so I'm sure they won't mind. I'll miss you guys.

I'm writing this while the world is still largely in lockdown. We don't know what will happen with bookshops, when we might be able to attend crime events, or meet with other authors beyond the internet. I hope it will all happen again one day soon; in the meantime, I wish you all well. An extra little bit of love to the following who have made me smile, laugh or given me a boot/boost: Joanne and MW-awesome-books-Craven, Elly Griffiths, Linda Regan, Ayo Onatade, Ian Rankin and Amanda Jennings.

When I'm teaching, I am often asked for advice on how to find a good agent. I say that it is important to find an agent you feel you will still be happy to work with in ten years' time, and to make sure that it is somebody whose opinion you respect, because they will be giving you bad news as well as good. I bamboozled Broo into representing me more than ten years ago, and Broo, I love you even when you give me a telling off.

Thank you to Lana, Dean, Natalie and Will, for being great company along the way, and for the hugs when I finished.

CRIME AND THRILLER FAN?

CHECK OUT THECRIMEVAULT.COM

The online home of exceptional crime fiction

THE CRIME VAULT

KEEP YOURSELF IN SUSPENSE

Sign up to our newsletter for regular recommendations, competitions and exclusives at **www.thecrimevault.com/connect**

Follow us

@TheCrimeVault

/TheCrimeVault

for all the latest news